The Unforgettable Mailman

The Unforgettable Mailman

A Novel

April Howells

alcove
press

Books should be disposed of and recycled according to local requirements. All paper materials used are FSC compliant.

This is a work of fiction. All of the names, characters, organizations, places, and events portrayed in this novel are either products of the author's imagination or are used fictitiously. Any resemblance to real or actual events, locales, or persons, living or dead, is entirely coincidental.

Published in the United States by Alcove Press, an imprint of The Quick Brown Fox & Company LLC.

Alcove Press and its logo are trademarks of The Quick Brown Fox & Company LLC.

Library of Congress Catalog-in-Publication data available upon request.

ISBN (hardcover): 979-8-89242-525-4
ISBN (paperback): 979-8-89242-526-1
ISBN (ebook): 979-8-89242-527-8

Cover design by Dawn Cooper.

Printed in the United States.

www.alcovepress.com

Alcove Press
34 West 27th St., 10th Floor
New York, NY 10001

First Edition: April 2026

The authorized representative in the EU for product safety and compliance is eucomply OÜPärnu mnt 139b-14, 11317 Tallinn, Estonia, hello@eucompliancepartner.com, +33757690241

10 9 8 7 6 5 4 3 2 1

For my grandmothers: Doris Hodgins and
Elizabeth (Beth) Burdick.
And my mother-in-law, Joyce Howells.
I hope all your memories came flooding back at the end.

1

Thursday, October 13, 1966
10:03 AM

A note on the counter prompted Henry to shave every day. Another told him in faded ink that he should not, under any circumstances, try to use the iron. And one, scrawled on the back of an old paper bag, screamed *CONNECTION IS CRITICAL TO KEEP YOUR MIND SHARP.*

None of them explained where he'd put the stamps.

The letter to his son languished on the kitchen table, its bare corner a constant reminder of the missing postage. Leaning his cane against the wall, he tugged at the middle drawer. A squeal filled the room, expanded wood groaning at the disturbance. Shoving items out of the way—rusting scissors, loose matches, three rubber bands—he searched for the roll.

At the bottom, a fork stared up at him, out of place. There were no stamps.

Henry's chest tightened. Someone had stolen them. They'd climbed in through the window and taken them in the night. All he'd wanted was a light breeze, and now he was paying the price. The window would need to stay closed permanently.

And he would need to replace the pilfered roll.

The post office spanned two Chicago blocks. Henry took the steps one at a time, careful not to trip. At the top, nine doors all led to the same lobby. He chose the third door from the left.

It was locked.

Moving over, he tried the next. By the time he'd checked all nine, his knee throbbed with the effort. Cupping a hand, Henry peered inside. Shadows floated through the expansive lobby, washing everything out. With a huff, he tapped his cane on the window. The ting of wood on glass sounded hollow. Gripping the handle firmly, he banged louder: ten quick raps that echoed down the steps.

There had to be someone inside.

Minutes passed, and a dull ache pulsed its way up his arm. He lowered his cane, jaw clenched. Turning his back to the building, Henry took the first step, placing one foot down and then the next.

Behind him, someone grunted. "What?"

Henry spun around to find a rotund man in a security uniform leaning halfway out the door, drops of sweat dripping from his brow onto the limestone in tiny bursts.

"I need to buy some stamps." Henry took the step again and moved toward the door.

The guard didn't budge. "We're closed."

"Closed?" Henry repeated. It was the middle of the day.

"Yeah, closed. Shut. Not open." Thick fingers wiped at a wet brow. Henry thought they looked like the sausages his wife, Elsie, liked to burn.

"I must be missing something," Henry insisted, knuckles turning white on the handle of his cane. "I just need stamps." It would only take a moment. No need to make a fuss.

"Like I said." The guard dragged the words out, rather unnecessarily. "The post office is closed. There's no one here to sell you stamps." Without waiting for a reply, the man squeezed his oversized body through the gap and slammed the door shut.

Henry watched him slouch away and tried to make sense of the news.

William,

I thought I'd be seeing you this week, but I understand if something's come up. You're such a busy young man, I know. You've always been flitting here and there with your friends. When you were young, you used to rile the whole street up and force all the neighborhood kids to play "war." There you'd be, proud as punch, wearing my old helmet as it practically fell off your head, a flag in hand, directing the actions of everyone else. Don had to keep watch from one end of the street, Billy the other. And poor little Ernest was always the attacking enemy. Though we both know there wasn't an evil bone in that scrawny boy's body. Oh, how they looked up to you, my boy. Wide-eyed and excited. Every game you concocted, they'd follow along.

I've been pacing a hole in the floor again, trying to fill my days. If only you were here to boss me around. Tell me what to do, William, and I'll do it. I'm bored out of my mind.

Hope to see you soon.

Dad

P.S. Someone came in during the night and snatched the stamps, so this letter may be a tad delayed. Don't worry. I've nailed the window shut with a hammer I found in the oven.

2

Thursday, October 13, 1966
10:44 AM

Roger bounced up the stairs two at a time, passing a man with a wooden cane. He would have stopped to say hello, even lend a hand, but he couldn't catch his breath. He'd sprinted straight here from Crane Tech. At the top of the stairs, nine doors stood proud. He paused, hands on knees, to collect himself before choosing the first door on the left.

It was locked. Strange.

He leaned to peer through the glass. At the far end of the hall, a large shadow turned a corner and disappeared. How could the post office be closed in the middle of the afternoon?

His mom had asked him to swing by on his way home from school to see if a letter had arrived, but Roger preferred to do things on his own schedule. No point waiting until the end of the day if he could sneak out under his science teacher's oversized nose instead. Mr. Tucker found more joy in having a postlunch nap than teaching. Every week he'd assign some random pages to read before propping his worn leather loafers on the desk and reclining in a chair that squeaked every time he snored.

Fast to sleep, Mr. Tucker also happened to be fast to rise if anyone so much as spoke. Roger would have already woken the beast if he'd been there. That much was certain.

He craned his neck to look at the windows soaring above each door.

"Wonder why it's closed?" Roger asked no one in particular, snapping his fingers and trying to decide what to do next. "We can either break in"—he chuckled at himself and looked through the door once more—"or we can tell Mom not to worry. Surely whatever letter she's waiting for will arrive soon."

With a shrug, Roger sauntered down the steps, determined to take the long way back to class.

2445 3rd Street,
Rapid City, SD 57703

Clyde,

I haven't asked for anything in seven years. Not a penny for the mortgage or the groceries. I didn't even ask for help when Sugar's vet bills became more than I could handle. I simply put my head down and made it work.

Well, guess what? I'm asking now. And I think I've earned the right to tell you straight.

Your son needs you.

Roger is struggling more than I've ever seen. It's like after you left, only . . . I don't know, a hundred times worse.

He's so aimless these days.

Ever since Pete moved away because his dad got a job at the Ford factory in Detroit, Roger hasn't been himself. I know he doesn't have many other friends, but still.

When he's not skipping school, he's disrupting the class. One of his teachers has started sending him to the back of the room for a "special project" if he talks. He only talks because he gets the work done so much faster than the other kids, but they won't listen when I tell them that.

I'm at my wits' end. It's your turn now, Clyde. You can walk out on us, but you'll never get very far.

As long as I can afford a stamp, I'll keep writing.

Tracy

3

Thursday, October 13, 1966
11:46 AM

The reporter was early. Reginald Stokes despised early. He was either slightly late or extremely late to everything. Feeling rushed made his eye twitch. The sound of his black patent shoes echoed off the walls of the expansive post office lobby and landed, with every heel strike, in a loud smack. Of the dozen possible options, it was the third set of elevator doors that opened to take him up to the top floor.

A deafening silence fell as he approached the end of the hall.

His assistant jumped up from her seat. "Mr. Stokes, sir." He wished she would stay sitting. "The reporter is in your office. I suggest—"

"You *what*?"

"I suggest you—"

"That'll be all, Brenda. I do not need my *assistant*"—he spit the word up toward her vacant face—"to suggest anything to me. I will simply tell the reporter that we have a slight backlog of letters but it's nothing we can't handle in-house."

She blinked. "He'll want to see the receiving platforms, I imagine, and the delivery division. To get a handle on just how *slight*. This could be a good opportunity to get the support we need. If we can get the public's assistance, we might be able to reopen in a matter of weeks."

Stokes glared at the middle-aged woman. She needed to learn her place. She also needed to learn the value of being put together. Streaks of gray had begun to take root in the dark hair she wore knotted at the nape of her neck, and her cheeks were a bright rouge painted by an inexperienced hand.

Had the reporter already judged him based on her appearance? He ran a hand down the front of his pin-striped suit. Appearances were everything to Stokes.

"No one will be seeing anything," he warned. "Everything is under control. It's barely even an issue, and yet, for some reason, you keep trying to talk about it. I do not pay you to have an opinion. I pay you to answer the phone and type up reports. Frankly, I'd be embarrassed if I were you. Always trying to save the day." He smirked, head tilted.

Brenda's lips got even thinner as she stepped aside.

Standing taller, Stokes sauntered into his office and greeted the *Chicago Tribune* reporter with a clap on the back. "Chuck, my friend. You're looking well. Now, listen, we're just a little backlogged."

He kicked the door shut with a bang, hoping it made Brenda jump.

4

Friday, October 14, 1966
8:44 AM

Bringing the newspaper in close, Henry scanned the fine print detailing a shutdown at the post office. The article was brief, with very little detail and even less reporting. There was a matter that needed sorting, though they were being rather tight-lipped about what the matter was. He reread the words, remembering the security guard's insolence the day before. The letter to William lay beside him on the table.

This won't do, Henry thought. *Not at all.* People needed their letters, and if he got another chance, he'd force them to explain exactly what they planned to do about—

His toast popped, making him jump. He crunched it over the sink.

Checking the clock, he wondered where Elsie was. It wasn't like her to leave the house so early. His wife of golden years was not one for early mornings. Henry sent the crumbs down the drain with a spray of water and looked around, news of the post office receding to the back of his mind. Aside from a dozen reminders scattered across the room, the kitchen felt the same as it always did. The wood-look table had been wiped clear. The tall chairs with their curlicue backs and their white vinyl upholstery were tucked in. The white shag rug was straight, hugging the floor. Nothing changed, day after day.

Beside him, a note said he didn't need anything.

Another asked if he had everything he needed.

Henry leaned on his cane and scanned the fridge, making a mental list of its contents. He ignored the pinned-up, underlined missive reminding him his memory wasn't what it used to be.

He didn't remember writing that one, so it couldn't be important.

The convenience store spanned the first floor of a two-story brick building around the corner from Henry's house. Wide windows stretched along the front, framing a glass-paneled door. Advertisements covering the glass told passersby they could buy two-for-one milk cartons, lollipops, and more. A worn poster spoke of an event that had already happened; a bright new flyer promoted an upcoming dance at the Hall.

Above the window, a white banner had *Jimmy's Food and Convenience* painted in foot-high navy letters. On windy days, it flapped violently.

As predicted, the sign flipped from closed to open as Henry shuffled up the street. The bell announced him as the first customer of the day.

His chest swelled.

"Good morning, Henry," Jim called as he walked to the till.

"Good morning, Jimmy."

Henry eyed the sparse wooden shelves. They were only half full as the seasons transitioned from one to the next. Avoiding a roughhewn edge known to collect thread from unsuspecting shoulders, he inched farther down a narrow aisle. He didn't know what he needed. Bread? Maybe.

Turning over a loaf, he pictured the cupboards at home. He could see bread. But was that because there was enough at home, or because he needed some? The soft crumb squished between his fingers as he worked to arrange the jumbled thoughts in his head.

They were hovering out of reach again.

"You don't need bread." The sound of Jimmy's voice made Henry drop his cane. Clinging to the goods, he stared down at the wooden stick, a slender crack forming along its shaft.

Jimmy reached for the cane. He traded it for the bread, placing the loaf back on the shelf. "Do you need something else? Eggs, perhaps?"

Eggs? No. Henry didn't think he needed eggs. He didn't like to bother with the yolk.

As Jimmy disappeared into the back room through the saloon doors at the end of the aisle, Henry moved farther down and scanned the shelves again, mind swirling. Tinned foods, household cleaning products. Three kinds of cereal to choose from. Rippled chips. Flour and baking soda and gravy granules. A row of Tide boxes formed a line across from him, the last one nudged out of place by a busy, unsnagged elbow.

He knew he didn't need detergent.

If only Jimmy hadn't seen him. He would have left the money on the counter. He was honest. So honest, in fact, it was his motto.

Honesty was the best . . . what was the word? It didn't matter. What mattered was he would have left the exact amount of change and been on his way. Who cared if he didn't need bread. He and Elsie would have eaten it, surely?

A mother and two young children bickering about who would get to stir the batter piled through the door. Their cries drowned out the bell. The youngest one tucked a doll under her arm and pointed at his cane.

"What's that stick for?" Light freckles dusted her nose. She looked about six, though she was shorter than she ought to be for that age.

Henry stared down at her. "It helps me walk."

"Don't your legs help you walk?" She didn't seem to notice her family had moved to the other side of the store.

"One of my legs needs a little help."

Her eyes glimmered. "Why?"

"Well, when I was in the war—"

"What's war?"

Henry looked around for the mother. She was distracted by the flour while the boy pulled at her hem. "It's like a fight," Henry replied, distant memories easier for him to recall, "only bigger. And during that fight I was hit by some metal. The cane helps my bad leg."

She broke into a toothy smile. "Like a third leg! I want a third leg! Mommy, I need a third leg!"

The mother's head jerked toward them, a frown creasing her brow. Henry smiled an apology and moved to the exit, hoping they would leave him alone. Behind him, he could hear the young girl telling her family he'd been in a bad fight and now had three legs and could she please have a third leg for Christmas.

As the door closed softly, he heard the mother's reply. "We'll write a letter to Santa and ask him, Jenny. How does that sound?"

A letter.

The morning's newspaper flashed into his mind, and with an eager limp, Henry made his way home. He had a letter of his own to write.

Dear SANTA and mRs. Claus,

Mom sed to rite to you for a 3rd leg. I saw an old maN in the stor and he had a 3rd leg and I need 1 to. It wil help me run fastr and beat Johnny in a race. I need to bet Johnny becuz I wood like to be better then him at something. I am not very good at things.

Pleas can I have a 3rd leg for Cristmas?

From

JennY L.

P.S. I kno it's only Octobr but I thot you mite need time to make the leg.

5

Friday, October 14, 1966
11:07 AM

Stokes called for her in a strangled voice. Brenda retied her hair and pushed away from her cramped desk, steeling herself for the conversation. No doubt he would reject everything she tried to say. She'd need to tread carefully.

Entering the smoke-filled office, Brenda swallowed a cough. A cigarette waggled between Stokes's lips as he muttered to himself. As anticipated, ash littered the floor beside him, grinding into the fibers of the carpet. His desire to look good had never extended to his surroundings, and Brenda had stopped trying to keep the place spotless. If he didn't care, neither did she.

Pursing her lips, she met his dark gaze. "Sir?"

"The men say ten million." He stubbed out his cigarette and narrowed his eyes at her.

"Ten million," she repeated, slightly surprised to hear the figure, though she'd known it would be high. For months, the crew had been sending red flags upstairs to land on deaf ears. The three jammed chutes? According to Stokes they didn't need to be fixed; the crew could walk the letters around the building themselves. The threats of a strike? He'd laughed at the idea of colored workers going without a paycheck.

He no longer toured the building. Refusing to stop on any other floor, he took the elevator to and from his office each day and instructed her that only certain individuals were allowed to get time with him—none of whom were the right people to deal with a backlog of this scale. It made her want to cry, working for such an incompetent man who had wormed his way into the upper echelons by schmoozing with the right people while she was left to spend her days typing out unintelligible directives on a Royal Quiet Deluxe from the fifties.

That would all be over soon. Now that the entire city knew about the issue, he couldn't hide behind his indifference. Surely.

"Do they have a plan?" she asked, her voice taking on a higher pitch. "Any idea how they'll shift it, or when we can reopen?"

He lit another smoke and leaned back. "Don't know. I haven't asked."

Right. Okay. She took a seat across from him. "Don't you think"—she crossed her legs at the ankle—"now that everyone is aware of the shutdown, we should try to handle the crisis?"

He was on his feet before she even finished the word. "Don't call it a crisis." The end of his smoke glowed as he jabbed it in her direction. "Like I told Chuck, it's just a little backlog."

"I mean, ten million isn't exactly little."

His voice lowered to a growl. "Brenda. I need you to do me a favor. Think you can do that?" He made her name sound like a disease. "Get the word *crisis* out of your head. This is not the disaster you, the crew, or even the *Tribune* are making it out to be."

She waited for him to continue.

"In fact, I say we ask for a correction. Yes. That's it. Call and demand they print a correction in tomorrow's paper."

"And what would you have them correct?"

"They said we're shut down indefinitely."

"We *are* shut down indefinitely."

"The people of Chicago don't need to know that. Call Chuck and tell him to say we're only going to be closed for a maximum of two weeks. That everything is under control."

Brenda fought the urge to roll her eyes. It would be impossible to clear ten million letters in two weeks. But what did she know?

6

Friday, October 14, 1966
11:15 AM

What did Brenda know, anyway? Stokes paced in front of his office window, flicking ash onto the floor and stepping over it with polished shoes. He made a mental note to comment on her lack of cleaning lately.

"Breakdown in management, my ass," he said to the now-empty room. He couldn't believe what the *Tribune* had reported. Stokes had been managing the facility for years, and there hadn't been a single issue the whole time. Suddenly a few extra letters got jammed and they wanted to blame him?

Clearly these things were beyond his control.

Now he had a target on his back. The postmaster general had already been on the phone, saying he would be flying in early next week from DC *to better understand the crisis and the cause of the shutdown*.

Stokes really needed people to stop using that word. Everything was fine. O'Brien didn't need to fly in on his governmental high horse. Brenda didn't need to sneak suggestions into every conversation. Chicago residents didn't need to climb the stairs to see if the post office really was shut.

If they would just leave him alone, Stokes could solve the tiny, insignificant matter of the backlog.

In his own time.

Until then, he had more important things to focus on. The latest Montgomery Ward catalog had arrived, and Stokes needed a new suit.

7

Friday, October 14, 1966
2:08 PM

In the row ahead of him, Jerry doodled the Batman logo in the corner of a paper, tracing over the lines to make them darker.

Roger leaned forward. "You messed up the wings. They should be rounder." He made a circular motion with his hands.

Jerry shot him a look and moved the paper to the other side of his desk, out of Roger's line of sight.

Roger tapped his leg. "Just trying to help. It's important the proportions are right; otherwise it looks like the 1944 version, with no head and sharper wings. They made the logo rounder over the years so it could take up more space on his chest. Did you know that? Also, they added the ellipse around the whole thing. If you ask me—"

From the front of the room, Mrs. Carmichael cleared her throat.

Roger looked up to find everyone staring at him.

"Do you have something you need to share with the class, Roger?" Mrs. Carmichael had a voice harder than the ruler she wasn't afraid to use. "It must be more important than learning about subjective pronouns." She raised an eyebrow at him.

"On no. I think subjective pronouns are just as important as creating an accurate representation of the Batman logo, Mrs. Carmichael." His leg jiggled under the desk.

Around him, his classmates sniggered.

Mrs. Carmichael bared her teeth. "Get to the back of the room, Roger. And do not disturb my class again." She turned back to the chalkboard and resumed the lesson.

An unkind smile spread across Jerry's face. Roger regretted trying to help him. Jerry was never going to listen to anything Roger had to say.

No one did.

He gathered up his notebooks and moved to a desk in the back of the room, facing the wall. Behind him, Mrs. Carmichael made an inaccurate claim about antecedents and Roger bit his lip to stop from correcting her.

The radio-making equipment remained where he'd left it the last time he'd been relegated to the corner. The instructions had long fallen down the side of the desk. It didn't matter; he no longer needed them. Once complete, this would be the fifth radio he'd made. A week ago, he'd overheard Mrs. Carmichael telling the secretary, Mrs. Walker, the whole faculty would be getting one for Christmas.

He reached for the wire strippers and removed insulation from the end of a wire, tongue poking out between his teeth.

"If I just cut a little bit back," he said, trying to keep his voice low, "and add you to the circuit, like that . . ." He used the red jumper wire to connect the hole directly above the seven pin of the op-amp with the nearest free hole in the top row of the breadboard.

The noise of the classroom faded away as Roger focused on the task.

The first thing his mom would say, after getting a call from the school, would be *What do you have to say for yourself?* If Roger could get the radio finished before class ended, at least he'd have something to show for the disruption.

And maybe, if she wasn't too busy, she would listen to him explain how it was made for once.

865 Blackwell Street
Chicago, IL 60611

My dearest Linda,

I've finished the credenza and it's a delight, if I do say so myself. You're going to love it. I know Stan wanted to keep it cherry walnut, the way his grandmother had it, but Goldie gifted it to me. And you know I prefer things that aren't so bland.

That's the Aquarius in me, I suppose.

How's Dennis, by the way? We just have to have you both over for dinner soon. I'll make that ham casserole you enjoy so much. And, of course, we'll invite Henry. To give him something to do; get him out of that house for a while.

Speaking of houses, have you decided on a fabric for your curtains? The turquoise you showed me last week would be wonderful against those plain white walls of yours. Much better than the gray that Dennis picked. I can't believe you even gave him a say in the matter. Men have no business trying to impart their design wisdom upon us. Or their ill-informed thoughts about the universe. (I haven't *quite* forgiven your brother for his opinion on what to do under a full moon.)

Anyhoo, let's get together soon!

Flo

8

Friday, October 14, 1966
4:48 PM

Henry knocked louder, feeling the door shudder under his insistence. Angling his body toward the hedges, he hovered on the small gray slab of concrete that doubled as a front porch, trying to keep his balance.

The door swung open midknock.

He stumbled back, knee screaming at the sudden movement. "Blasted hell—" He caught himself when he saw it was Flora standing before him.

Flo Byrd's staunch belief in the power of the planets, her flowing dresses, and her delight at multicolored wigs left Henry uneasy. She had a way of getting straight to the point in a lyrical voice that left Henry wondering whether he was being praised or admonished.

He had first met Flo at the Berghoff. He'd been there with Stan, enjoying a quiet beer and engaging in a mild debate about whether Peter Woodward's new girlfriend was a distant Kennedy (Stan for, Henry against) when in stormed a crazed flamingo. At least, that's what Henry's first thought had been. His second had been why said flamingo (who was actually a tiny wisp of a woman with shockingly pink hair) had reached for Stan's beer, taken a large gulp, and proceeded to tell them that the current aspect of Mars meant they should be extra careful not to get injured, as everyone was more prone to disaster just then.

Stan had fretted over the possibility of being hit by a car. Henry had worried savage pink birds were out to get him.

"Henry," Flora sang, reaching a delicate hand out to grab him before he fell onto his back. "Come in." Her pencil-thin eyebrows, drawn on every morning, were raised and her hair, now a soft brown, was parted in the middle and curled in at the chin. It was, Henry knew, her newest wig and gave her the bookish look of an erudite librarian. It was a stark contrast to the lemon-sherbet hair she'd had last week, and Henry was glad for it. One needn't always look like they had alopecia, in his opinion.

As she helped him inside, Henry caught the faint whiff of orange-scented cleaner.

"Come through to the kitchen," she said, floating down the hall.

The assault on his eyes when walking into the Byrd residence was something Henry had never become accustomed to. Interlocking strips of teal and fuchsia covered the walls, and a gaudy gold mirror hung above a sponge-painted credenza that had recently belonged to Stan's grandmother. Henry cringed to think what Goldie would say if she could see what Flo had done to it. Henry was glad he and Elsie preferred the calming hues of white and cream.

He squeezed his eyes shut briefly before heading past the grand piano (his friend's pride and joy) and down the hall.

In the kitchen, Flo handed him a glass of tepid water. He could see Stan in the garden through the glass doors, bending over a pile of stacked logs, pulling at something in the ground.

"We have a mole," Flo said, following his gaze. "In August, I told Stan he'd better block that hole right up to stop the vermin coming back; otherwise it'll be wanting to get into the house to keep warm from the early frost. You think he listened to me?" She took a sip from her own glass. "Now, just because I don't want it in the house doesn't mean I can't appreciate it. Moles symbolize journeys of self-exploration and inner investigation, you know."

Henry stared at her.

"They have a capacity to remain undetected and avoid notice, even in difficult circumstances. It's fascinating."

"Mmm, I see she's filling you in on the mystical attributes of our little badger." Stan shook the dirt off his boots as he came in the back door. Flecks of mud landed in a spray around the coir mat.

"It's a mole," Flo corrected as she rinsed out her glass and left the room, skirts billowing behind her.

"Mmm, right. A mole." Stan slumped into a chair and leaned back on two legs, hands behind his head. Henry pulled out the chair across from him and sank down onto the orange plastic. Not wanting the water but not wanting to be rude, he wrapped his hand around the glass.

"This weather sure has settled into my bones," he said.

Stan's eyes were closed, chin tilted toward the ceiling. Anyone else and Henry would have assumed they weren't listening to him. Not Stan. Ever since meeting more than a decade ago, they'd been close, despite their seventeen-year age gap. "Your knee?"

"Yeah. And just about every other bone in my body. I could entertain a crowd for hours with cracks and creaks. You could add the harmony."

"Mmm, we'd be a sellout act."

Henry rubbed his knee absently. "The doctor told me not to think about it. He says the more I focus on the pain, the more pain I feel. I told him I'd show him what pain felt like if he kept talking like that."

Stan chuckled. Henry continued. "He's only a child. Barely out of med school, and he thinks he has wisdom he can impart to me? No way. I told him all about my war, and you know what he did? He nodded along, wrote a few lines in my file, and then told me once more that I should try to focus less on the pain."

"And have you?"

"Have I what?"

"Thought about it less?"

Henry twirled the glass between his hands. "I don't know, I can't remember."

A smile tugged at the corners of Stan's mouth. He leaned forward until his chair leveled out. "Easier said than done. Not thinking."

"Exactly. So, tell me about this critter you've got."

Henry listened as Stan told him about the trap he had finagled that hadn't worked and the three new holes that had appeared in the garden overnight. So far, Stan had tried overwatering and underwatering. Cheese had been used to lure the creature out, only for the birds to get there first. Stan had suggested poison; Flo suggested flowers. Now he was on the hunt for marigolds in October because she wouldn't let him dig up the ones in the front yard to plant in the back. It had been weeks, and all Stan could think about was the damn pest.

"And don't tell me not to think about it," Stan said with a wink. "That doesn't work."

"What?" Henry thought he had missed something.

Stan shook his head, glancing away. "Never mind." He rose from his chair, joints popping as he stood.

"Boy, this weather is really settling into the old bones. Have I told you what the doctor said to me?" Henry asked.

"Yes." Stan sat down slowly with a fresh glass and took a sip. "You told me. But why don't you tell me again."

"Oh no. I hate when people repeat themselves. Say"—Henry couldn't read his friend's expression—"has there been any news?"

"Mmm, 'bout what?"

"I read about the shutdown in the paper," Henry said. "Have you heard anything?"

Stan's gaze shifted to a calendar on the wall that hadn't been changed. A nondescript field of flowers depicted the month of September, where Flora's messy handwriting detailed dates to remember. "Yes, I know about the shutdown."

Before the Zone Improvement Plan had been implemented, Stan had managed the receiving division of the post office. His team was the largest in the building, making sure everything ran smoothly throughout the process, from when a letter arrived in the building to when it left.

Long receiving platforms were accessed by ramps on Harrison Street. Stan's floor handled oversized parcels and money orders. Local letters were sent to the fourth floor for sorting. Damaged parcels got rewrapped on floor six, and anything foreign went up to seven. The eighth floor focused on first-class mail, circulars, daily papers, and out-of-town deliveries. On the ninth floor, the Nixie Section deciphered addresses that were illegible or incomplete. The Dead Letter Office was the keeper of undeliverable mail.

When they announced the Zone Improvement Plan, or ZIP, as Stan liked to call it, he'd been first choice to lead the transition. With such an innate familiarity with the whole sorting process, Stan understood how the new system would improve the speed of mail delivery. He also understood, long before upper management, how long it would take to get people on board.

"People are slow to change," Stan would say. "They need time to adjust."

No one was ready to add a five-digit number to the front of their letters. So Stan starting prioritizing mail that included a ZIP code. If it had a code, it got delivered first. This meant that all around Chicago, people were getting government correspondence, magazines, and advertising flyers faster than a note from a neighbor. Flora used to joke she could deliver a letter across town faster than her husband could. She wasn't wrong.

That was three years ago, and the Zone Improvement Plan was still a work in progress. Stan was their very own Mr. ZIP. Except a little less orange.

He would know what to do. "They haven't called me in yet. I don't know why. I must be needed," Henry said.

Stan sighed. His long fingers tapped a tune into the table impatiently. Even when he wasn't at a piano, Stan was playing music. "You aren't needed—"

Henry slammed down a shaky fist. Water splashed, and he swiped at it with his left hand. "You're telling me the post office I dedicated forty years of my life to doesn't need me during the biggest crisis it's ever seen?" He had time to spare, and even with a bad knee, he could move around faster than anyone gave him credit for. He should be the first person they called in to help during a crisis.

Didn't they know how eager he was to lend a hand?

Stan's fingers stilled midtune. "Henry." His voice was soft. "You weren't . . . Ah, you never . . . Never mind. Look. There's nothing for you to do. They don't need you at the post office during this mess. Hell, they've basically said they don't need me there. They don't like that I've been telling them for months we can't shift this much mail. Stokes has refused to see me the past two times I've tried to get a meeting with him, and Aldo said they're only letting a few people into the building right now. Aside from the obvious"—Henry didn't know what the obvious was—"I don't see how you can help. Unless you're going to break in and deliver the letters yourself." Stan's laugh was like a motorcycle engine, rumbling through the kitchen as he resumed an imaginary song with his hands.

Henry puffed out his cheeks, unsure why Stan was being so cryptic.

There were so many things he wanted to say. Questions he wanted to ask. Nothing was solid enough to speak aloud. He took a sip of water he didn't remember pouring. Outside the window, leaves blew from the old maple and swirled to the ground in slow circles. He thought about what Flo had said about the animal. *They have a capacity to remain undetected and avoid notice, even in difficult circumstances.*

A bright leaf pulled away from a branch as an idea started to take shape.

9

Saturday, October 15, 1966
8:09 AM

A crumpled piece of paper littered the floor. It lay a few feet from the garbage can, as if it had bounced off the rim. With a grunt, Henry inched to the edge of his seat and reached for it with his cane. The address on the front of the envelope was written in his own hand.

Addressed to the post office.

With a butter knife, he tore open the flap and scanned the contents, the day-old memory flooding back. The post office was overwhelmed, unable to deal with a backlog. The newspaper had been unclear, leaving gaps in the story he couldn't fill. They shouldn't have been so vague. He reread the choice words he'd written the night before, demanding someone take responsibility for the issue and fix the problem. The words were slanted, as if they'd been written in a rush, the page filled with spelling mistakes he hadn't noticed. At the bottom, he'd signed his name.

Tucked behind the letter, on a small sheet of scrap paper, he'd mapped out a plan. Rereading his words, Henry's heart began to pound. Would it be possible?

There was only one way to find out.

Black ballpoint pens, lead pencils, and a lone eraser whose soft pink nub was now stained a deep metallic gray were spread around him in a bric-a-brac sea. Beside Henry, lined and smudged drawings done in an uneven hand detailed a large building. A half-eaten sandwich had been forgotten on a plate by the window. A worn trunk sat open beside the couch. The brass hinges were tarnished, the leather inside cracked.

It was filled to the brim with letters.

Henry pushed the contents aside, searching for one in particular—his hiring letter from the post office. He tried to recall the words, but they floated just outside his vision. If he found it, he knew the memory would come back.

Things were a little hazy at times. Ideas died on his tongue. Speech swirled in his throat. The very core of his being felt just out of reach.

As if everything, and nothing, mattered.

Henry shifted the top of the pile and dug deeper. The trunk had been deteriorating in the attic for years, covered in a thick layer of dust. There were other things up there he hadn't expected to find. The fabric bust donning Elsie's lace wedding dress, the crisp white now faded to an aged amber. His father's old phonograph, the manivelle hanging at an odd angle. A train set from when William was a boy, missing the caboose. An old copy of *The Adventures of Huckleberry Finn*, well loved and worn.

It had taken hours to lug the trunk downstairs, first down the precariously thin ladder he had pulled from the ceiling with a long, slender rod they kept tucked in the upstairs linen closet, and then down the staircase to the front room.

It was only a few feet wide, and he'd tried to tuck it under his elbow, but that made his arm stick out at an awkward angle so he couldn't see the steps. He'd thought about tossing the trunk from the attic onto the landing but worried about the damage that would cause, inside and outside the box. Rigging a pully system was out of the question when he couldn't remember where the rope was. And going through the contents in the attic would have been impossible with so little light.

In the end, he'd nudged it to the edge of the attic door, climbed onto the top step, tugged at it with one hand so it rested against the crown of his head, and taken the ladder rung by rung until he was close enough to the ground to lower it with care.

He then sat on top of it for the better part of an hour to catch his breath.

Blowing a raspberry into the empty room, Henry kept searching. Near the bottom he found a birth certificate as old as he and a photograph of William when he was a baby, in a little white bonnet that made his ears stick out.

There were multiple letters from a candy factory—some place called Ferrara Pan—including a newspaper clipping honoring him for a Lifetime Achievement Award and calling him a true confectionary hero.

Confectionary? It sparked something in his mind, a niggling that wanted to break free, but it was gone before he could catch it.

Oh well.

Beneath them he found a letter from his mother, written on brittle paper. The chemicals mixed in the air, hitting his nostrils with their acidity, and he breathed through his nose, enjoying the musty aroma.

He reread the words she'd written all those years ago. Words of pain and duty and adventure. Was he up for another journey? Forcing himself up, Henry picked his way from the room on the balls of his feet.

He would need to enlist Stan's help.

✉

April 14, 1918

My dearest Henry,

You're off to do your duty, though I hope you realize now it won't be everything you expect it to be. Beauty may be hard to come by at first glance. I imagine you will have to look at everything very closely to see something that might spark inspiration. Perhaps you will find it in a stranger's kindness, or a soldier's rare smile.

I fear the world is slowly turning black. All we have now, my dear boy, are letters. Making their way across the Atlantic from my hand to yours and back again. Please don't forget to write. To us, and to Elsie. Your father says I've already started to pace a path in the floor.

Letters will connect us, always. I look forward to reading your words and hearing your voice on the wind.

Never forget life is an adventure. Even in the darkest of times.

All my love,

Ma

10

Saturday, October 15, 1966
6:17 PM

Stan pushed his roast around the plate. He didn't have an appetite—his nerves were taking up too much space—but he knew if he said that out loud, a frown would drag the corners of Flo's mouth to the floor. The last time he'd skipped a meal, she'd buzzed about the movement of the earth and its axis.

He certainly didn't want to start *that* conversation again. Taking a small bite of potato, he forced himself to swallow. Bursts of garlic and Parmesan filled his taste buds.

He wondered if Henry had eaten anything other than plain toast all week. His friend went through more loaves than anyone else Stan knew. Was he getting enough nutrients? Stan didn't understand enough about vitamins to know.

He stabbed a carrot with his fork.

Across from him, Flo flipped through the most recent Avon catalog, painted eyebrows knit together in concentration. A large pink jar graced the front cover, filled with a miracle concoction only women cared about. She'd be wanting to put in an order soon, if all the downturned page corners were anything to go by.

"Mmm," Stan exhaled, pushing his plate away. He wasn't in the mood to pretend. Flo looked at the half-eaten meal and opened her mouth at the same time a knock came at the front door.

"I'll get it." Stan jumped up and hurried away from her admonitions. Henry stood before him in a rumpled shirt, gripping his cane tightly.

"Henry," Stan said, surprised to see his friend out so close to nightfall. "Come in."

By the time they entered the kitchen, Flo had cleared the table and started the dishes, suds kissing her elbows.

"Morning, Flo," Henry said as he sank into the chair and leaned his cane against the wall beside him.

"It's evening, Henry dear." She set a glass on the sideboard. "Have you eaten?"

"I had some toast earlier. With grape jelly. Do you happen to know why Elsie needs so much grape jelly? We must have thirty jars of the stuff."

Stan covered a laugh with a cough.

"No," Flora said. "No, I don't . . . right." She spun around, brushing her wet hands across the front of her star-print apron. "You'll be needing more than toast." She piled roast beef, mashed potatoes, and boiled carrots onto a plate before slathering it all in gravy. On the side of the plate, she added a thick slice of corn bread.

Henry's eyes lit up as he took a forkful.

Flora left the room, no doubt heading to her vanity to see what bottles of lotion needed refilling. Stan knew that Avon order was imminent.

Henry pushed the carrots to the edge of the plate and ate around them. Definitely not enough nutrients.

"How was your morning?" Stan set a glass of water beside Henry's plate and took the seat opposite. "Do anything exciting?"

"Yes," Henry mumbled around a mouthful of food. "It was excellent." He moved another carrot out of the way. "I caught up on some sleep and found some memories in the attic I forgot were there. Elsie has always loved hiding things away, hasn't she. There were so many surprises above our heads this whole time." He finished the last bite.

"Mmm, how did you manage to get up there on your own?" Stan asked. "You could have fallen off the ladder, or gotten stuck, or passed out from the lack of oxygen at the top of the house . . ." He ticked the worries off on slender fingers. "You know you can always call me over to help."

Henry smoothed out a crease in the tablecloth. "I think it's pretty foolproof," he said after a moment.

Stan rubbed the back of his neck. "What's foolproof?"

"My plan. Well, your plan, actually." Henry waggled his eyebrows. "To deliver the letters."

Stan felt as if his lungs might fall in on themselves. He never knew what parts of a day Henry would cling to. "Oh—"

"Just listen." Henry leaned forward. "With Elsie visiting William . . ." Stan shifted in his chair. This couldn't be good. Henry pressed on. "It's the perfect time to focus on what our next steps should be. Now, of course it will be easier if you agree to help—don't look at me like that—and I think the cops will be thrown off if—"

"The cops? What the devil are you talking about?"

"You've still got that black coat, right? We're going to need it."

Stan twisted his wedding ring round and round as Henry detailed his plan. He glanced at the door to make sure Flo wasn't listening in. He knew what she would say if she could hear them now.

The planetary advice would be endless.

Henry finished, after doubling around and back on himself when he forgot one thought and half remembered the next, the ghost of a smile on his lips. Stan eyed his friend. He had hoped—no, expected—that Henry would forget the flippant joke he'd made about delivering letters on his own. It was preposterous. It was unheard of.

It was so typically Henry.

"But . . . I just . . . why?" Stan asked, trying to wrap his head around the idea.

Henry shrugged. "That old trunk I got down from the attic—stop fidgeting, I was fine—it was filled with letters. Ones from when William was learning to write. All his *e*'s were backwards." He chuckled. "And ones that Elsie and I sent each other during the war. She used to write me every day. Did you know that?" Stan hadn't. "Anyways, I saved them all. These little pieces from my past. I can't imagine never having received them. And all I can think about are all those letters stranded in the post office. What happens if they never get delivered?"

"They will."

"You don't know that. You don't. And I just . . . I need to do something to help . . . not just the post office, but those people too. All those people waiting for their letters."

Stan wanted to protest. To drone on endlessly about how it was a terrible, impossible, wild notion Henry would never achieve. To spill the fear that clawed at him, painting a picture of everything that could (and probably would!) go wrong.

Despite the eagerness on his friend's face, he wanted, more than anything, to say no.

"Mmm," he sighed, gagging on apprehension. "What do you need me to do?"

June 12, 1918
Private Henry Walton

My dear beloved husband,

Just a line, my darling, in answer to the two letters I had yesterday morning. Thank you very much for the photos from the front. They're quite nice but not so good as the first one you had taken. The sweater doesn't look too bad on you. I'd have thought it would be wider, but it looks okay.

I do think you look as if you have gone a lot thinner. It seems as if this party is getting us both down, because you look too thin and everybody tells me I'm like a shadow.

But never mind. I'll make up for it when you're home. I'll feel a lot happier when we're together again and then I'll be found to put on weight.

I'm glad, darling, that you're feeling better, but I wish you were here. Then I could look after you. I'm longing to see you and hold you ever so tight in my arms and kiss you. You mean the world to me. Without you, life wouldn't be worth living.

Bye for now. I'll write again in the morning.

For always,

Elsie

11

Saturday, October 15, 1966
8:32 PM

Roger rolled a pair of marbles in his hand, feet banging against the side of his bed. The Batman logo on bright yellow, with its perfect curves, contrasted with a green cat eye. A full jar sat on the small wooden table beside him. On the top was his favorite taw—a clear shooter with streaks of indigo and ocher inside.

He'd used it to knock Pete out of the ring the last time they'd played, claiming a hard-fought victory he wasn't used to. He could still remember the song he'd made up on the spot; could still hear his friend's laugh.

That had been more than a year ago.

Roger's shoulders sank. He held the cat eye up to the light and wondered what he could trade the collection for. "Maybe Jerry will swap something for the Batman one?" he said to the room. "It would help him get the logo right on future drawings, that's for sure." A small smile formed at the thought of Jerry pulling out the marble in class and having it confiscated.

His mom popped her head around the corner, hair already in a satin bonnet for the night. "Oh." She scanned the room. "I thought I heard you talking to someone."

"No." His feet picked up their pace.

"Why don't you go out, Rog. You could take your bike? Go see what's happening at the Hall. I saw a poster for a dance the other day; I'm sure it's tonight."

"I've got two left feet." He jiggled his left leg in her direction. "Remember the time you tried to teach me the Mashed Potato and I kicked over the vase? We were picking up shards of porcelain for weeks, and every time you found a new one you waved it at me and said I was never to dance again."

The vase had been a wedding gift. He'd heard her tell a friend one day she was glad it had been destroyed.

She laid a hand on her chest before lowering it quickly. A small smile didn't quite make its way up her face. "I know. I just thought you could go make some new friends. New memories." Her fingers worried at the hem of her nightgown. "You can't spend your whole life in this room."

They'd had this conversation before. Or, at least, a version of it.

Ever since Pete's dad had been relocated to Detroit, it had felt like his mom was trying to get him *up and out!* every day. What didn't she understand? He didn't want to make new memories. And he especially didn't want to make new friends.

Her gaze landed on the marbles in his hands. He dropped them back in the jar before she could suggest they play a game.

"It's all right." He rose. "I've got some homework to catch up on. Tonight is not the night for an adventure."

12

Sunday, October 16, 1966
10:00 PM

Henry pulled the scarf tighter around his neck. Beside him, Stan was dressed head to toe in black. The fabric strained against his stomach, and a strip of skin showed at irregular intervals between the bottom of one garment and the top of another.

As they passed Lexington, they could just make out the shadow of their destination.

At this time of night, only a few headlights were making their way home, passing under one side of the imposing building and miraculously coming out the other. When the post office first expanded, there had been uproar across the city as people heard the plan to block the new Congress Expressway. Hundreds lined up in the streets outside the construction zone, holding signs that cried of injustice and political corruption. A compromise, they had called it, when finally, after days of protesting, the decision was made to leave a gaping hole at the base of the building. For two decades it had sat that way: a massive building perched atop an empty hole. Nowadays, the road passed straight through. Henry still couldn't wrap his head around it.

Above them, a crescent moon nicked the night sky.

"Flo says the moon's in Virgo," Stan had mentioned as they set off. "It means we need to be more organized, apparently."

Henry had laughed him off with a shrug, but now, as he looked up, he couldn't help wondering if Flo's obsession with the movement of the planets might just come in handy. Organization was, after all, the mark of a good crime.

Plus, his motto was *Preparation is key.*

They continued the last few blocks in silence as the city fell asleep around them. Henry tapped his pocket to make sure he still had the paper. A block later, he tapped it again. When they stopped in front of the building, he pulled it out, flattening the creases. He held it at an angle, under a streetlamp. Parts of the paper were smudged where he'd had to erase and go back over the page with thick new lines. Half the building was missing because he couldn't fit it all.

"What's this?" Stan whispered.

Henry turned the drawing around so Stan could see it better, his thumb covering a note in the top corner that reminded him what he'd drawn. "The post office. We'll go in here." In contrast to the real doors before them, his image looked like wet noodles. He leaned his weight to one side and held out the paper. "We'll get in with your key," he said, nodding to the first of nine doors in a long row of brass and glass. "I'll keep watch a couple of steps down to make sure no one is passing by on . . . what street is this? Never mind. When you've got the door open, you whistle a little tune, nothing too complicated, and I'll know we're good to go. And then *you'll* know we're good to go when I appear at the door, because I'll have double-checked the coast is clear."

Stan looked from Henry to the drawing to the building.

Henry looked from the building to the drawing to Stan.

"Henry, your drawing—"

"I know, I know." Henry waved the paper under the soft light. "It's not a hundred percent accurate. But it should do."

"What's this?" Stan pointed to a large rectangle etched onto the page in thick lead lines, covered in small round circles.

"The elevator bank. We'll make our way across the lobby, quiet and slow, towards the elevators. Then we'll—"

Stan interrupted. "The elevators aren't here." He jabbed at the drawing. "They're here." He moved his finger to a spot across from the door they would enter through, which was not at the opposite end of the long marble lobby as the drawing suggested. Instead of turning left, Stan had them going straight.

"No, they're here," Henry snapped, "where I've drawn them." He squinted his eyes shut and tried to picture the inside of the building.

"They're not. Look, Henry, your memory—"

"Is fine!" he cried. "I know this building inside and out, so unless they moved the elevators . . ." Of course. They'd moved the elevators. In a recent remodel, or perhaps because they were too far away from the doors to begin with and people had complained.

He let out a soft laugh.

Stan vacillated. At his side, his fingers played out a rapid string of notes. "I don't know about this."

"It's fine. Look, you whistle. I'll check the street and follow. Then we'll head up in the elevator." Henry's plan had them going to the second floor, a receiving area for the whole building, and loading up two bags he'd found in the attic nestled between other long-forgotten wares. There was no logic to the things Elsie saved. He couldn't think of a reason to ever own large burlap bags. Until now.

He crumpled the paper with one hand and shoved it back into his pocket.

Stan didn't move. "They hired a new security guard a few years back. This guy, Fletcher, he never sits down. He spends the whole night shuffling around the building to make sure everything's okay. We're going to have to be silent." He gave a warning glance at Henry's cane.

Henry tucked it under his arm to prove he could move without it. He swayed only slightly.

"That elevator is going to make too much noise," Stan continued. "We'd better take the stairs. Unless you want to turn back."

Henry shook his head and narrowed his eyes at his friend. They glanced at the building one last time. It was darker than the sky behind it and looked as if it had been cut from the fabric of the universe. A car honked a few blocks away, reminding them they weren't alone.

"Think of the badger," Henry hissed.

"The what?"

"Your badger. Flo said they avoid notice. She said even in difficult circumstances they're sneaky. We can be like the badger. Just think about it. We can get in and out undetected. And when we do, we'll be heroes. Bringing letters to those who need them most. Delivering words that are meant for someone at the very moment they're needed. Watching people's faces light up at being united with something that is meant just for them. Oh, we can definitely be like the badger, Stan. This is our chance to do something *different.*"

Stan didn't say anything. Henry thought he muttered "mole" under his breath, but it must have been the wind.

Pinching the bridge of his nose, Stan took a deep breath. He climbed toward the door, pausing occasionally to look around.

In the back of his mind, Henry could hear Elsie's dismay at his plan. She would have waggled a finger at him, letting him know in a loud, clear voice that it was none of his business and he didn't need to get involved and didn't Henry realize there were other people who could save the day?

Leave it, she would plead. *Let someone else deliver those letters.*

Stan stopped at the door, fiddling with the key. He twisted it around and tried again. His shoulders were hunched in concentration. Minutes passed, and as his friend struggled to open the door, Henry questioned everything they were about to do. Who would deliver the letters if they couldn't get in?

Elsie's voice pulsed in Henry's ears.

When it came, the whistle was soft, floating on the night air, and Henry felt a tingle dance up his spine. Never had he felt so needed, so certain this path had been laid out before him for a reason.

With a hasty glance to the left and the right, he pushed Elsie from his mind and stumbled up the stairs, passing under an etched bronze sign.

They were in.

13

Sunday, October 16, 1966
10:26 PM

If the lights in the lobby had been on, they would have seen tiles stretching out before their feet in alternating shades of cream and white. In the center, black, white, and brown tiles formed a compass pointing in every direction. The ceiling soared high above them. Huge windows spanned entire walls.

Stan relocked the door behind them. They crept past the shuttered windows of the Postal Savings Bank, an empty information counter, and a row of drop boxes.

The door to the stairwell was beside the elevator bank. Henry kept his cane tucked under his right arm and held his left arm out at an angle to balance his weight. He trundled forward, cringing at the scuff of his shoes on the tile. The sound felt amplified in the open space. Ahead of him, Stan tiptoed on the balls of his feet, tapping out a silent tune as he moved.

Henry huffed and shuffled faster.

Step by step, they ascended two flights, stopping every so often for the noise to disperse when either a foot or a cane hit a creak in the stairs. Henry gripped the railing as they moved, coming to a stop as Stan inched open a door.

The receiving room was vast. And everywhere, there were letters.

Huge metal bins on casters were lined up along every wall, overflowing with mini mounds in five-foot intervals. A wide conveyor belt snaked its way through the open space, now a river of mail swallowing everything in its wake. Dozens of mail slots on floor-to-ceiling wooden shelves were full to bursting. In the far corner, desks and chairs were lined up in uneven rows. One desk was piled so high the top was an invisible apex. Packages were stacked on top of packages along the far wall, more precarious than the china cabinet Elsie forbade Henry from opening lest he cause a stack of porcelain bowls to topple at an inopportune moment. Only Elsie could open it properly and retrieve something from its depths when their more particular guests came for a visit—namely, her mother, who would have been criticizing Henry's every move if she'd been there.

White envelopes coated the floor under his feet like the first snowfall of the year, each address lost under the letter on top and the one on top of that.

"Holy hell," Henry breathed.

"I know," Stan said. "It's been like this for months. We can't keep up with the pace. Nothing is being received properly anymore; the men are just sending anything they can into random chutes for the other teams to deal with." He picked one from the top of a pile and read the front. "No ZIP code." He tossed it back down. "Where do you want to start?" Stan handed Henry one of the burlap bags. Their half-baked plan, less organized than the Virgo moon would have predicted, was to fill the sacks with as many letters as possible and return to Henry's house as fast as they could.

Henry looked around, eyes still adjusting to the dim light of the overhead bulb. "Anywhere, I guess."

"Mmm, right. Chicago addresses only?"

Though logical, Henry knew it would take too long. "No," he countered. "Don't worry about that. Let's just load up and get out of here."

They set off in opposite directions. Stan left, Henry right.

He weaved around the conveyor belt and made his way to the stacks along one wall. Each one was higher than the last, as if they'd been in competition when operations stopped. He started with the stack in front of him, not bothering to read what anything said as he shoved them by the handful into the burlap sack's greedy mouth. He moved as fast as he could. When he'd lobbed the top off several piles, he turned to the conveyor belt, trying to make a dent in the river of white.

For every envelope he grabbed, another slid into its place.

There was no method to his choosing. He climbed over one pile only to grab two from the next. He took them from desks and chairs. Rescued them from underfoot before they were trampled. One from here, another from over there. One in a sky-blue envelope, one in light pink. From up high and down low, from this side and that. He heaved them from hoppers and rescued a handful from the mouth of a chute.

Little by little, Henry filled his bag until it was almost too heavy to lift. He looked around the space, breath hitching when he saw he hadn't made an impact in the chaos. It looked the same as before.

With a sigh, he dragged the bag behind him toward the door.

He stopped to catch his breath only twice. The second time, as he inhaled deeply through his nose and the bag rested against his leg, a letter caught his eye. It lay on a bare shelf, probably the only uncluttered space in the entire building. Was it important? He turned it over. On the back, a gold seal gave it an air of superiority. Henry rubbed a thumb across the raised edges.

Tossing it into the bag, he made his way to the door.

Stan's bag heaved. Henry pulled his up beside it and leaned over to slow his heart. "How many do you think we have?"

"Mmm. A few hundred or so."

Henry stood up, hips creaking, and eyed the bags. Three hundred letters (give or take) for him to deliver. Three hundred letters he would get into the hands of their rightful owners. He felt a flutter in his stomach. A growing responsibility he hadn't fully thought through. He would need to go to all these houses, talk to all these people. Explain that he was . . . what, again? He shook his head and scrubbed a hand over his face. It would be fine. He would just say whatever came to mind. No one was going to interrogate him.

Stan asked if he was ready to go.

Henry didn't know. He was torn between wanting to stay and collect more, oh so many more, and dumping the bag out at his feet before hightailing it out of there. He scanned the room. A white sea spread out before them and crashed into every wall, swelling above every surface, pooling in every corner.

There was no end. This would have to do.

Stan switched off the bulb and was reaching for his bag when Henry's hand shot out to stop him. Their eyes met. Footsteps echoed in the hallway outside the room—each footfall louder than the one before.

Someone was coming.

14

Sunday, October 16, 1966
11:52 PM

No one was coming. Flora flicked the curtain closed with a sigh. She'd known their little escapade would take time, but she hadn't expected it to take quite this long.

Sinking into an emerald armchair with a tufted back and rolled arms, she opened her diary. It was a habit she'd started as a young girl, writing about each day before it ended. As she grew older, she cherished the memories more and more. On bad days, she would find old diaries and devour past entries.

All it took was one interaction with Henry to know writing things down made a difference.

She scribbled the pen across the paper, though she knew her recollections were only half the story. Stan would need to fill in all the details when he returned. Flora pictured him falling into his BarcaLounger, closing his eyes, and telling her about every moment. She pulled a single sheet of paper from the front of her diary, the one Stan had left on the credenza in the front hall before slipping into the night, and read it for the dozenth time.

He'd been worried before he left, coming into the hall wearing a buttoned-up beige jacket and brown loafers. Flora had taken one look and sent him back upstairs to change. He couldn't break into such a monumental building looking like John Wayne.

Folding his note, she glanced again at the clock and reached for her pen. When she'd committed everything she wanted to say to paper, she closed her diary and tucked it into the bureau's little drawer.

Then she paced in front of the window as one day ticked over to the next.

Flo,

(Forgive the pencil, I couldn't find the pen.)

Don't read this until I'm around the corner and out of sight, or you'll come running after me and I don't have the strength to convince both of us it's a good idea. I know it's not. But what else am I to do?

Henry needs me. It may not make sense to anyone (even us) what he's trying to do, or why he's suddenly so consumed by this purpose. But I do know it's the first time in a long time I've seen him so passionate.

Every time I mention the factory, his eyes glaze over. But a single reference to the post office and it's as if life has finally flooded back into his system. Who am I to stop that?

The least I can do is make sure he doesn't get caught mid-heist. You should see how much (and . . . okay . . . also how little) he's planned out! It makes my stomach do somersaults, but at least it's something.

I'd better go. My palms are too sweaty to hold the pencil, and my knees already feel too weak to stand for long.

Don't wait up.

Stan

15

Monday, October 17, 1966
12:02 AM

They pushed away from the bags and waddled along the wall to hide behind a sorting bin. Four knees cracked in unison as they lowered to a crouch.

The footsteps grew louder.

Henry dipped lower, head sinking onto aging shoulders. He reached for his cane and realized, with a shudder, he'd left it by the bags. He was about to look for it when the door swung open.

A golden light pierced the dark room, scanning left and arching right.

On the other side of a sorting bin—one they hoped was piled high enough to hide them—a man let out a low whistle. Technically speaking, it was more robust exhale than whistle, and before it had a chance to crescendo, it caught midthroat and caused whoever it was to cough violently. Deep and guttural, a noise Henry didn't think he could make even if he tried, the sound nestled itself between nooks and inside crannies.

Henry sank lower. He didn't want to find out what would happen if they were caught; he didn't have the energy for such an interrogation. Just the thought of it made his head throb.

For a moment, the light danced up and down, filling the space with a bouncing golden ball they couldn't keep track of. When the door slammed shut, darkness descended once more, the sound of heavy footsteps and heavier coughs retreating down the hallway.

Henry held his breath. Beside him, Stan's shoulders held their tension. "Let's give it a minute, hmm?" Stan murmured. Nodding in agreement, Henry shut his eyes and leaned back on a twenty-pound paper pillow.

And waited for his hands to stop shaking.

They were halfway down the stairs when a door opened above them.

They froze.

Henry looked at Stan, eyes wide, and braced his old bones to run. Leaning his full weight on his cane, he hefted the bag higher. The burlap scraped at his cheek. Footsteps landed like thunder in the stairwell, echoing off the plain walls. A flashlight pierced the darkness, illuminating the two geriatric thieves.

"Hey!" The shout was strangled, distant, followed by words Henry wouldn't repeat.

They didn't wait to hear what else was said. In shoes that were better suited for dawdling than dashing, they raced down the stairs and into the lobby. Henry's cane bounced off the marble floor, landing with a thump on the intricate compass design. They careened toward the closest door.

"Hurry," Henry pleaded. His breath came in short bursts as a cramp made itself at home in his side. "Let's get out of here."

"Mmm, I'm trying," Stan hissed. "The key is stuck." The same key that Stan had struggled with on the way into the building was now refusing to turn on their way out. Behind them, a door slammed and heavy steps pounded the floor.

"What are we going to do?"

Stan turned to face him. With a wink, he reached for Henry's cane and smashed through the glass at the same moment the guard turned the corner and barreled toward them.

16

Monday, October 17, 1966

12:19 AM

Vincent Fletcher couldn't breathe. A wet wheeze escaped his lungs as he stopped, bent in half, in the middle of a tile compass. Wind whistled through the broken door as glass littered the floor of the lobby.

With a huff he pushed himself up. In all his years as a security guard, nothing out of the ordinary had ever happened. He walked the halls, checked the floors, secured the locks. He protected the building, and in return, the building remained an uneventful space.

Quiet. Calm. Until tonight.

They must have been pushing eighty, surely? It wouldn't do to admit two old men had outrun (and outsmarted) him. No. Everything was under control. There was no need to think too much about the matter. He'd just pretend it never happened. He couldn't get in trouble if he hadn't seen anything, right?

Moving to the elevator bank, Fletcher pressed a thumb into the call button. There was a Reuben sandwich on his desk, calling his name.

On the receiving platform, a shaky pile toppled without making a noise, letters cascading to the floor. A hand-scrawled note surfed along the top and stopped, faceup, a few feet from the door.

South Chicago Community Hospital
8012 S Crandon Ave, Chicago, IL 60617

Dear Dr. Stewart,

I tried calling your office but your receptionist informed me I would need to make an appointment at least six weeks in advance. That's an awfully long time for a phone call.

So, I'll get straight to the point. It's my son, Vince.

I'm afraid he's still letting the silly mishaps from his youth slow him down in life. I know he was picked on (terribly so!) but he's a grown man now. His security job should give him a sense of purpose. Of pride. He should be walking around with his head held high, confident to make his own decisions.

But that's not the case. He's still just as withdrawn and morose. And his weight is getting worse.

Is there a tincture he could try? Something that will perk him up a bit and give him a voice?

I'll await your timely reply. Perhaps a letter back won't require *quite* as much wait as a call.

Sincerely,

Virginia Fletcher

17

Monday, October 17, 1966
6:47 AM

Henry poured coffee into a chipped porcelain mug (following self-produced instructions that he preferred it, like most things, plain). He brushed aside a hand-scrawled memo that said he needed to ask for help sometimes and that was okay. The burlap bags sagged against the wall, filled with stolen letters. The sight of them made him feel light-headed.

He couldn't believe they'd really done it. Just the thought of having to break the glass before the security guard caught them made his fingertips tingle with pleasure.

Sitting down, Henry reached for a fresh sheet of paper to leave Elsie a note. He so wanted to tell her what he'd done. It wasn't like him to have such an adventure. The mixture of pride and worry had him tossing and turning all night, and it wasn't until the faint light of a new day touched the horizon that he'd remembered Elsie was visiting William. No doubt she'd be gone for a few days. Better to write a little note than call and worry her. He'd be done with his mission in no time.

So yes, a letter was best.

A little whisper of a memory prompted him to save the letter for William as well. He tucked it in the drawer, the top right corner still bare, awaiting postage.

He'd deliver it when he returned.

* * *

It took three trips to load the old Ford. As he climbed behind the wheel, he wasn't confident it would start. When was the last time he'd driven it—last month? Last year? He wondered if he still had a valid license. Probably not.

The Ford started on the fourth try, engine revving to life slowly. Reversing at a crawl, Henry scanned the address on the top letter, made a mental plan, and headed west.

18

Monday, October 17, 1966
7:57 AM

Henry's hands gripped the wheel as he slowed to a stop in front of the small house. Nestled on a quiet side street, it sat waiting, like a beacon he'd never known to look for.

It had taken him almost an hour to locate, doubling back on himself three times as he navigated the city. How did anyone find their way around all these confusing streets? Especially the ones that claimed to be one-way, and if you just *happened* to go the wrong way, everyone and their neighbor would let you know how they felt about that. A lot of people had shared their opinions with him this morning: a car horn symphony making him sweat.

Never mind. He reached for the first envelope. Small, tight letters in perfect penmanship floated across the front, as if someone had painstakingly spelled out the address so it wouldn't get lost. It filled him with a determination, that impeccable writing. An eagerness to deliver it to . . . he double-checked the name. A Mr. Roger Knight.

With the letter in one hand and his cane firmly in the other, Henry clambered from the car, his only audience a squirrel intent on flicking its bushy tail like a metronome.

Flo would take that as an omen.

He wished his legs would stop shaking. He could do this. All he needed to do was walk up the gravel path, avoid stepping on the errant ninebark, and ring the bell. Then he'd hand over the mail with a full-wattage smile and be on his way.

Oh, the thrill.

He gave a stern, silent message to his appendages and told his heart to relax. Everything would be fine. Nothing would stop him from uniting this Roger fellow with the messages inscribed just for him.

Ignoring the questions at the back of his mind, Henry pressed a finger into the doorbell. A long chime sounded on the other side of the door. He cleared his throat and waited.

Behind him, the squirrel got bored and raced up a tree on the opposite side of the road. Minutes felt like hours, and just as he was about to give up and slide the letter through the brass slot, the door swung open. A middle-aged woman with a robe wrapped around her waist and curlers in her hair raised an overplucked eyebrow in his direction. "Can I help you?"

"Oh, yes." Henry forgot how to form words. "I'm just . . . you see."

She brushed a wayward curl from her forehead and started to close the door. "I'm afraid I'm going to be late for work—"

"Wait." Henry panicked. "I have a letter. For . . ." He glanced at the envelope again. "Roger."

"Oh." She opened the door fully, coming to join him on the porch. The sun bounced off her ash-blonde hair. The curlers were a soft shade of pink, matching her robe. "Rog left for school already."

Henry's face fell. His very first delivery and it wasn't going to plan.

"I'm his mom," she explained. "I can give it to him. I've been waiting for it, actually." She reached out a hand with cuticles so neat Elsie would be proud.

"Okay," he said, his grip on the letter tightening involuntarily. He passed it to her with a shaky hand.

She stepped back into the house without reading the front, pink fading into the darkness. "I'll make sure he gets it. Thank you, Mr. . . . ?"

Henry stood straighter. "Henry. My name is Henry Walton." He thought about giving a salute, but that felt too formal. And he couldn't shake her hand, because his palms were wet and she was already inside.

Baring his teeth, Henry wished her a fine day. He waited until she closed the door before pumping a fist into the air with a hoot.

Delivery number one, complete.

2728 W Cortez St
Chicago, Illinois 60622

Hey Rog,

It's been a while.

I hear things have been a little tough lately. Ever since, what's his name . . . Paul? Pete? moved away.

Look, why don't you come out here for a visit? We can let bygones be bygones and talk, man to man.

It'll do you good to have a little adventure. We can go into the Badlands. Drive around, or even do a little hike? Remember that time we camped up by North Bay? It could be like that. Though we should probably bring tent poles this time. Your mom never did forgive me for forgetting them and making us sleep on the ground. Says that's where her fear of spiders came from.

Anyways, what do you say, Rog? You up for it?

Dad

19

Monday, October 17, 1966
8:11 AM

"Speak up." Spit flew from Stokes's lips.

The security guard stepped to the left and repeated himself, voice muffled. "I didn't . . . didn't see or hear nothin'." He wrung his hands in front of him, twisting swollen fingers around and around.

Stokes rolled up his sleeves, ignoring Brenda, who hovered nearby. "'Didn't hear or see nothin','" he said, adopting Fletcher's tone. "What the hell are we paying you for?" He kicked over a pile of letters to his right and watched it fall. Beneath his feet, a dozen or so had already been trampled on the platform, crumpled and edging toward illegible.

He wanted to stomp on them all. Why was this happening to him? Stokes had done nothing but support everyone in the building, and now he had to deal with a break-in on top of the staggering accumulation of mail he had absolutely no control over.

"I was doing my rounds." Fletcher crossed his arms. "As you instructed. I checked every floor . . . walked . . . walked the whole building. I didn't hear no break-in." His eyes were glued to the floor.

"I bet it was that goddamn reporter." Stokes pictured the man slinking into the building in the middle of the night. Had he broken the door with his camera? "I wouldn't let him look at the receiving platform, for obvious reasons, and now he's broken in. To . . . what? Snap some pictures? Write up a more accurate article for tomorrow's front page?" He let out a string of expletives, pleased when it made Fletcher recoil.

Brenda stepped in. "We're wasting time. O'Brien is going to be here tomorrow. We need to talk to him about the backlog."

"We?"

She cleared her throat. "You, sir. Need to talk to O'Brien about the backlog. What happened here is done. There's no way we're going to catch whoever broke in, and even if we do, I really don't see the point—"

"The point, Brenda, is that someone has made a fool of me." Could he just walk into the *Tribune* office, demanding Chuck come out and confess? Maybe he could grab a camera off a desk and threaten to destroy it. Or smash up the printing press for tomorrow's run. The man had refused to print a correction, and now this?

The break-in had become his number-one priority.

"But the mail"—Brenda pointed to the sea of white—"we need a plan."

Stokes balled his fists. "The plan is to find whoever did this. Everything else can wait." He spun around, toppling a pile of letters as he turned. They would find the young man responsible. And Stokes would make him pay.

20

Monday, October 17, 1966
9:43 AM

Double-checking that Stokes's office door was closed, Brenda reached for the phone.

They needed a plan. Since the postwar mail boom, the Chicago Post Office had been running out of space. Year after year they struggled to keep up with the demand. It wasn't just letters for residents of Chicago either. Because of the size of their facility, mail came from all over the country to be sorted and redirected to dozens of states. Five years earlier, O'Brien had pushed the idea of a master post office, and without a thought for the future, Stokes had agreed. Even the Zone Improvement Plan had done little to help with operations.

A voice answered on the third ring.

"Stan? It's Brenda. We need to talk."

At the end of the hall, the elevator doors slid open. Aldo emerged, breathless.

"Is Stokes in his office?" He brandished a scrap of paper in her direction.

Brenda rose. "Where else would he be?"

Stokes had instructed Aldo, alongside a handful of letter carriers brought in to help deal with the crisis, to search for clues. When Brenda left him on the receiving platform an hour earlier, Aldo had been elbow deep in letters on the conveyor belt.

"We've found something."

She followed him into the office, ignoring his curious glance, and closed the door behind them.

"Sir." Aldo stopped in front of Stokes's desk. The paper in his hand fluttered.

Stokes touched a foot down to stop midspin. He lit a smoke and tossed the lighter onto the desk with a clang. "Spit it out," he said, taking a deep pull.

"The break-in . . . we believe it was a man named Henry Walton." Aldo held out the paper with a shaky hand. "We found this."

Stokes snatched it away. He read the contents before throwing it onto the desk. From where she stood, Brenda could see *bread, toothpaste, jelly (preferably grape)* listed in pencil. *Carrots* was crossed out at the bottom. "It's a grocery list," Stokes fumed. "What use is this to me?"

"Read the back," Aldo replied.

Stokes reached for the paper and turned it over. His eyebrows knit together; he rubbed a hand over the dark stubble that had started to spread across his jawline before flinging it back down.

Brenda picked it up to read the back.

Step one: break into the post office.

Step two: steal letters (no packages, too heavy)

Step three: deliver letters

If at any point you feel yourself losing courage, repeat this: I am Henry Walton and it is my sworn duty to deliver these letters to their rightful owners.

"Who's Henry Walton?" She reread the words, turning them over in her mind.

"I have no idea," Stokes snapped. "Where's Fletcher?"

"I think he's—"

"Get him. Now." He spun his chair around, effectively dismissing her and Aldo until they returned with the security guard in tow.

21

Monday, October 17, 1966

10:07 AM

Fletcher called the elevator. He'd been summoned to the top floor. Normally he could visit the upstairs offices only at night, when the building was vacant. But now he was actually being invited up.

They must want to praise his outstanding work. Stokes would pull out a chair for him and offer a cigarette. Fletcher would politely decline (smoke made him cough). Then his boss, tossing ash around like confetti, would tell him he was an excellent security guard. Top notch. Best of the best. And Fletcher would dip his head and say *No, no. I'm only doing my duty to the building and its letters. It's nothing, really.* And then Stokes would—

"You lied." Stokes's sharp voice cut through his thoughts. "Get in here, you useless—"

Fletcher dipped his head and entered the office. Behind him, Brenda closed the door with a click. Aldo hovered by the window, not meeting his gaze.

"Who's Henry Walton?" Stokes cracked his knuckles.

"Who?"

"Who. Is. Henry. Walton?" He split the name in half with his tongue.

Fletcher looked around the room for a clue. That was the wrong thing to do.

"Look at me," Stokes hissed. "And tell me who—"

"I don't know! I don't know any Henrys. I know a Herbert, but that's it." He crossed and uncrossed his arms. They hung limply by his side, heavier than normal. Should he make a joke about the time Herbert had fainted at the sight of blood and Fletcher had tripped over him and ripped his pants straight down the back? He smiled at the memory.

Ash fell to the floor. "You think this is funny?"

Okay. Best not to joke. "No, sir."

"Want to tell us what actually happened last night?"

"I didn't—"

"Shut up. Aldo found a note." Stokes stabbed the scrap of paper with his cigarette, marring the words with a burn mark. "And we know it was someone named Henry who broke in. So, Fletcher, it's time for you to tell the truth. Unless, of course, you want me to throw you out? What's two broken doors, at this rate?"

Fletcher stared at his feet. Or, rather, he stared in the direction of the feet he hadn't been able to see for years. Stress eating, his mother called it. Boredom, the doctor said.

He trilled his lips.

"Okay," he started. "I might have seen something. There was a man . . . an old guy."

"Old? How old?"

"Eighties, maybe. Old. He had a cane. Anyways, there I was, doing my nightly rounds. I walked the whole building, as I always do, and everything was fine. Nothing out of place. No unusual sounds. I checked the receiving platform—all in order—and then I took the elevator up to the third floor. The guys in the print shop asked me last week to start making sure the machines were shutting off properly. So I checked those. All good, machines are off and the floor is quiet. And since I've already checked the other floors, I decide it's time to do another sweep of the lobby. Except, this time I think I should take the stairs. Because . . . you know . . . Anyways, I start down the stairs and I'm using my flashlight, and suddenly my light lands on an old guy with a bag full of letters." No need to mention that there were two old guys with two bags of letters. "So I start chasing him. I run down the stairs as fast as I can and head into the lobby after him. But by the time I get there, the door has been smashed and he's gone."

Stokes stubbed out his cigarette. The ashtray overflowed. Didn't Brenda ever empty it?

"A guy in his eighties?"

"Give or take a few years."

"Broke into the largest post office in the world and ran away with a bag of letters?" Fletcher could hear the manic glee in his boss's tone.

"Well, yes. It would appear that way. And I'm sorry I didn't say anything earlier; it's just . . . I . . ."

"It's just you didn't want to admit you're incapable of protecting the building from a decrepit thief?"

Fletcher pulled on his fingers. The man wasn't *that* decrepit.

"How many?"

"What?"

"Goddammit, Fletcher. How many letters did the old man steal?"

"Oh. I'd say a few hundred, give or take."

Aldo tried to cover a low whistle with a cough.

Stokes lit up again. "We'll deal with your profound ineptitude later," he said. Fletcher felt heat creep up his neck. "First, we need to find this guy."

Brenda leaned forward. "Sir, O'Brien will be here tomorrow, and I really think we need to—"

"I don't need you to think. I need you to let us men do our jobs."

Fletcher didn't dare look at Brenda. If he was going to redeem himself, he needed to do what Stokes asked of him.

The backlog, it appeared, would need to wait.

22

Monday, October 17, 1966
1:45 PM

Brenda ran her finger along the edge of an envelope before setting it down on top of a wobbly pile. In front of her, Stan tapped a tune out against his leg, taking everything in. She knew he hadn't seen the receiving platform since everything had ground to a halt.

"Stokes is refusing to deal with it," she said, massaging her temples. "All he cares about is a break-in that happened last night. Though whatever the thief took, it doesn't compare to what's here."

All morning Stokes had been trying to figure out who the thief was and where he lived. Last she'd heard, he'd sent Fletcher around to several stores in the area asking about old men buying grape jelly.

Meanwhile, she couldn't see the floor where she stood.

Stan turned away from her and picked up a letter. "There's just so much, isn't there?" He set it back down on an identical pile. "It's frustrating that I haven't been called in to help."

Brenda shrugged. "You know Stokes. He needs to be the smartest man in every room. He's not about to bring someone in who could actually . . . you know . . . help." She scanned the space. "I wish we had a way to properly sort it all, but there's not enough space."

"Mmm. We need to magically reduce the amount. By . . . say . . . I don't know, destroying things that aren't critical." His laugh made Brenda think of a car backfiring. He flicked through the pages of an Avon catalog. "Like this."

The last makeup order Brenda placed had been a waste of time. The rouge came as a thick red goop, and every time she tried to apply it, her hands got covered and her face looked worse.

They should definitely get rid of Avon catalogs.

Stan moved to a stack by the door and cleared his throat. "Maybe it's a good thing someone is trying to deliver some of them?"

Brenda threw her hands up. Why couldn't anyone focus on the massive problem in front of them without getting distracted? She was tired of dealing with people who couldn't see the bigger picture. "We don't need a man with a cane delivering letters." She walked to the door, careful where she placed her feet.

She'd thought Stan would be able to help. That he'd make a suggestion or take the time to strategize with her. Clearly, he only wanted to focus on the break-in too.

"What we need"—she opened the door—"is for management to do their jobs for once."

23

Monday, October 17, 1966
2:13 PM

Stan took the elevator to the lobby. It felt strange being back in the building. Thoughts of their heist mixed with the enormity of the crisis made him giddy. Thank goodness Brenda hadn't caught on to his little joke. Imagine the post office destroying mail! It was unheard of.

The doors opened, and Stan exited the elevator slowly. He knew they wouldn't invite him back in to help with the backlog, and he wanted to linger a little longer. He would have stayed to run his hand along the letter drops, but Stokes hovered by a window with a security guard. It couldn't possibly be the same guard, could it? Stan dropped his head as he passed them.

"I know what neighborhood this Walton guy lives in," the guard said.

Slowing his pace, Stan strained to listen.

"Over on Dearborn, or in that area at least. I talked to a guy who owns a corner store over there. James something or other. He said a guy named Henry comes in every day to buy a loaf of bread and grape jelly. Gave me a description of him and everything."

"Good," Stokes said. "Will you recognize him if you see him?"

"I think so. I bet I could spot him on the street if he so much as walked past. Both of them."

Stan froze.

Behind him, Stokes sounded perplexed. "Both?"

"Oh . . . you know . . . um. The old guy and his cane. I'd notice both him and his cane."

Stan bit his lip and moved away while Stokes told the guard not to say idiotic things that confused him. How did they know it had been Henry? If they knew where he lived, they'd go after him. Stan needed to warn him before it was too late.

24

Monday, October 17, 1966
8:06 PM

Roger didn't recognize the writing. The envelope lay on the counter, his name written in neat block letters on the front.

"What's this, then?" he asked the empty room. Pulling a can of soda from the fridge, he kicked the door closed and opened the letter with his teeth. A single sheet fell onto the counter. Roger took a swig. His Adam's apple bobbed.

He had nothing to compare it to. No other correspondence to let him know if the tone of this letter was common or out of place. He looked at the scrawl of his mom's shopping list pinned to the fridge, the chaotic penmanship similar to his own. This perfect writing was not something he recognized. The formation of each letter was deliberate. Calculated.

The first thing his father had sent him in seven years.

"No," Roger said to no one. "I don't need you; I never have. I have my mom and . . ." The sight of Pete's name made his thoughts swirl. How did his dad know about Pete? Or that his friend had moved away, and that ever since, Roger had felt weightless. Untethered.

Like a tent with no poles. He could hear his mom on that trip, complaining about sleeping on the hard ground with nothing above them but a sheet of stars. His dad had laughed and tossed another log onto the fire. Watching it burn, Roger had started to talk about the chemical reaction and the energy being produced, but neither wanted to listen. His mom had cried about spiders and his dad had cracked open another beer, and Roger had bit his lip and tried to match the jiggling of his leg with the flicker of the flames.

No. He did not need to relive that, man to man.

Tearing the letter in two, he tossed the scraps into the garbage under the sink and placed the can on top. He stared at the return address on the envelope for a moment before throwing that away too.

25

Monday, October 17, 1966
8:42 PM

As Henry parked the Ford, the possibility of his mission stretched ahead of him. Technically speaking, the day had been a success. He'd delivered thirty-five letters and could feel the thrill of every interaction in the tips of his arthritic toes.

There was only one tiny problem: He'd spent the day following a chaotic route that had him driving in circles and doubling back on himself.

It wasn't sustainable. He needed to dump out both burlap bags on the living room floor and organize everything. It would make the whole process easier if he had a system. A plan.

An organized mind is a clear mind was his motto, and he was kicking himself for not following that pearl of wisdom earlier.

Coming through the front door, Henry lunged for the phone before it stopped ringing.

"Hello?" He nudged one of the burlap bags with his cane so it wouldn't topple over.

"Mmm. Henry. Good, you're back." Stan's throat sounded constricted.

"Just walked through the door. It's been such a whirlwind, but in the best way. I feel . . . I don't know. As if this might be the making of me."

Henry knew that sounded silly. He was well past his expiration date, and he wasn't getting any younger. But doing something of value for the first time in a long time made him want to throw his hands in the air and shout.

If Elsie were home, she would have filled the hallway with balloons to celebrate a successful first day. She also would have burnt his favorite meal, but that was neither here nor there.

He couldn't wait to tell her all about it.

"That's great. Look, I need to—"

Henry interrupted. "I drove down a little street earlier lined with trees. I was looking for an address, so I slowed right down to read the house numbers, and guess what I saw? A young woman delivering her own letter." His voice got higher as he pictured her. "She wore a bright-yellow hat, like a canary, perched on top of chocolate-brown curls, and she was clutching a white envelope between her mittened hands. Do you wear mittens? I think I prefer gloves, but now I actually can't remember. Anyways, I watched her look left and right, and then she slipped it through the door of a tall brick house and dashed down the road, around the corner and out of sight."

"I like gloves."

"What?"

"Never mind."

"Whatever that letter contained, it mattered," Henry said. "To the recipient, and to the woman in the hat. It mattered so much she didn't trust anyone else to deliver it." Oh, he wondered what it said.

"That's lovely, but we need to talk." Why did Stan sound so worried? If that woman could deliver letters, he could too. He would have said as much, but Stan kept going. "I went to the post office today."

"What?"

"Look, it's a long story, and I'll explain when I can. But as I was leaving, I overheard Stokes talking to that security guard."

"The one from the other night?" Henry could still hear the man's lumbering footsteps chasing them.

"I think so. Either way, whoever it is, they know who you are."

"Didn't think the big guy had it in him."

Stan chuckled, and Henry's chin lifted ever so slightly. "Me neither," Stan said. "Though if I were you, I wouldn't hang around too long to figure out what else he's capable of."

Henry stared at the overflowing bags as he wished Stan a good night. If he wanted to finish what he started, he'd need to move quickly.

3944 California Ave
Chicago, IL

Lucy,

I need help.

Charlotte asked me to iron her wedding dress because my ceilings are taller than hers and she said that the dress could hang at full length in my house better than it could in her house. All I needed to do was press it out, slip it back onto the hanger, and drape it from the hook in the ceiling that my pothos normally hangs from.

And I did all that.

Everything was fine, the dress was all ready to go for Charlotte's big day, and I was feeling so proud of myself for having lent a hand during such an important time.

But then last night . . . oh, it's almost too terrible to write. I made spaghetti for dinner, and I was just on my way to the couch to watch Bewitched when I tripped on those black patent pumps (which Charlotte forced me to buy because she said they make my feet look smaller) and fell off the step towards the window and of course some landed on the hem of her dress.

It's just my luck that this would happen.

Luc, how the devil do I get tomato out of a white dress? I've tried everything. Can you come over in the morning and please, pretty please, lend a hand?

I couldn't bear to have Charlotte overhear it on the party line, which is why I slipped this letter through your door and will await your response in the same fashion.

I know I can trust you to keep mum.

Nothing good will come of upsetting Charlotte before her big day and I know if anyone can help me put this right it's you.

May as well bring a bottle of sherry when you come. We're going to need it.

Ethel

26

Monday, October 17, 1966
11:48 PM

Three white shirts, two pairs of black trousers, four pairs of plain black socks, four pairs of underwear (color undisclosed), one pair of black leather loafers, two ties, three felt-tip pens, one warm wool sweater, the compass Elsie had given him on their tenth (or was it eleventh?) wedding anniversary, one toothbrush and its accompanying paste, one comb, one razor, six Marathon bars, one pad of lined paper, and one pink patterned handkerchief Elsie had found in a small side-of-the-road shop years before and said she must own because pink was her color.

Henry surveyed the items, ticking off a mental list one by one.

It was his third time taking inventory. The first time he forgot to count the socks. The second time he wondered why he needed a map and had to sit down for quite a while to consider why so many items were laid out in neat rows across his living room floor.

Now he whistled as he tucked everything into the overnight bag he'd found under the bed, making sure to protect the compass as he pushed the contents down and secured the zip. The sides of the bag bulged. He could have packed lighter, he supposed. But his motto was *It's better to pack it all than to be left wanting.*

Or something like that.

He carried the bag to the front hallway and set it by the door. When he left in the morning, he wouldn't be coming back until the job was done. He knew Elsie would understand.

She always did.

Returning to the living room, he tipped the burlap bags out and unfolded the large map. Time to create order amongst the chaos.

A swelling tide rose around him. White hills of varying sizes were spread out around the room, each representing a neighborhood or town. Seventeen in Avondale so far. Three for Lincoln Square. Old Town's pile had thirty, while Dearborn Park had thirty-one. Big Oak didn't have any (which was surprising), but Union Ridge had twelve. And North Mayfair had two compared to regular Mayfair's one.

He scanned the addresses of three letters before going over to the map to locate them. Two he placed on existing piles; a third he used to start a new pile before heading toward the door and starting the process all over again.

Back and forth he went, the stacks rising slowly with every added envelope.

On one pass he stopped to right a toppled pile. The pass after that he righted two more. Little by little, the mess under his feet started to diminish.

Save for a scattering of letters here and there, everything had been organized by location. Most of the letters were for homes in Chicago and the surrounding neighborhoods. There were a handful for over Rockford way, one for an address just west of Davenport, six for Minneapolis, one for Fargo, one for Winnipeg (Canada!), two for Sioux Falls, one for Sioux City. Then there was Kansas City, Hannibal, and finally Springfield.

He rubbed at the stubble spreading across his chin in patches. He would need a shave before leaving in the morning. It wouldn't do to look like a blue-collared man. *A shave a day keeps the dirt at bay* was his motto, after all.

27

Tuesday, October 18, 1966
8:46 AM

Stokes looked even worse today. Brenda wished he'd thought to shave before O'Brien arrived. The stubble across his chin had thickened overnight.

Oh well. If he wanted to look like an incompetent fool, that was on him. She needed him to act the opposite, though. "When he gets here, you need to focus on the backlog, not the break-in."

"Everything is under control. That's all O'Brien needs to know." Stokes blew a smoke ring in her direction. Brenda stepped out of its path.

"Nothing is under control."

Stokes slammed the cigarette into the ashtray she'd emptied earlier and jumped up. His lips curled into a sneer. "Everything. Is. Under. Control. If I hear you so much as imply something different, to anyone, not just O'Brien, I will make you pay."

Brenda blinked. "Sir, O'Brien needs—"

"What O'Brien needs is to hop back on a plane and return home. We don't need him here. In fact, all he's doing is slowing down our efforts to locate Walton."

Oh, for the love of . . . Brenda bit her lip. If he refused to talk to O'Brien about the crisis, she would need to find a way to talk to the postmaster general herself.

28

Tuesday, October 18, 1966

9:01 AM

Larry O'Brien carried the assassination of JFK around everywhere he went. The event wrapped itself around him, producing an air of authority he didn't know he exuded. It was one thing to be an adviser to a president; it was quite another to be in the motorcade with him when he was killed.

Also wrapped around his neck today: a tie.

A ghastly pattern of lilac and burgundy flowers covered its skinny gold surface. Stokes couldn't understand why a grown man would wear flowers around his neck.

"Nice tie, sir," he said, offering the postmaster general a chair.

O'Brien tugged on it and remained standing. "Thanks. Elva ordered it from a catalog." Thick black glasses framed his face. "Now, Reginald, what exactly is going on around here?"

Stokes leaned against his desk and shrugged. "Everything's under control, sir." The sooner Stokes could get O'Brien to believe the crisis had been exaggerated, the sooner he'd be able to focus on the actual issue: Henry Walton. He'd sent Fletcher to patrol Dearborn this morning. If they could catch Walton leaving home or making his daily visit to the corner store, they could put this whole mess behind them. "There's no need to worry."

"How many?"

"What?" His fingers itched for a cigarette.

"How many letters are you backlogged?"

Stokes raised his palms. "You have to understand," he said. "It's all those damn flyers. Add the overtime charges on top of that . . . the ones you refuse to talk about because you actually think those *men* deserve overtime pay." Stokes would never understand the desire for equal rights. What a waste of time. "And suddenly we've got a situation on our hands. We never could have prevented this shutdown. *Never.*" He didn't mention the warning signs his team had been flagging for weeks.

O'Brien straightened his tie. "Shall we invite some of the staff in? Perhaps they could give a more articulate answer to my question. If you don't know how many letters are clogging up your facility, we have a problem."

Stokes rocked forward. "No, no. Let me look at the latest report from the team." He rounded the desk and grabbed a file from the top drawer. It contained magazine clippings. Ignoring brightly colored pocket squares, he said, "The estimate is ten million."

A paperweight narrowly missed his head, slamming into the wall behind him.

"What the—" Stokes flinched. The paperweight rested on the carpet, under the window.

"Ten million is not *a little backed up*. Do you understand what will happen if this post office closes?" O'Brien hemmed him in. "It's the hub of the entire nation's postal service. Almost every single piece of mail traveling east and west comes through your doors. So being backlogged here isn't just impacting mail in and around Chicago, you insufferable little man."

Stokes bit back a retort.

O'Brien's voice lowered. "Your ill-managed backlog has the potential to shut down postal services across the entire country. So, I want to know every single detail, and I'm not leaving until I'm satisfied you have it within you to sort this mess out. If you can't, *Reginald*, I will replace you with someone who can." The postmaster general pulled out a chair and sank down heavily. "Tell me, what's your plan?"

It would have been fine. Stokes could have explained it all away and instilled confidence in his superior abilities if Aldo hadn't chosen that moment to arrive.

"We've made a new discovery," Aldo said, tripping over his feet as he hurried into the room without pausing to see who was inside.

The receiving team had their own systems, he explained in a rush. When they received different-looking letters, they would set them aside for further inspection. It was important for everything to get the appropriate attention. A note from a son to his mother wouldn't get a second glance, but one with a presidential seal on the back? They paid attention to those, he stressed.

O'Brien spoke first. "A presidential seal?"

"Yes, sir." Aldo said, turning toward the postmaster general. "Recently, just such a letter came in, and the boys downstairs set it aside. There's a shelf by the door they use for all special-looking pieces of mail, ones they want to examine further. Even in the chaos, they pay close attention to the correspondence they're handling. They're very good at what they do, always reading and rereading everything so it gets sent to the correct floor for sorting. Anyways, this letter was intended to go to the eighth floor today to be handled as first class, only now it's missing."

"Missing?" O'Brien asked.

Aldo nodded. "It looks like it might be one of the ones Walton stole."

Stokes felt all the air escape his body. "O'Brien," he cut in. "It's nothing. We have everything under control. Look, why don't I send you a full report by the end of the day." He moved around the desk to usher his boss out.

O'Brien held up a hand. Looking at Aldo, he said, "Who is Walton, and what do you mean by *stole*?"

Aldo shifted from one foot to the other. "Well, sir," he stared at the carpet. "We believe a man named Henry Walton broke in and stole hundreds of letters. Including the one with a presidential seal."

O'Brien lips pressed in on themselves. He looked the young letter carrier up and down. "Thank you, . . . ?"

"Aldo, sir."

"Thank you, Aldo. That will be all for now."

With a small nod, Aldo backed out of the room. O'Brien turned back to Stokes. "Well, Reginald. It looks like you have *two* little problems to sort out." He raised his eyebrows. "Which means I need *two* reports by the end of the day."

As O'Brien left without another word, Stokes lit a smoke and inhaled deeply. He couldn't wait to prove everyone wrong. Once he found Walton and solved the issue of the break-in, O'Brien would realize nothing else mattered. The backlog would sort itself out in time.

In the meantime, he needed to focus.

29

Tuesday, October 18, 1966
9:34 AM

Brenda hovered outside the door, twisting a bracelet round and round her wrist.

She hadn't caught every word, but she'd heard enough to understand how dire the situation was. If they didn't sort out the backlog, the entire nation's postal service would grind to a halt. They couldn't let that happen.

O'Brien rubbed the back of his neck as he exited the office. Brenda wondered if his wife had picked out his tie. It really brought out the flecks of amber in his hazel eyes.

"Sir," she said, resting a hand on his arm and then yanking it quickly away. "I wonder if you have a moment?"

O'Brien's face looked blank.

"I'm Reginald's assistant," Brenda explained. "I'd love to talk to you about the backlog and ways we might move through—"

O'Brien moved toward the elevator. "Talk to Stokes."

Brenda hurried to keep up. "I have, sir. That's the point, he's not listening."

He pressed a thumb into the call button. "Look, Stokes needs to handle this. I suggest you keep bringing him coffee and cigarettes so he can do his job."

Brenda balled her fists. "Certainly, sir," she said, forcing a smile as the elevator doors closed.

She slipped into the ladies' room to think. Peering into the mirror, she was glad to see no lipstick marks on her teeth. The latest tube she'd ordered was strangely flaky. She kept licking her teeth, paranoid she would make a fool of herself. Nothing she'd purchased lately had been worth it. She should throw out the catalog and cancel her subscription. She certainly didn't need another tube of this lipstick, or more rouge . . .

The thought made her pause.

What had Stan joked about yesterday? Destroying things that weren't critical? Like magazines and circulars and catalogs.

That was it. If they could get rid of unnecessary pieces of mail, they'd have more space to properly sort through everything else. Brenda beamed at her reflection and adjusted her hair. All she had to do now was convince her boss to give the go-ahead.

6400 Kimbark Ave, Apt 103
Chicago, IL

Vera,

I could strangle Stokes. Wrap one of his ugly, plain ties around his neck and watch him squirm. He's obsessed with an issue that doesn't even matter and, no matter what I do, I can't get him to focus on the disaster at hand. Though I can't even get his boss to pay attention either, so perhaps the problem is me.

There's a screaming in my head I can't turn off.

I should have known this job would be a disaster the minute they told me it wasn't possible to type sixty words per minute during my interview. They called the typewriter faulty and made me retake the test. Do you remember that? I should have listened to your sisterly advice at the time and looked for work elsewhere.

Oh Vera, I cannot stand having small men look up at me, mouths caught in a sneer, as they bumble around searching for non-existent solutions. It makes me sick. I can't just sit around idly waiting for these incapable men to figure things out. I have a plan that I'm going to put into action, with or without their support.

Throw this letter on the fire tonight. We have to make sure everything burns.

Love,

Brenda

30

Tuesday, October 18, 1966
3:44 PM

Roger sat hunched outside the principal's office, waiting for his mom. "You've really done it this time." He picked at a pimple on his cheek.

"What's that, dear?" Mrs. Walker, the secretary, called.

"Pardon?"

"You were just saying something. I couldn't quite catch it."

"Oh," Roger mumbled, "it was nothing." His leg danced up and down while he waited, unable to sit still. His mom would have something to say about him skipping class again. A small frown would form between her plucked eyebrows, and she would give a small sigh. And then she would launch into one of her monologues about how his grades were slipping and school was important and did he want to end up in a dead-end job like her? "No, I don't."

Mrs. Walker raised her head in question. Roger lowered his.

When his mom finally arrived in a puff of perfume, she sailed past him into the office and shut the door. He heard her muffled voice mingling with the principal's. His leg picked up speed. After several minutes, she flew back out and nodded for him to follow her. He saw the shake of Mrs. Walker's head before he ducked under the doorframe and left.

"You can't keep doing this." His mom sat so close to the steering wheel it was as if she were trying to climb through it. "They'll kick you out."

"They won't." Roger sat pretzeled beside her, tapping his leg.

"They will." She signaled to turn. "Mr. Henderson and I both agree it's time for a change of scenery."

Roger felt the presence of his principal filling the car. "A new school?" He tapped faster.

"No. Just a little . . . break." She turned onto their street and slowed. "A trip, of sorts."

"A trip," Roger repeated under his breath.

She sighed. "I can never tell if you're talking to me or yourself."

"What kind of trip? Where are we going?"

"No. This is a trip for you to do on your own, Rog." She turned into their driveway. The engine stilled to silence. "I think it's time you go see your father."

"My . . . what?"

"Your father. I saved the envelope with his return address. The one you threw away." She twisted in her seat. "Don't look at me like that; I didn't read the letter. I don't even know how it arrived, since you said last week the post office is closed. But I saved the envelope. So you know where to go."

For once, Roger didn't have words.

"I know you don't want to see him."

"You think?" He waggled his eyebrows at her.

"You need to do something different, Rog. I know it's been hard since Pete left. And I know the kids here aren't really . . . well . . . they're not nice. Let's leave it at that. But you can't keep skipping school and disrupting class." She tried to meet his gaze, but he looked away. "You can get out of here, Rog. Be anything you want to be. But first, you have to graduate. So I think you should go see him, and when you get back, you can focus on your studies. You can move forward."

Roger wrapped his arms around himself as she climbed from the car. His mind filled with a dozen questions, each vying for an answer he didn't have. Closure? Sure, he probably needed some. To graduate and make something of himself? It was possible. A visit to the father who had left him and his mom when he was ten years old? No chance.

31

Wednesday, October 19, 1966
6:58 AM

Where was he? Henry stared at a pair of water marks snaking across an unfamiliar ceiling. Only a thin, worn blanket covered the uncomfortable bed. It was impossible to tell if it had been manufactured in such an unfortunate shade of brown or if it had faded drastically over the years. The lamp, atop a scratched nightstand, was missing its shade. In the morning light it looked naked and forlorn.

Where was the clean, white linen with the embroidered roses? Or the Tiffany lamp Elsie loved so much?

Henry scrunched his eyes shut and willed the night before to come into focus. He remembered zigzagging his way through neighborhoods all day, getting lost and found and lost again. After that he'd driven in circles while the moon crept higher and his eyelids had grown heavier.

And then? Sherman House. Henry remembered the glowing letters advertising comfortable beds to all passersby. A haven in the middle of a raging (albeit self-made) storm.

He let out a breath as the rest of the memory flooded back. It had taken him three trips to bring everything up from the car the night before. He would have asked the receptionist for help, but she looked up from her magazine only once as he paid for the room.

"I'd like a room with a view," Henry had said to the top of her head.

"We're just about all booked up." She'd waved to a few sad-looking keys on the wall, which, Henry supposed, was a gesture to inform him only sad-looking rooms remained.

"Whatever you have is fine." He needed a bed.

"I can give you room twenty-seven. It's on the second floor. Not much of a view, but the bed is big." Scribbling on a note pad, she had done fast math and told him the total was twenty-two dollars a night.

He'd nearly choked on his tongue.

"G-golly," Henry had stammered. "Includes breakfast, does it?" A single shake of her head confirmed the opposite before she handed him the key and returned to her reading.

It had taken him an hour to settle into his room. His cane kept getting in the way on the stairs as he lugged the bags up, and on more than on occasion he'd had to pause for his lungs to relax. By the time everything was upstairs, he'd been too tired to register anything in the room.

Now he could see the light of a new day was not enough to make it look habitable.

The burlap bags rested against the far wall beside a television set that showed only static. Inside the bags, all the letters had been carefully organized by location. He still couldn't believe he would need to travel so far to deliver them all.

With a stretch that hurt more than it helped, Henry ambled to the bathroom (also brown) to get ready for the day.

32

Wednesday, October 19, 1966

9:35 AM

It was a regal house. White siding draped its way around the exterior of the house like an oversized coat. Shutters the color of an Ajax tin framed each window facing the street. A long, straight drive cut a path through the yard and ended at the foot of a large, two-car garage, its doors painted the same vibrant hue.

The concrete path was lined on either side with small round shrubs, each a perfect sphere. Spaced evenly apart, they created a polka-dot pattern guiding each visitor from the drive to the (also blue) front door.

Henry checked the address again. With a shaking hand, he gripped the letter and knocked. Two loud raps in quick succession.

A moment passed. Then another.

When the door finally swung open, a woman as beautiful as the house stood before him. A paisley dress hugged her curves, clinging dramatically to her waist. Light-brown hair sat in a neat coif atop her head, and her eyes shone bright, rivaling the color of her exterior accents.

"Yes?" Her voice was honey. "Can I help you?"

"I'm looking for a . . ." Henry paused to reread the name. "A Mrs. Taylor."

She nodded ever so slightly to confirm she was the Mrs. Taylor he was seeking. Henry nodded back. "I have a letter for you." He handed over the crisp white envelope, and a smile filled her whole face.

"Oh," she squealed, "it's from Elinor." He didn't know who Elinor was. Should he?

Before he could back away and wish her farewell, she ripped it open with the vigor of youth. Henry gasped. Letters were private. She should read it alone, behind closed doors. In case it made her cry. Or—

She let out the highest-pitched laugh he'd ever heard. Doubled over, her small frame heaved with every titter. The humorous letter shook with delight.

"It's her daughter," she said, pulling herself up and wiping the corners of her eyes. "She gets into the most delicious trouble for such a young girl."

"Oh my," Henry said, wishing he could leave. He didn't need trouble right now. He had a job to do.

She folded it back up with a chuckle. "Thank you."

"My pleasure." He turned back to the Ford.

"Wait," she cried, reaching out a hand to stop him. "Where's Arnold?"

Henry felt himself shrink under the scrutiny. He didn't know an Arnold, he said.

"He's my regular mailman. Is he off sick?"

His vision blurred. He wanted to flee. "I don't know . . . I'm just . . . I wanted to make sure you got your letter."

Why was he here? Was there something he needed from her?

"Well, thanks again," she said with a wave.

The door swung shut, leaving Henry with more questions than he knew how to answer.

2244 North Franklin Street
Chicago, IL

Ruth,

You're never going to believe what happened on the weekend. I took the girls to the pool for some afternoon fun. Just a little splash around, you know.

Well, Annie didn't want to go in. She claims she's afraid of the water now, though all summer long she couldn't wait to go to Dave and Sue's for a swim.

Anyways, Annie doesn't want to go in, but Carol does. So, I send Carol off to the shallow end and Annie and I find a seat so we can watch.

I think Carol was happy not to have her younger sister around for a bit.

Well, after a while Annie gets bored (like always) and asks if she can have a little wander around. The pool is enclosed, and she can't go anywhere, so I agree. Go entertain yourself, I say.

Ten or so minutes pass and suddenly the fire alarm is going off. All the kids get bundled out of the pool, dripping wet, and have to leave the building and stand outside in the cold.

Meanwhile, I'm searching for Annie to make sure she's safe. I find her hiding behind a pillar by the front door, tears in her eyes.

It's okay, it's just a false alarm, I say. Carol is safe, everyone is okay.

And she looks at me, with those big blue eyes, and says SHE WAS THE ONE WHO PULLED THE ALARM. Want to know why? Because we've been teaching her to read, and she saw a bright red box that said "Raise Cover, Pull Lever."

Can you believe it?!

Next thing I know, all the swimmers are shivering outside and a little boy comes up to Annie and I and says, "Some kid pulled the fire alarm."

I nearly died!

Needless to say, I've now had many conversations about the meaning of words and context with my five-year-old.

I hope this brings you a little laugh.

Love,

Elinor

33

Wednesday, October 19, 1966

3:04 PM

Stokes paced in front of the window. They still hadn't found Walton. Fletcher had spent two days hanging around Dearborn, but according to him, he hadn't seen a single man with a cane.

Stokes was beginning to think the cane was fake. That Walton had carried it on the night of the break-in just to crash through the glass. The man could probably walk no problem.

The door opened and Brenda edged her head around the corner, keeping most of her body in the hall. Her cheeks were pale. It would be just like her to get sick when Stokes needed her most.

"Sir," she said. "I've been thinking."

Oh, Christ. Stokes could not handle another mention of the backlog. A leather-bound Motorola Ranger sat on the corner of his desk and he reached for the dial, cranking the volume before she could keep going.

"This is WCFL news," the familiar voice of Jimmy Stagg crackled. "We're interrupting those soulful tunes with a breaking update on the Chicago Post Office."

Brenda came into the room.

"It appears the backlog at the post office has been cleared up and residents are once again receiving their mail. A young woman named Julie called into the Stagg Line earlier to give us the good news, saying a man had brought a much-anticipated letter to her front door earlier today. There you have it, folks; the problem's been taken care of in record time. Now, don't go anywhere. We've got some of the best love songs of the year coming up . . ."

Stokes switched off the transistor. "What are they talking about?"

Her eyes widened. "Henry Walton."

"You can't be serious. Fletcher said the man was nearing ninety. There's no way an old geezer's going around town delivering mail."

"He must be. Because it's not us delivering it."

Stokes bent his head back and laughed. "Okay, fine. Maybe Walton is delivering mail. So what? We don't need to worry about that. Leave him to it."

"And what happens when he's delivered all the letters he stole and people stop receiving their mail?"

"Dammit." She had a point. The last thing Stokes needed right now was an old man delivering letters better than him. They needed to find him. "We need to find him. I can't have him out there causing all this chaos."

"Well," Brenda said, taking a step closer. "We could let him keep delivering. It won't hurt to have people believe we're back up and running. It would give us time to deal with the issue at hand . . ."

Why could she not let it go? She should be out there typing out the reports O'Brien had demanded yesterday. Not in here, making time slow down.

"No," he said, turning away from her. "A wanted poster. That's what we need. Henry Walton's face pasted all over town." He could picture it now. The man's smug expression overshadowed by *WANTED* in block letters above his head. "Make it happen."

34

Wednesday, October 19, 1966
6:36 PM

Henry wanted to turn right, but a man in a hard hat wouldn't let him. The roadwork on Polk Street had forced him down a series of detours. Convincing himself he wasn't lost, he kept going only to make things worse. Now he couldn't turn back onto Plymouth, because it had been blocked off.

What a nightmare.

He inched forward, gripping the wheel. A large white van, driven by an even larger man, cut him off, causing him to swerve into the left lane. As he did, the pile of letters flew off the seat and landed in disarray. Course-correcting as fast as he could, Henry leaned into the horn.

Swallowing a curse, he pulled over.

The noise from the construction grated on his nerves, and a headache began to wrap itself from one ear to the other. He looked down at the not-so-neat pile and took a deep breath. Kicking himself for not bringing the master list of deliverables (which he'd inscribed that morning using the brown nightstand as an awkward desk), he reached down to retrieve the scattered mess. He had the map spread out on the back seat, but he didn't know what order everything should be delivered in. There were twenty left to distribute for the day, and while they were all close together geographically, different routes would take much more time than others.

His sigh filled the car.

Reading the addresses aloud, Henry shuffled through them. He knew where he was headed next, so he placed that letter facedown on his lap. One by one he arranged them in an order that made the most sense, given the unexpected construction.

It was a far cry from his original plan, but he couldn't get stuck in the past.

Time to wing it.

Okay. Winging it had been a bad idea.

He drove in circles for the rest of the day, trying to navigate his way around the city with no help from anyone. A large family who didn't speak English all tried to give him different directions to the next address with wild gestures he couldn't decipher. A child on a tire swing told him she couldn't talk to strangers and if he said another word she'd scream. Two teenage boys had laughed in his face when he asked for help. And an old woman who looked like a toad said she didn't believe he was delivering letters to help with the backlog and demanded to see official postal certification.

He had none.

By the time he arrived at the last address of the day, Henry was struggling to keep his eyes open. The outside of the three-story walk-up seemed rather dismal. Just looking at the brick made it crumble, and the rusty front door hung open on its hinges. Multiple units appeared to have broken windows, and an abandoned shopping cart lay on its side in what could hardly be described as a front yard. Garbage spilled from its hollow metal interior, filling the air with a stale, putrid scent.

He could hear music blaring from one unit and loud shouts echoing from another. The darkening sky wasn't helping the appearance of the place. For the first time, Henry noticed the lateness of the hour. Apprehension clogged his throat, and he inhaled deeply to calm his nerves.

He double-checked the address. *Unit 17.*

Under his feet, weeds wound their way up through cracks in the sidewalk. An intercom hung loosely beside the broken door.

It buzzed loudly. An intermittent squeal off and on. After ten rings, a voice crackled through. "Hello?"

"Hi," Henry said, speaking to the wall.

"Hello-o-o-o-o?" the deep male voice called again.

Henry moved closer. "I have a letter for a Mr. Frank Harrington." A brief silence hung in the night air before a loud buzz signaled the fact that he'd been granted permission through the already-open front door. He used his cane to limp awkwardly into a foyer that wasn't really a foyer and made his cautious way up the stairs.

Unit seventeen was on the second floor at the far end of the hall. Through a small rectangular window, he could see the Ford parked on the street. Relieved that no hoodlums had broken in to steal priceless paper artifacts and buoyed by the fact this was his last letter of the day, he raised a hand to knock.

"Open." The yell came from inside the apartment. It was the same tenor that had called down to him through the intercom. Henry hesitated. It went against his nature to enter a man's house unannounced. Except, of course, it seemed he *had* been announced. Although not to his face, or in his general direction at all, for that matter.

Oh, what a mess. He tried the door and found it was, in fact, open.

He couldn't see anything in the entryway. There were no windows, and with all the lights turned off, it was difficult to make out his surroundings. Henry looked down at his shoes. He could hear Elsie reciting her firm no-shoes-in-the-house policy. Did that apply to every house or just their own? he wondered.

He leaned against his cane and reached down to slip the left one off at the heel.

"Leave your shoes on. Come on in; it's just starting to get good."

Henry followed the voice to the end of the hall and stopped short. From the building's outward appearance, he would have said the apartments were run-down and crawling with cockroaches and covered wall to wall in crude graffiti slogans no one except the person who did the artwork could read.

This was anything but.

Beautiful black-and-white photos hung on crisp white walls. A long leather sofa sat low to the ground over a clean, white shag. In front of the sofa sat a modern glass coffee table lined with *TIME* magazines.

From the large television set in the opposite corner, Henry could see a woman in a crisp white skirt having her hand kissed by what appeared to be a matador. A middle-aged man sat on the sofa, eyes intent on the program. His salt-and-pepper hair was trimmed short, and a five o'clock shadow graced his square jaw. Dressed smart in cleanly pressed trousers and a button-up shirt, he matched the feel of the room perfectly.

Save for the two buttons that were left undone to expose a mass of dark chest hair.

"Man, sit down." He gestured to the sofa, and Henry obeyed, stealing a glance at the envelope in his hand to get a name. Frank. "April has just entered the bull ring and is trying to distract the men while Mark locates the designers."

Henry didn't have a clue what Frank was talking about, and he said as much.

Frank laughed. "*The Girl From U.N.C.L.E.* That's April Dancer." They turned their attention back to the show for a while longer. Henry couldn't keep track of the story line, which involved both bullfighting and space rockets. When it finished, Frank crossed the room and switched the television off.

"So, who are you?" he asked, finally giving Henry his full attention.

Henry explained himself. "I have a letter for you." He held it out and watched the color drain from the other man's face.

"Where did you get that?" Frank's voice was a low rumble that made Henry want to recoil. Not waiting for an answer, Frank leaned forward and snatched the letter from Henry's outstretched hand. Mumbling to himself, he stormed out of the room. A loud crash filled the apartment, followed by a string of curse words.

Henry perched on the sofa, not sure if he should stay or go.

"It's from my wife," Frank said, stalking back into the room. He stopped by a small window and looked out. "We haven't spoken for years. She left me." He made it sound like a question. "My mood was like a black cloud hanging over our marriage. Dark. Relentless. It was always there, every second of the day. From the moment we woke up until we fell asleep, it sat between us like an uninvited dinner date who wouldn't leave." He paused, jaw tense. "She used to beg me to get help, to talk to a doctor. But I never did. Back then, I couldn't get myself out of bed, let alone string a sentence together about how I was feeling. It took me a few days to even realize she'd left."

Henry couldn't picture what he was describing. The man in front of him didn't match the image of someone who was so defeated they couldn't move. He looked around at the black-and-white pictures again, and for the first time he registered what they were of. A close-up of a woman crying. A fallen tree being cut into logs. A third showed the edge of a broken glass. At first glance Henry had thought them artsy. Now he saw them differently.

The letter lay faceup on the coffee table, and Henry registered the return address. It was less than a fifteen-minute drive away.

"Will you open it?" Frank's question startled Henry from his thoughts. He wanted to say no. He couldn't possibly; it was none of his business.

Instead, he reached for the envelope and slid a finger under the flap to loosen it. Pulling the pages out, Henry scanned the contents. "I think . . ." He rubbed the back of his neck. "Sometimes people need to save themselves before they can help save others."

Frank's shoulders slumped. He took the letter and read the words his estranged wife had written down just for him.

He didn't notice when Henry said goodbye.

It struck Henry, as he climbed back into the Ford, that each letter he carried brought with it an unexpected piece of humanity. A sliver of life folded neatly into a rectangular envelope.

Was there anything more important? Henry didn't think so.

A restlessness coursed through his veins as he thought about all the people who touched a piece of correspondence on its journey. He'd known, before he'd started, that delivering this stack of mail was important. But he hadn't quite grasped the fact that he would be stepping inside the lives of others, completely unannounced.

"I can't forget this," he said to no one as he started the engine. "I can't forget why I started."

#17 4902 Northcote Ave,
Chicago, IL

Dear Frank,

I'm sure the first thing you'll notice is the postmark of this letter. You always have had a keen eye for detail.

I'm in Chicago.

I have been for a number of months now, getting a job and settling in. I sell Avon on weekends, and during the week I help a family with three small children. The mother, Agnes, is ever so kind and patient.

I wanted to tend to things before writing. It wouldn't have done either of us any good if I'd reached out when I first arrived . . . I wasn't in the right mindset to say what I've been wanting to say for a long time.

I'm sorry for leaving.

Life has felt long, up to this point. Do you ever feel that? As if the years both drag and fly; time at odds with itself.

Frank, your darkness consumed us both. I don't know if you ever realized that. It hung over our lives, suffocating everything in its wake. Once, when you couldn't get out of bed for days, I sat in the corner of the room—in that old rocking chair that belonged to Ellen, the one with the ripped leather I've always wanted to fix—and stayed there. Back and forth I rocked, hoping against hope that you would realize how loved you are. I wanted my presence to be a small light you could cling to, a reminder of what was waiting on the other side of the darkness.

Five days. That's how long you stayed in bed, and how long I stayed there with you.

Do you remember what you said, when the episode was over?

You told me it would have been easier to get out of bed if you hadn't seen my face looming over you every goddamn day.

I thought I was helping, but . . . I wasn't. And before long, that darkness consumed me, too.

It wasn't your fault. It's never been your fault. It's just the way your mind works. But I couldn't let it bring me down too, Frank. I owed it to myself to find the light.

I hope you understand. And I truly hope this letter finds you well. I was thinking (hoping) we could meet up. A coffee in the park while we trade stories?

Well, you know where to find me now. I'm just on the other side of town.

All my love,

Marjory

35

Thursday, October 20, 1966
6:03 AM

In three days, Henry had delivered seventy-three letters. To men, women, grandmothers, and children. To retired old soldiers, moody adolescents, and unopened doors. He felt like he'd already seen the whole spectrum of human emotion. He'd met happy people and sad. Been yelled and cursed at. Had two doors slammed in his face; been offered one whiskey and three pieces of pie. He'd been swallowed by hugs eighteen times and slapped once (it hadn't hurt, but it had taken him by surprise; she was such a tiny old lady). He'd been laughed at, frowned at, and questioned. Some ridiculed him.

Many said thank you; others did not.

Henry reached for his cane, pulling himself up to start a new day. He rubbed at his bad knee. The back of his hand had collected age spots. When had he acquired so many?

Steam fogged up a mirror above a sink he didn't recognize while he shaved (a note had told him to, and he hadn't wanted to disobey himself so early in the morning), and he wiped at the mist with a towel.

"Only two hundred and twenty-seven to go. Give or take." His reflection didn't comment.

Scanning the master list, Henry made a mental note of his route for the day. It would take him in a zigzag across town. If a more efficient way to do it existed, he didn't know what it was.

As the clock moved the day forward, he gathered his wits. When a reasonable hour chimed, he knew there was no time like the present.

"Day four, here I come," he sang as the door closed behind him.

Different salutations filled his day. *Who are you? Whaddya want? What do you mean, it's closed? Hey! Old man!* No one expected Henry, and their surprise rang true with every encounter. After an hour he had mastered the art of deflection, and by noon he was skilled at avoiding people altogether.

He didn't have the stomach for pastries so early, or the time to take his shoes off. No, he didn't need a hug, and thanks but no, he didn't need more coffee.

As the Ford inched closer to empty, Henry took a break. Pulling up to the gas station, he switched the engine off and cranked the window.

"Regular?"

Henry had to crane his neck to see the young man's face. With a long brown beard and a scar across his eyebrow, he was the spitting image of an escaped convict. He repeated the question with a grunt.

Henry nodded.

By the time the Ford was filled and the attendant had moved on to the next car in line, Henry had imagined four different crimes he appeared capable of committing.

Not that he was being judgmental. His motto was *Never judge a book by its . . .* something or other.

The final Chicago addresses passed in a blur as he navigated lanes and crossed busy roads. Calluses were beginning to form along the ridges of his palms, imprints from the steering wheel marking his skin.

When the last local letter dropped through the mail slot of a small boarded-up bungalow, Henry's stomach growled.

Alan Forsythe
3100 N. St. Louis Ave
Chicago, IL

The National Republic Bank of Chicago
1201 West Harrison Street
Chicago, IL

Loan Number: 34900000BH29421000LL

Dear Mr. Forsythe,

I regret to inform you that after repeated attempts to contact you, with no response on your end, we must start legal actions to foreclose your property. You must vacate the property by end of day October 9, 1966. If you fail to vacate the property by the stated date, we will be forced to call the authorities on you and any member of your family who remains.

Sincerely,

Peter Wright

Account Agent

The National Republic Bank of Chicago

36

Thursday, October 20, 1966
11:59 AM

Henry spread the map out. Pushing the salt and pepper shakers to one side, he ran his finger along the route he would take, memorizing the curves in the road. Rockford first, eighty-seven miles away. After that: Davenport, Minneapolis, and Fargo.

Then Canada.

He wasn't looking forward to crossing the border. The last time he'd done so had been in 1936, when Elsie had decided they needed to attend her great-aunt's fourth wedding, even though neither of them had seen hide nor hair of the woman in a decade and knew nothing of her betrothed. He hadn't been back to Canada since that dreadful wedding (the groom's father had too much sherry and spilled wine down the bride's dress and punched out the bartender like a schoolboy). A wave of displeasure washed over him at the memory.

He hadn't really been anywhere since then. He and his wife weren't big adventurers. Their home was their comfort, filled with everything they loved, and traveling felt so . . . intimidating.

For Henry, Elsie was the world. One look at her made his love span the vastness of the ocean, pulling on his heart like a tide. Each freckle was a new destination he wanted to explore, connecting the dots across her fair skin, making her laugh when it tickled too much. Her hair was volcano fire. Her smile the sun.

Where else could he possibly need to go? Nowhere.

Until now.

The food arrived without warning. Before Henry could fold the map, the waitress dumped it on Des Moines. Sauce splashed a lake across western Iowa. Henry wiped at the stain. Pulling the map out from under the plate, he could see the faint smear of sauce through the page.

He thought of asking for a discount, but by the time she came to clean his table, he'd forgotten.

37

Thursday, October 20, 1966

1:30 PM

Flora arrived in such a huff, Stan's mind immediately went to the worst place. He turned scenarios over in his head as his fingers tapped out a tune on the table. The remnants of a half-eaten sandwich sat before him.

"Did you know?" She slammed her purse onto the counter. Two loose coins rolled out and landed with a ping on the floor. "It was at the grocer, pinned up on the noticeboard for all to see. I didn't notice it at first, but Elizabeth pointed it out. Of course she did. Holier-than-thou Elizabeth with her sly grin and her crooked teeth just had to point it out, knowing full well I would come racing home to tell you."

She sank into the chair opposite Stan. His fingers moved faster than his mind.

"Now everyone will be talking about it, and about how I reacted to it in the middle of a crowd. What an embarrassment."

"Flo—"

She fiddled with the tablecloth. "Have you heard from him? I wonder if he's seen it yet. He'll be in a tizzy when he does. Oh yes he will." She reached for his discarded lunch and took a bite. Flora was never one to waste food, what with all the starving children in parts of the world she'd never heard of. "I can imagine what that smug woman is saying to her John now. And he'll be nodding his head and laughing as if he were there." She finally made eye contact. "Well? Don't you have anything to say?"

"I would, dear"—Stan's fingers stilled—"only I don't have the foggiest idea what you're talking about."

"The poster."

"What poster?"

"The wanted poster at the grocer with Henry's face plastered on the front." She finished his lunch and pushed the plate away.

"Wanted?"

"Yes, wanted." Flora raised a penciled eyebrow in his direction. "Did you know?"

"Well . . . I . . . no. I didn't actually. Did it mention . . . am I?"

"Are you what?" She snapped the last word in two.

"Am I mentioned?" His fingers resumed their melody. "Is my name—?"

Flora rose and took his plate to the sink. With her back to him, she gave it a light rinse and set it on the sideboard for drying. When she finally spoke, her voice was ice. "No, you're not mentioned. Just Henry. And now everyone's going to think he's the one at fault and not the post office, instead of realizing the bigger picture."

"Oh. Yes, the bigger picture . . ." He stopped midsentence.

Flora spun around. "His mind, Stan. Sometimes he's completely there, and other times he doesn't know up from down. We're used to it. We've been watching it get worse, and more sporadic, for years. Except now we've let him go off on his own with all these letters, to all these random addresses, and he's stopped calling. So who knows if he's safe or where he is or whether or not he even remembers where he is and why he's there. I told you Virgo demanded a plan."

Stan tried to picture Henry successfully completing his mission, like the mole he'd fixated on. Remaining undetected, slinking in and out, a sight unseen. He knew his friend's memory had been . . . changing . . . but surely he at least knew where he was at all times and why he'd set out on the adventure in the first place.

It was something new.

Something to shake off the routine and brush away some of the cobwebs of his mind. He was off doing something he cared about, and that's what had mattered so much to Stan. It was why he'd helped him in the first place.

But a wanted poster? That certainly changed things.

38

Thursday, October 20, 1966
2:00 PM

Brenda folded the poster in quarters and shoved it into the top drawer of her desk.

The police artist had meticulously etched the fine detail of every wrinkle, spot, and crease on Walton's face. She'd never seen the man, but she could imagine him from the charcoal drawing. Stokes had called it sheer luck that Walton's picture had been printed a few years before in the *Tribune*, celebrating him for something to do with candy.

Stokes had pinned up the poster by his desk so he could blow smoke rings at it.

When the police had asked how Walton had come to be in possession of three hundred letters, Stokes had shot her a look of warning before saying the man was a disgruntled employee, upset about the backlog. The officer hadn't batted an eye at the lie. Mishandling mail was a federal offense. Rest assured, they would find him.

With the police focused on Walton, Brenda needed Stokes to return his attention to the actual problem. He couldn't keep ignoring the issue. Right?

Pushing open the door without knocking, she entered Stokes's office. There he sat, as always, looking like a child in a suit. Smoke billowed above his head.

"Sir, the backlog—" Why was she the only one bringing it up every day?

"Stop worrying so much, Brenda. It's giving you wrinkles. No man wants a woman with wrinkles." His eyes traveled over her body.

Her fingers curled. "I have an idea."

Stokes barked out a laugh. "You? An idea? Go back and type up my reports, Brenda. O'Brien is waiting for them."

She refused to back down. "Of the ten million." Stokes rolled his eyes at her. "At least a million, maybe more, are garbage."

"What do you mean?"

"Magazines, circulars, catalogs. That sort of thing. If we were to get permission to destroy those, we could clear up some space and start sorting."

"And how are we going to do that?" He spun a lighter between yellowed fingers, light glinting off its stainless steel.

"We're going to run an ad in the newspaper, asking people to give us permission to destroy unnecessary pieces of mail. Like circulars and magazines."

She watched as her idea landed like a flicker of hope.

Stokes stubbed out his smoke. "You can start with this." He handed her the Montgomery Ward catalog from the corner of his desk. "I've already ordered the lambswool/alpaca suit in cognac from page five hundred seventy-six."

She didn't tell him brown made him look shorter. He deserved to find that out himself. "I'll write the ad."

39

Thursday, October 20, 1966
5:08 PM

Grease coated the window beside their booth. Roger wanted to run his finger through it, though he knew if he did, his mom would tell him to sit on his hands and stay still.

His leg bounced.

"Did you know grease comes from microscopic drops of oil suspended in the air?" he asked, grabbing a napkin from the metal dispenser and wiping the table. He set the napkin beside him. It looked out of place on the empty table, so he stuffed it into his pocket and opened the menu.

"Is that right?" His mom didn't look up from her own menu, brows knit together in concentration.

He knew she'd get the steak Diane.

Roger decided not to keep talking about volatile organic compounds and tried to focus. Rows of options filled his vision. Burgers, old-fashioned chicken, seafood platters that couldn't be fresh this far from the ocean, spaghetti with garlic bread, chopped liver, soup of the day (undisclosed), corn dogs, and something called a fishwich he didn't want to know anything about. Not to mention milkshakes in seven different flavors and fresh strawberry pie with whipped cream.

"Whatcha havin'?"

She appeared as if from nowhere, red hair matching red lips. Smacking at a wad of gum, she tapped a stubby pencil against a lined notebook and raised an eyebrow.

His mom said, "Steak Diane."

Without enough time to make an informed decision, Roger said, "I'll get a burger."

"What one? We've got plain burgers, cheeseburgers, and Al's Ultimate Chicago Burger."

Roger blinked. "Who is Al, and what makes his burger the ultimate?"

"It comes with cheese, bacon, lettuce, pickles, and Al's special barbe-cue sauce." Tap. Tap. Chew. He was about to repeat the first half of his question when she tossed her head back and said, "Al's the chef."

Roger looked up at her and noticed the lipstick had bled past her lips, leaving a faint ring around her mouth. He could see her molars when she chewed. He ordered a plain burger and a Coca-Cola. When she called his order to the back of Al's head, he swore he heard a grunt.

His mom stabbed a mushroom with her fork. "Have you thought more about what we talked about?" She dragged it through a pile of mashed potatoes and spoke around the bite. "Visiting your dad?"

Roger shifted in the vinyl booth. In the far corner, a jukebox held court. He wondered how many songs it contained. "Yes," he said, taking another bite of his burger and wondering if he should have gone with Al's version. "I've already packed my bags. I'm leaving in the morning."

"Rog . . ."

He shot her a wink. "I can't go. I need to finish all the radios." He couldn't let the faculty go without at Christmas. "I'm up to seven now."

She sliced off a strip of meat, shoulders slumped.

Roger finished his burger. "Honestly, though. I'm not going. I'm not interested in camping or talking or doing anything with him." People streamed past the greasy window. Roger tapped his leg, imagining where they were headed. Did that young girl still talk to her father? What about that man in the unfortunate brown suit?

His mom threw her napkin on the plate, meal unfinished. When she spoke, her voice had a slight wobble. "You need to do this, Rog. Not just for you. For me too."

Roger tilted his head from side to side. "Oh yes, sure. With uncharacteristic speed and resolve, I'll head off into the night, ready to face the joker." He smirked, but she wouldn't meet his eye. "Mom, stop focusing on him. He doesn't deserve even a single thought from us. We're fine."

She slammed her hands on the table; the clank of cutlery echoed through the diner. "Nothing is fine. Look." She yanked her hands into her lap. "I wrote to him. I told him he needed to reach out to you. I'm sorry I didn't tell you, but you need a male role model, Rog. And he's the only option."

He couldn't read the look in her eyes when she finally looked up. His leg moved faster, and he felt as if his whole body might float away, through the roof and into the sky. Another volatile compound in the air.

They paid for the meal, and for once, Roger stayed silent.

40

Thursday, October 20, 1966
5:57 PM

The house was tiny, crammed so tightly up against its neighbors on either side that Henry didn't think he could stretch his arms fully between the dwellings. Weeds were winning the battle, sprouting up across the small front yard in pockets. The overgrown grass looked as if it had stopped trying a long time ago.

Henry parked on the street under a low telephone line.

Narrow steps led him to the covered front porch. In a corner, a ladder leaned against the house, blocking one window. Three buckets were stacked beside it. A rusted shovel lay on the ground, fallen over and discarded. Next door, a dog tied up in the backyard barked incessantly. On the next block over, a car backfired.

Henry knocked, two soft raps.

The dog whined, pulling on its chain. He was glad he couldn't witness its struggle. He jumped as it barked again. Could it read his mind? He hadn't spent enough time with dogs to understand what they were capable of. Maybe it had spent years loosening its chain, waiting for an unsuspecting stranger to turn up next door so it could pounce. He wouldn't be able to fend off a rabid dog, even with a cane.

Henry tried to peer through the window, but he couldn't see anything through the thick lace. Glancing at the letter, he considered how important it was. There were millions that wouldn't get delivered anytime soon. He'd seen them, clogging up the chutes and lining the walls of the receiving platform in unimaginably high towers. So many would get lost, discarded. Perhaps this one too?

Henry shook his head, admonishing himself, and shoved it into his pocket. He was here. He was in . . . whatever this little town was called, and he had a job to do. He couldn't give up before he'd even begun. Squaring his shoulders, he knocked louder.

The door opened a crack. Henry couldn't see anything. "Can I help you?" A low voice filtered out.

Henry peered into the space, catching the dull white of the man's eyes. He towered over Henry, his skin fading into the darkness behind him.

"Can I help you?" the voice repeated, taking on a new edge.

Like a punch, the weight of the situation sank in. The neighborhood he was in, the magnitude of a white man pounding on the door of a Black man. Henry wasn't naive. He knew what had been happening across the country. All those riots and protests; the walks Martin Luther King Junior had organized.

He reached into his back pocket as the door started to close. "Wait!" he cried, pulling out the envelope. "I have a letter." He tried to show it through the crack. The name on the front read *Lewis*. "I'm looking for a Mr. Lewis."

He took a step back, creating space between himself and the door, holding the letter out in front of him. No one would come to his rescue if he got into trouble here. He was the outsider. The intruder. The dog kept barking, louder, angrier. Henry's palms were sweating as he gripped the letter in one hand and his cane in the other.

A lifetime passed before the door opened with a creak.

"What you done doin' bringin' a letter here?" The man's voice was gravel in a blender. "We got our own mailman. Big Steve a' reckon he gone be out of work now."

"I'm not. I. Sorry," Henry stuttered, keeping his gaze lowered. "I'm sure Big—what's his name? I'm sure he still has a job. It's just that the post office in Chicago has shut down, and—"

"The post office done what?" the man asked.

"Closed," Henry said. The wind was stronger here, whistling through the covered porch. It wrapped its icy fingers around his legs and he shivered, cane wobbling in a crack on the porch.

The man looked up and down the street. "You'd better come in and 'splain yerself." He opened the door. "Leave yer shoes on," he hollered as he walked into a corner that doubled as a kitchen. "Shirley'll be home any minute, and she'll kick us both out if she sees you sat at her table with bare white feet."

Inside, the walls were happy, a shade somewhere between lemon and chartreuse. A colorful cloth covered a round table, its edges beginning to wear from the ritual of being removed and returned every day. Four mismatched chairs were tucked in. The faint hint of a roast lingered in the air, mingling with the smell of stale tobacco. Henry tried to picture the man sitting down to dinner with his wife, a half-smoked cigarette between his lips as he listened to her stories. He felt like he could feel the sum of their whole lives just by being in this one room.

"Right, then," the man said, leaning back, lighting a cigarette and tossing the letter onto the table. "Why don't you tell me what's goin' on?"

Gaze fixed on the tablecloth, Henry told him everything he could remember.

About the post office closing and his break-in with Stan. He talked about the people he'd delivered to—the man with the television and crippling sadness; the elderly couple who never opened each other's mail but couldn't agree who should open the letter he delivered, since it had no first name on the front. He told the man about the big houses filled with sorrow and the small houses filled with joy.

The laughter, the tears, the anger.

The man smoked three Lucky Strikes, not uttering a word as Henry told his story in bits and pieces. He didn't prod when Henry forgot a key detail, circling back around when it entered his mind. He didn't ask questions, get mad, or smirk. He listened as Henry recalled what he could. And when it was clear the story was over, the man lit a fourth cigarette, watched the tip glow, and laughed.

His great frame rolled up and down as he doubled over, smacking at his knee wildly. Ash fell around him. Henry's shock lasted for half a second before he too was doubled over.

Their laughter danced around the room and united them.

Wiping tears from his eyes, the man inhaled a final drag before stubbing his cigarette out. "So, you're some kind of rogue mailman?" He chuckled. "Here to save the day with a letter?"

Henry hadn't thought of himself as saving anyone's day. He said as much.

"How many you done delivered so far?"

"About a hundred, give or take."

The man let out a low whistle. "An' how many more you got?"

Henry squeezed his eyes shut and tried to picture the map spread out on the back seat of the Ford. He could see circles inked around the names of cities, a thick line heading north. "I have another handful or so for here . . ." Henry didn't attempt to name where here was exactly. "Then I have some more . . . close by. And some more after that in. Oh, what's it called? It starts with an M . . . Minneapolis. And then Canada." Henry exhaled, mind swimming in fog.

"Well, I'll be damned." The man reached for the discarded letter and scanned the front before tearing it open. Henry shifted in his seat while he waited.

When done, the man crumpled it in his large fist and tossed it toward the garbage. Hitting the rim, it bounced off and rolled to a stop under the table. "Ain't nothin' but hate mail you done come all this way for," he said.

Henry pulled his gaze from the ball on the floor and met the man's eye. "Hate mail?"

"I marched with Dr. King in August," he said, his voice an octave lower than before. "Moved here after Marquette Park 'cause no one wanted nothin' to do with me. Done lost my job. Lost e'rything." Henry held his breath. "That letter you just traveled all them miles to deliver? Nothin' but an ol' work fella spitting hate across the city at me. Tellin' me he's gon' come over here an . . ."

Time stopped, the seconds crashing to a halt. The smoky air hung around them like the faux-fur coat of a long-gone aunt—soft, warm, and completely stifling. Henry tried to process what it meant to go out of your way delivering hate mail to someone in their own home. Sitting at their table, serving up atrocities like afternoon tea. He couldn't breathe. He felt the meaning of it all slipping away, into the recesses of his mind, and he clung to the knowledge of what he'd done, what he'd delivered, grasping what he could from the fragments of reality.

Across from him, the man said nothing. When Henry met his eyes, a slow smile stopped before it even started. He inhaled with a shrug.

Henry stood, the legs of his chair scraping against the worn floor. The man made to rise, but Henry motioned for him to remain seated. Bending down with the help of his cane, he reached for the crumpled ball and held it firmly in his right hand. He could almost feel the anger and hate oozing into his palm. The lines around its edges matched the ridges of his skin.

Henry crushed the ball in on itself, arched his arm, and lobbed it into the garbage where it belonged.

824 Island Ave
Rockford, IL

Lewis,

In view of your low-grade, abnormal personal behavior, I will not dignify your name with a *Mr.* You know you are not equal to us—you do not belong in this country AT ALL. You are sub-human, and immoral. Your children rob and rape our little girls. Your wives steal from our wives.

And YOU marched alongside an evil, filthy fraud.

Now your end is approaching. Yes, your end is fast approaching. YOU KNOW WHAT TO DO. Just tie the noose already. If you don't, we will come do it for you. We know where you live. We will find you no matter where you go, you disgusting animal.

You are not welcome anywhere on this planet.

When you are gone we will rejoice on your grave. We will not stop until all your kind are wiped from this earth and the righteous are the only voices left. You claim to be a man of God, but it was Satan who created you. Now to Satan you must return.

DIE ALREADY.

41

Friday, October 21, 1966
9:07 AM

Stokes's outburst bounced off the wall. "Where's that goddamn folder?" A once meticulously organized stack of folders sat in a heap of loose paper as Stokes pulled files out of his top drawer in random order. Papers of significance fluttered to his feet to join the growing pile of debris.

The folders were color coded. Burgundy for human resources, brown for finance, black for the Blacks, blue for the personnel matters no one was allowed to disclose.

He chewed a hangnail as he surveyed the room. "Brenda. Where is that godda—"

"Folder?" His assistant swept into the room and stopped short.

"Yes. The brown one." Stokes pushed his chair back, wheels rolling over paper under his feet. "I need the finance folder."

"Sir, it's not brown, it's green." She pointed to the corner of a folder on the edge of his desk. "There."

Sliding it closer, Stokes cursed. "You can barely read the writing on this file. How was I supposed to know this is the right one?" Why did everyone keep changing things without consulting with him first? It was as if they thought they could run the place better than him.

"It's your writing."

"What?"

"You said it has to be *you* who writes on the files so you can read them, because apparently my perfect penmanship is not good—"

"Shut up."

He examined the folder's contents, plucking his collar as he read. Halfway through, he spotted a ledger he didn't recognize from a company he'd never heard of: Blue Shield Association. "What company is this?"

"The health insurance company."

"No it's not. Our insurance is with Blue Cross."

"Ours is, yes," she said. "But the receiving staff have a different policy through Blue Shield. You know, the . . ." She pointed to a line showing how many employees were on the Blue Shield Association plan.

"They have insurance?" He didn't pay much attention to the receiving staff. He could care less about their hours or their pay. Or their insurance, obviously. All he knew was they threatened to strike on a monthly basis and were a huge pain in the ass. Especially now, after all that Freedom Movement noise. He was glad to see the momentum they'd gained in the summer was beginning to wane and lose focus.

"Yes. They always have. Used to be with Empire Green, but they went out of business last year. Now it's with Blue Shield. It's been that way for months—you signed the agreement."

A knock at the door cut through his muttered complaint.

"Sir. Do you have a moment?" Aldo leaned into the room.

Stokes responded with a grumble.

"It's just, well, you see—"

"For Christ's sake, spit it out, Lombardo." Stokes spit a sliver of nail onto the floor.

"Right, well." Aldo hesitated. "It's the men downstairs, sir. The receiving crew."

"What about them?"

"They've found something."

Stokes sat up straighter. "What?"

Aldo mimed that he needed a minute and left the room. When he returned, he dragged a young man behind him.

Stokes frowned. "Who are you?" Why did everyone keep interrupting him? He needed to focus on finding Walton and sort this whole mess out. He didn't have time to listen to receiving team grievances.

"Denny, sir."

"Who?"

The young man shot Aldo a glance. "Denny. D-E-N—"

"I know how to spell," Stokes snapped. "What do you want?"

Aldo cut in. "It's the letter with the presidential seal, sir. Denny's been out sick."

Out sick? Stokes would need to deal with that. He should cancel their insurance. That would teach them a lesson.

Denny explained that when he'd arrived today, deeming himself well enough to return to work, he'd asked about the letter.

Aldo nodded. "And I asked how he knew about the letter."

"I'm the one who put it aside," Denny said.

"And?" Stokes didn't have time for this. Brenda frowned and signaled for him to pay attention.

"I remember the address."

A slow smile spread across Stokes's face. He rose and came around the front of the desk. "You know the address?" He'd been screaming at the receiving crew for days, trying to learn more. And now this kid strolls in with the biggest break of all.

"Yes, sir."

Stokes dismissed them with a backhanded wave and told Brenda to call for Fletcher.

If they knew where Henry Walton would be heading, they could find him and put this whole mess behind them in no time.

42

Friday, October 21, 1966
11:14 AM

Brenda leaned in to listen. Stokes had spent all morning locked in his office with Fletcher mapping out a plan of attack. That's what he'd called it—an attack. She'd tried to show him the ad she'd been able to get printed overnight, but he refused to pay attention. Now she strained to hear his muffled phone conversation with O'Brien.

"Like I said," she heard him say. "Everything is under control." She pictured him spinning around with a self-satisfied grin on his face. "We know where Walton is headed, so we'll be able to stop him before he causes too much trouble. Yes. Yes, I know. But it's an address in town, so not too far. No. Yes. I understand."

Brenda wished she could hear what O'Brien was saying. Was he making it clear the backlog took priority?

Stokes's voice went up a notch. "It does matter. Look, we know where to find him, so that is going to be the focus right now. Yes . . . yes. About that. I've had a genius idea. We've run an ad in the paper. I was able to get it printed overnight, to ask people for permission to destroy unnecessary pieces of mail. Yes. Magazines, circulars, that sort of thing. Thank you, sir. I agree, it's a good idea, and it will give us a chance to shift some of the excess and start sorting."

Brenda scrambled to understand what he was saying. She felt light-headed.

"Thank you, sir. I appreciate the praise. It means a lot coming from you. No, no. Unfortunately, everyone else has proved incompetent. But don't worry. I'll make sure I continue supporting them. We'll get through this."

She heard a roaring in her ears. Tripping away from the door, Brenda clenched and unclenched her hands. Had he honestly taken credit for her idea? And for Denny's discovery?

She'd clearly underestimated just how calculating the man was. Well, two could play that game. Composing herself, Brenda strode toward the elevator and jabbed at the call button.

If Stokes wanted to take credit, she'd give him something big to put his name on.

43

Friday, October 21, 1966
7:02 PM

Situated on a grassy plot outside town, his last house of the day was neither large nor small. It sat, proud of its middle-class size, at the end of a long driveway curved in two directions like an exaggerated S. Henry drove slowly, making his way up the pavement, conscious of how much attention an unknown car drew in the countryside.

He rang the bell and waited, leaning on his cane for balance. The door opened in a burst, and he gripped his cane tighter. The woman before him filled only half the doorframe. She looked to be in her seventies, though she had aged exceptionally well. Which might be on account of the small dumbbells she was pumping. Raising them one at a time, she punched the air above her head, keeping with the beat he could hear from inside the house and closing the height difference between them.

"Yes?" *Up, down, switch.* Her voice was like a song. A gray permanent curled around her heart-shaped face, and thick, round, mahogany glasses framed bright eyes.

Up, down, switch.

"I'm Henry," he said, eyes traveling in time with her movements.

"Hiya, Henry. I'm Delwyn. C'mon in." Arms still pumping, she turned away and disappeared into the house.

What was it with people inviting him inside? He was the mailman. The mailman was known to stay on the doorstep, never to cross over the threshold. His feet felt like lead, and he was about to place the letter under a corner of the front mat when, above the sound of the music, she told him to close the door because he was letting all the heat out and did he normally come to people's houses only to waste what precious energy they had?

Henry followed the rhythmic melody through a wide, open foyer, past a kitchen where everything was white (he hadn't known they made white toasters; Elsie would love that) to a sunken den in the back with thick shag carpet. She was squared in front of the television, arms moving in sync with a young girl on the screen shouting out positive affirmations with a voice dipped in sunshine. *You're doing great! That's it! Keep going!*

The on-screen woman continued to speak in exclamation points while the real-life woman in front of Henry dripped from the effort of trying to keep up with an instructor forty years her junior. "I want to keep up my physique," she panted between sets. "Almost done, grab a seat."

He perched on a dark suede armchair, peeled his eyes away from the aerobics, and noticed, for the first time since entering her house, the clocks.

They were everywhere.

There were two imposing grandfather clocks on either side of the bay window with intricate carvings etched into their wood. One had geometric designs, the other an animal totem topped by an eagle spreading its wings. Three grandmother clocks lined the opposite wall, and seven small clocks of various shapes and sizes lined the fireplace mantel. A large one hung across from the television, its pendulum ending in an exaggerated disk and swinging left and right in a heavy sideways motion. Henry slid silently from the arm of the chair into its soft berth, drawn into the sounds. Under the cheery sound of the program and the heavy breathing of his host, he could hear the soft ticking of each clock. While they were all set to the same hour, their individual mechanisms caused them to tick forward in time in an uneven musical dance.

He closed his eyes and listened.

When she said "All done," the symphony faded into the background.

Henry peeled one eye open and watched her place the weights on the ground and smooth out her pantsuit. It wasn't a traditional aerobics suit, like the one Flo wore when she was doing her steps beside Stan as he watched baseball. This one, rather, was made of some sort of velvety-cottony material. With a smile that filled her whole face and woke a dimple in her left cheek, she turned to him.

"Cuppa tea, love?" She didn't wait for him to answer.

Henry stifled a yawn and followed her from the room, the clocks ticking their farewell. In the kitchen, windows spanned one whole wall and showcased a darkening sky. He could make out an expansive garden, edged by tall cedars to the back and sides.

She gestured at a stool tucked under a crisp white countertop. "Fancy telling me who you are?"

Henry climbed on, feet dangling awkwardly, and rested his cane between his knees. Her accent was stronger now that the house was quiet (save for the clocks; there were three in the kitchen), and he tried to place it. Scottish, perhaps?

"Sorry. I'm Henry." Had he already told her? "Henry Walton."

He had. "I know your name, Henry love, but I don't know who you are or why you're here." Her dimple made another appearance.

"Oh, right." He reached up to cover a yawn as it escaped and gave her the abridged version: post office, letters. "I'm looking for a Mr. Joseph Davies," he finished, gripping the mug she'd handed him.

"Davies," she said, not pronouncing the *e*. The steam rose from her tea and swirled around her face. "Welsh, it is."

"My apologies, a Mr. Joseph Davies," he corrected himself, and took a sip, the tea warming his throat. She opened a packet of Peek Freans and offered him one. Henry selected a delicate butter biscuit and took a bite.

"Right, then," she said, taking two for herself before dunking one into the hot liquid. "I'm afraid you've wasted a trip. Joey's dead."

Henry's chest constricted.

He reached for the edge of the counter as a memory sharpened. His heart threatened to stop, hammering itself into his mouth, choking him. As his mind swirled and broke open, reality crashed to the surface with a slap.

Elsie wasn't at William's. William wasn't . . . it was too much. Henry felt as if the world had stopped. His cane fell in a clatter by his feet.

44

Friday, October 21, 1966
7:52 PM

Elsie was gone, and Henry was drowning in half-formed visions, unable to see anything with clarity but knowing deep down it was true.

How many times can a heart break from the same pain?

Low and vicious, a groan escaped his throat. Animal. He gripped the counter tighter, vision blurring. His ears rang with the dying echo of a forgotten life.

From far away, a hand on his arm, a slow dimple.

Gulping at the air, Henry resurfaced in a daze. He rubbed at his eyes, shoulders shaking, and tried to sit straighter. With a bottomless exhale, he regained some composure.

Time passed, and she downed the rest of her tea without a word. Henry peered into the bottom of his own mug and wondered if there was anything to what Flora had shared recently about tea leaves. He didn't see any divine messages; just a few brown bits clinging to the porcelain. "She's been gone nearly ten years now, my Elsie," he heard himself say. "A car accident, the night before our anniversary. She was out buying balloons." He sucked air through his nose. "I forget, you know. That she's gone. I find myself talking to her—about her—as if she's just in the next room. It's as if all my memories are locked in a trunk I can't open. They're there, just out of reach. But they aren't tangible. I can't unlock the life we had."

She took his mug and placed it alongside hers in the deep white basin. With her back to him, she stood gazing across the yard. Henry peered at the closest clock, squinting to read the delicate black numbers. It was getting late. He was about to tell her as much when she caught him off guard.

"Fancy a bonfire?"

45

Friday, October 21, 1966
8:13 PM

Loud crackling filled the night air. It took them two trips to lug the bundles of wood from the shed to the stone-ringed fire pit. Delwyn carried more than he did. She also built the fire. Though, in his defense, he did hand over the matches that were out of her reach. She'd invited him to stay the night. Insisted, really. "No sense driving around town for a hotel room when I have a perfectly good spare room here," she'd said. Henry, grateful for the chance to rest, had accepted.

"I'm sorry about Joey," he said as a faint glow from the flames crept over the ground and up their legs.

Delwyn sat across from him in a lawn chair that was more rust than metal, a wool blanket spread across her legs. It had taken him four tries to get his chair open in the dark. In the end, Delwyn had to help.

"Thank you. It's been a few months now." She twisted a ring in her lap. "I'm slowly getting used to the idea, though I reckon it takes a little longer to get used to someone not being around after fifty years of marriage."

"More like the rest of a lifetime." Henry rubbed at his knee.

"What was Elsie like?"

"The life of the party," he said, sinking deeper into the chair. A spark struck the ground beside his foot. The air smelled of cedar. "She loved to host. Anytime we were in public, she would invite people over for dinner. I swear she went for walks just to find strays and bring them home to feed." The embers flickered. Henry could see patterns in them. Faces and shapes.

"She burned everything," he continued with a trembling laugh. "Her invitations came fast and furious, but once she poured a drink, she never stopped talking. She'd spend an hour tittering on about a dress Lee Remick was wearing and forget all about the roast beef. I can't count the number of times our house almost burned down. She would've saved the world if she could."

A bat flew overhead, its high-pitched echo tracing a line through the darkened sky.

"Tell me about this letter then, love." Delwyn's hands stilled. Henry pulled it from his pocket and leaned forward, using the light from the fire to read the crisp black writing spelling out Joey's name and the address of the house behind him.

"I don't know much," he said. "It was in the pile of letters I happened to take. Judging by the fact it has no footprints on it, I'd say it was on the conveyor belt, in a river of identical envelopes."

Coming around the fire, she collected it from him. Henry could see her staring at the return address. The light of the fire filled the creases of her frown, and he hoped, with a worsening knot in his stomach, it wasn't hate mail.

"It's from his brother," she whispered, before tossing it onto the flames.

Henry cried out, but it was too late. He watched as the paper curled in on itself and disappeared. Tears pricked his eyes and he wiped at them, hoping the darkness would hide the sudden emotion. It wasn't his letter. It wasn't his life. The wood cracked and popped in the cool air, and he folded his arms across his chest. He tried not to wonder what words had been contained inside.

"Sorry you came all this way for nothing, love."

Henry didn't respond. He was too tired to deal with all the feelings folded into the envelopes that sat on his passenger seat. Feelings he was carrying around and dropping at the feet of unsuspecting strangers. They ran through his veins like lead. He could feel his eyes closing, the warmth lulling him to sleep. The last thing he saw was a tunnel of smoke dancing in the air. And Delwyn's shadowed face on a glowing, velvet-clad body.

46

Saturday, October 22, 1966

7:24 AM

The faint smell of smoke lingered in the air as Henry made his way down an unfamiliar hall. In the kitchen, his host sipped a mug of tea, steam rising around her face.

"All right, love?" she asked as he stood on the threshold.

Henry rubbed a hand over the stubble that coated his jaw, trying to remember the night before. "I have to ask," he said, motioning around the room. "About the clocks."

Delwyn smiled, dimple springing to life, and told him to follow her. They descended a narrow set of stairs into a cool, dark basement. She tugged on a cord, light filled the space, and his breath caught in his throat.

There were clocks everywhere.

Full clocks, broken clocks, bits of clocks. There were more tools than he'd seen in his life lying this way and that on every surface. A long worktable had been constructed out of an old barn door, its peeling paint mingling with old springs and loose numbers. Along one wall, three shelves were lined with more tools and various clock-building equipment than Henry had a name for. On one end of the highest shelf, a heavy mantel clock was missing its face, making it look more like a gothic metal statue of a woman lying in wait than a timepiece.

Down there, under the earth, the ticking was amplified.

Crossing a sea of haphazard numbers on the floor, she said, "Clocks were Joey's hobby."

Henry stepped over a flowery *4* only to land on a thick, brass *9*. She led him to the center of the room, beside the worktable, and picked up a small pocket watch. "His father was a horologist. The best in all of Wales. He taught Joey how to make them when he was a lad, and that passion never faded. He used to sell them at fairs and markets every so often when we were first married. He once helped a woman repair a clock she'd been gifted by the Queen. It was the ugliest thing I'd ever seen." She wiped a layer of dust off the pocket watch with her thumb before setting it down. "He spent all his spare time down here, tinkering away. It was where he was happiest." She closed her eyes and inhaled deeply. "He always said clocks were a little like people. When clocks get too wound, their power needs to be let down so they don't get damaged. It's something to do with the energy they hold and what happens if you try to fix a clock that's holding pent-up energy. If I got upset over nothing, Joey would tell me to 'let down the power,' and it was my cue to unwind a little, relax. As humans, we get so caught up in our own stresses and worries, winding ourselves tighter and tighter. Sometimes letting down the power is what we all need."

Henry looked around. There were so many intricate designs and details. He stepped over a toppled pile of tools to study the most beautiful cuckoo clock he'd ever seen.

It was hanging low on the wall, and he could just make out its features under the dim overhead bulb. It was carved from a solid piece of wood into the design of a mountain chalet. Two evergreens framed the round face, boughs of needles ending in a pointed treetop. Above them, a mountain cliff had been carved with rock details and two more trees. The chalet had a little wooden door, where presumably the cuckoo bird would pop from if the piece were in working order, and five etched windows. A pile of firewood was carved into the side of the house under a tall chimney. Beneath the clock face—a dark hazelnut brown with white roman numerals—a small deer looked out as if to make sure someone in the real world was there to keep time. Below the deer, two weighted chains hung down into empty space.

"It's funny, isn't it? Time. We always think we have more than we do." Delwyn turned a complex metal wrench over. "Joey held time in his hands. He made it seem so tangible, so alive. A ticking heart around every corner, tucked into every crevice, placed on every shelf. When we were first married, I warred against those clocks. I didn't want the incessant ticking reminding me all day, every day, that time was passing me by. I tried to ignore the magnitude of it. The breath between seconds, the slow momentum of one hour rushing into the next. And then one day, he brought me down here. He led me over to a broken grandfather, and he asked me to fix it. 'I can't fix a clock,' I said, 'I can't repair time.'" She set the wrench down and met Henry's gaze. "We're bound by time. All of us. That day, in front of a clock I couldn't fix, I realized that by not paying attention to time, I was inadvertently throwing so much of it away. It's not infinite, but it's important. How we use it, whether or not we go after our dreams. Joey repaired that clock, of course. And me? I learned to clutch time between my trembling fingertips and hold on tight."

Her smile wasn't enough to wake her dimple in the low light. Uneven ticking echoed around them from half-finished clocks.

Henry ran a hand over the tools in front of him. He thought again of her words: *We're bound by time.* Picking up an *8*, he traced the edges. "Do you wish you had more?" The metal rasped his fingertip.

Delwyn bit the inside of her cheek. "I don't think I have an answer for that." Above them, a clock struck the hour: eight loud chimes seeping through the floorboards and landing at their feet.

3902 Whitfield Dr
Rockford, Illinois

Joey,

It's been a few years, hasn't it, mate? I was surprised to receive the letter from Delwyn. Mary told me to toss it away without even opening it, but what use would that be, I said. If someone takes the time to sit down and write to you, the decent thing to do is read what they have to say.

I'd say I'm sorry to hear about your heart. But I'm not.

I reckon it serves you right, having a ticking time bomb in that chest of yours. No point sugar coating my feelings after all this time. You followed your heart, no matter how much it hurt anyone else, and claimed whoever and whatever you wanted. Bold, handsome Joseph Davies who could've had any girl he wanted.

You just had to choose the love of my life, didn't you?

So that failing heart of yours, I'm not that sad to hear about it. Thirty years hasn't been enough time for me to forget. Perhaps in another three decades, with you underground, I'll find it in me to forgive. Mam always said our stubbornness would be our ruin. Don't want to prove her wrong now, do we?

You turned your back on your family and your homeland. Now we're finally turning our backs on you.

Gareth

47

Saturday, October 22, 1966
9:14 AM

Fletcher ambled onto the receiving platform to do his rounds. He'd been so distracted by Walton lately, interrogating shopkeepers and staking out the neighborhood, though he had yet to see the man who'd broken in.

To be fair, he had to go off the police sketch more than his own memory. He'd only seen the back of the man, fleeing the scene with a cane in hand.

Fletcher had started daydreaming about catching him. In his mind, he was fifty pounds lighter and able to keep up with two men double his age. He'd take the stairs three at a time, gaining on the thieves before they could enter the lobby. Spinning them around, Fletcher would lean in close to get a sense of who he was dealing with. They would cower under his glare, arms out, ready to be detained. In his imagination, Fletcher saved the day every single time.

Coming onto the platform, Fletcher looked up and stopped short.

A van had reversed on Harrison Street, its back door open wide. Stacks of mail were being funneled into the van by receiving staff.

Brenda stood to the side, supervising the efforts.

"Hey," Fletcher called, lunging forward. "What's going on?"

Brenda spun around and wrapped her arms around herself. "We're destroying unsolicited mail. You know, magazines, circulars, flyers . . ."

"But there are letters in there." Fletcher saw a bag of mail get tossed into the van, followed by another.

Brenda shifted her weight onto her left foot. "Vince, just ignore it."

Fletcher tugged at his fingers. "Ignore what? The crew need to be more careful." He pointed to another load of letters being thrown around. "They're making mistakes."

She puffed out her cheeks and came to stand beside him. Fletcher wasn't used to feeling so small. He wondered how Stokes felt next to the woman.

"Like I said," she hissed, leaning toward him. "Ignore it. There's nothing to see here. We're just disposing of things, like Stokes asked."

Fletcher rocked on the spot as he realized what she was doing. "Brenda, you can't burn actual mail."

She looked away. "I'm not."

"You'll never get away with it."

Her face pinched in on itself. She really could use some rouge. "Stokes has already taken credit for my grand idea. Since he wants to bask in all the glory, I'm merely giving him something to bask in."

Fletcher swallowed thickly. He knew once Brenda set her mind to something, there was no convincing her otherwise. He'd once tried to suggest they add extra security to the lobby, given the location of the Postal Savings Bank and the special-delivery windows. He'd wanted her opinion before taking the idea to Stokes. She'd looked down her nose at him and said the information desk, handling more than thirty-five thousand calls a month, was understaffed and if he even so much as mentioned extra security over desk staff, she'd get him fired.

The crew loaded more mail onto the van as Fletcher trundled off the platform, lips sealed.

An hour later, a chimney of smoke appeared in the afternoon sky.

1930 Carpenter Street, S
Chicago, IL

Brenda,

You do seem to get yourself into sticky situations, don't you, dear girl.

It's no surprise. You've always been trying to prove yourself in a world full of men who won't listen.

It doesn't help you're taller than so many of them.

I remember the time little Larry Butler tried to steal your idea (for a tool pouch with attachable straps so it could be customized by the wearer) in class and you knocked him clean out. I had to collect you from school, and wouldn't you believe you kicked that boy's shin on the way out the door while he sat in the hallway bleeding. An extra dose of suspension came for that one.

I'm glad you're finding a way to work the system and still maintain a modicum of control.

Just be sure to cover all your tracks, if you know what I mean.

Lots of love,

Vera

48

Sunday, October 23, 1966
2:11 PM

Roger closed his eyes as thoughts engraved themselves on the backs of his eyelids like an Etch A Sketch. The envelope from his dad threatened to overwhelm him from the corner of his desk. He'd turned it over so he couldn't see his name written on the front, but that hadn't helped.

"I'm not very good at knowing what to do," he whispered to himself.

It hadn't always been that way. When he was young, his mom said, he would talk to anyone and everyone, making decisions and directing people around. They called his fidgeting endearing, his talkative nature an adorable quirk. And then his dad left, and suddenly Roger's quirks weren't so appreciated. He could remember the time his mom snapped at his endless questions, throwing a mug against the kitchen wall in exasperation. It wasn't him, she'd pleaded later, tears salting her cheeks. She was just . . . sad.

Roger still saw that sadness flit across her face every now and then, no matter how hard she tried to be strong.

He swung his legs over the side of the bed. "I need to be strong *for* her. Even if I don't feel strong and don't want to go see the man who walked out on us and have literally nothing to say to his face. Or behind his back, for that matter." He paced his small room, touching objects as he passed. His new Cubs hat, a gift for his seventeenth birthday from his mom; a signed picture of Don Kessinger; a binder that held the extra homework he'd accumulated; the trophy he'd won playing T-ball. It was the only year he'd played. After that, all the other kids told him he wasn't wanted. Apparently, he couldn't stand still long enough to catch a ball.

On his third lap, Roger's hands picked up a tremble he couldn't stop. What if his father turned him away? What if he drove all the way to the Badlands and got told to get lost? He didn't think it was possible to get any more lost than he already was.

With a sigh, Roger resigned himself to the trip. For his mom and his future and maybe, just a little, for himself.

But definitely not for his father.

49

Monday, October 24, 1966
9:30 AM

On Monday, it took Henry three hours to get to Davenport. The sun crested the horizon as he drove off, Delwyn in his rearview mirror waving the handkerchief he'd gifted her like a beacon of hope. He had thought, rather optimistically, that some rest was all he needed to clear his mind and shake the ever-present feeling of forgetfulness.

He'd thought wrong.

He took the wrong exit at one point and didn't notice he was heading in the wrong direction. By the time he realized his mistake, he'd wasted hours of precious morning light, and he practically threw the three letters he had to deliver in the area at their unsuspecting recipients—including one to a wisp of a woman who hid in the shadows, barely making eye contact. She accepted the letter with an unsteady hand, as if it meant to bite her fingers clean off.

She looked, to Henry, like a defeated housewife in need of a break.

A break would do him some good as well.

His aim for the day was to get to Minneapolis and find a place to rest. He estimated it was going to take seven hours to get there, and another three to Fargo. If he could stop off in Minneapolis to rest and regroup, he'd be in Fargo by the morning and be halfway through his trip this time tomorrow.

All Henry needed to do now was keep his head down and his foot on the gas.

He was just past Cedar Rapids when things started to get strange. The first person to shoot him an odd look was a gas attendant.

Everything seemed normal when he asked for regular and the attendant filled up the Ford. But when the young man came back with his change, he leaned right in close and squinted at Henry through heavy lids.

Henry took the change and sped off, forgetting to say thank-you.

An hour later, near Cedar Falls, a woman in the grocer's did a double take when she saw him. In a small bathroom, tucked behind the meat counter and a stack of boxes marked EXPIRED, he peered into the mirror above the sink. The right half of the mirror was cracked in so many fine lines that there were multiples of him. Too many. Aside from the still-there disgraceful layer of stubble and the wrinkles he couldn't erase, there was nothing on his face to indicate why people kept staring.

He hurried out of the store without purchasing anything.

The tank of gasoline disappeared as the odometer crept higher, each mile indicated by the spin of a little white number. He'd stopped counting the total number of miles some time ago and couldn't remember if he'd started on 23,013 or 21,330.

He swung into an Esso.

Its red-and-blue sign shone against a sailor's favorite sky. Shifting into park, he bent to wind down his window as a young man approached the car. When Henry looked up, the kid did the same double take the woman had done in Cedar Falls, his mouth falling open as though a screw had fallen loose.

Henry narrowed his eyes. "Regular," he said with a grunt.

The young man with no manners didn't move. With a sigh, Henry thrust the bills out the window. "Will you pump it?" he asked. "Or is this one of those newfangled ones I do myself?"

"Is your name Henry?"

With a start, Henry pulled the cash back into the car. He always hated it when people he couldn't place knew his name. Every time Elsie had a party, he dreaded having to be reintroduced to husbands he'd already met and whom he'd forget by the time they got their coats. Name tags, he'd once suggested. She had shot him down.

Now he peered at the boy. The kid didn't look familiar, but there was no way for him to know for sure he'd never met him. He thought about saying *No, I'm not Henry.* Instead, he confirmed the query and asked through gritted teeth, "How do you know my name?"

The kid turned and walked into the station without a word.

"Goodness," Henry muttered, pulling himself from the car and turning to face the pump. It didn't look like a do-it-yourself version, but what did he know. Twisting off the gas cap, he told the machine he wanted regular petroleum and inserted the wand into the gas tank.

Shuffling into the gas station, Henry tapped his cane on the ground. "I figured it out," he said to the kid who hadn't returned, "no thanks to you."

Without a word, the young man pointed to a small television propped up on a shelf in the corner behind the till. On the screen, in black and white, was a drawing of Henry's face. The rough charcoal sketch made his ears look bigger than they really were. Above his face was the word WANTED in thick black type. Below it were his name and the phone number that should be called anytime if someone happened to locate him. He was not dangerous, the notice said, but chances should not be taken, as his behavior up until that point could only be described as erratic.

Henry stared at the screen. The kid moved from one foot to the other, and Henry wished he would stop. Fidgeting made it hard to think.

Studying the image on the screen again, Henry scanned the fine-print details and realized, with a sinking stomach, why the kid looked so nervous. They were offering a reward. He looked at the boy and saw a line of sweat starting to form along his hairline.

Henry knew he had two choices.

He could pay for the gas and wait for the police, who had undoubtedly already been called, to arrive. Or he could hightail it out of there.

He did the latter.

703 Wilson Ave
Sterling, IL

Maisie,

I didn't know where to send this. My best guess is you'll have gone to your mother's in Sterling, but you could also be hiding away with Lila up there, too.

Where are you, Mais? It's time to come home to Springfield.

I know you're feeling embarrassed after last week's dinner party. But a few burnt rolls is nothing to get upset over. Yes, I yelled. But that was just in the heat of the moment because I was disappointed in how we were coming across to Neil and Georgia. Did you know Georgia once served a dinner party of 30 guests (including the Governor of Illinois) and still gets rave reviews over it? Of course, I was mad that you couldn't even handle a roast for four.

But you know I never mean anything I say when I'm upset. You know that, Mais! Those are just silly words said in the heat of the moment. They don't count. And I didn't mean to grab you like that. You know I didn't, right, Maisie girl?

And, yes, sure, I was also upset about the curtains. I still don't understand what possessed you to try and unhook them from the rod with the fire poker. You should have known you were never going to reach high enough. You're too short! Maisie, you must know all of this. I sometimes wonder if you even have a brain inside that tiny head of yours. If you do, it doesn't get much use.

Come home and we can put things right. I've already had Mrs. Clark around to mend my trousers, the curtains, and that white shirt you stained. So, you see, everything is fine again. You just need a little extra support around the home to aid you in your duties before you officially become Mrs. Blythe. I have no doubt the rest of your wifely duties will be up to scratch.

Also, I heard they can get you into the Tupperware club starting next month. That's a nice thing for you to do on Wednesdays, while I'm at the club.

Come home darling,

Phillip

50

Monday, October 24, 1966
1:22 PM

Brenda rubbed her temples as Stokes lifted his chin and repeated the question. By the window, Aldo stayed unnaturally still.

"I don't have an answer," said Fletcher, employing the exhausted tone of someone used to being blamed. He stood hunched in the corner, blinking at such a rapid rate that the sweat that would have been pooling in his eyes was instead bouncing off his short eyelashes and landing on every surface within a three-foot radius. Brenda wished he would grow a backbone. "My job is to patrol the floors," he said, "not investigate the happenings at every level. And I can assure you, no one is confiding in the lowly security guard as to why they're quitting such a fine establishment."

The adjective fell like a lead balloon.

Stokes muttered in front of the window, biting at the raw edges of a nail. "We've brought in more workers to help sort. We've started paying minimal overtime, though if you ask me, those *people* don't deserve overtime. They should be grateful for what they're given. It's not like they're slaves." Brenda flinched. Stokes continued. "And O'Brien has set up a goddamn task force . . . Right." He surveyed the room. "What's the latest news? How many magazines are we destroying?"

She stepped forward. "We've been able to get rid of nearly half a million, give or take, sir."

Stokes whistled. "That's more than I expected. I'm surprised we had so many magazines in the first place."

Fletcher shot her a look, but Brenda ignored him. “Yes, I was surprised too. It seems we have a lot of catalog readers in town.”

She hid a smile as she pictured the van driving away, turning into a green space, and navigating narrow lanes. Passing by thousands of etched granite tributes, it would have come to a stop in front of an old stone building, money and bags passing hands in silent procession before the van drove away as fast as it had arrived.

“That’s great news,” Stokes said. “I can’t wait to update O’Brien.”

Brenda’s smile dissolved as Aldo, head shaking, interrupted. “You don’t understand.”

Looking at the carpet intently, Aldo explained that while permission to destroy thousands of circulars *was* a great start, the way people were giving their permission was less than ideal. “They’re dropping off letters,” Aldo said with a groan. “They’re writing letters to say it’s okay if we destroy the circular they ordered in the mail because they want to do their part and help with the backlog.”

The color drained from Stokes’s face. “Mailing in permission?”

“Yes. In addition to getting permission over the phone, we’re also getting letters. Letters that are now stacked on top of the millions we’re trying to get rid of. That’s why the receiving room staff are quitting,” Aldo explained.

They were being swept away, quite literally, by a landslide of correspondence.

To the Chicago Post Office

I’m writing to formally give you permission to get rid of the Avon brochures and magazines I receive in the mail.

I’m an Avon representative; that’s why I get so many. And they expect me to cart them around to everyone’s house with a smile on my face, flicking page by page while women in multiple shades of pink order beauty products they do not need.

It's a service of the highest order, they said once in a letter. And that I'm to shower my neighbors in the good ol' Avon Attitude.

Fine! But stop sending me so many damned magazines, I say.

So yes, you can definitely destroy those. You have my permission. I hope this means the backlog will get cleared up soon. I'm expecting an important letter from my aunt (there's money involved!), and I do hope it's not lost in the fray.

Please let me know if I can be of more assistance.

Augusta (Auggie) Day

51

Monday, October 24, 1966
7:41 PM

By the time Henry checked into a hotel that night, he'd received two more strange looks: one from the receptionist on the front desk, another from a businessman pacing the lobby. Head lowered, he'd lugged his bags up to the fourth floor and unlocked a wooden door so thin he could put a fist through it.

Tossing everything against the wall, he sat on the edge of the bed. The springs pushed up through the comforter, waging a fight against the mattress and trying to break free.

He rubbed a hand across his jaw, stubble scratching at his palm. It felt foreign to him, but he knew he'd have to keep it if he was on the run. A beard was the only way to disguise himself from the Henry who had started this journey.

Lying back, Henry stared at a crack weaving its way along the ceiling. Dark water stains circled it in one corner and wound a separate path toward the light.

It would be just his luck to have the ceiling cave in while he slept.

He leaned over and flicked on the small wireless that sat atop a wooden bedside table. "The fire raged into the night last week," a man's voice crackled, "and a reported twelve firefighters were killed in the blaze that engulfed the Wonder Drugs on Twenty-Third Street. Moving on, more people are reported missing after an earthquake struck Peru—"

So much death and sadness; he didn't know where to store all that pain. He waited for the next story, already forgetting how many had perished in the fire.

"The Chicago Post Office announced this morning they will be back up and running"—Henry dove for the radio and turned the volume up—"within the week. A Mr. Reginald Stokes, manager of the Chicago Post Office, held a press conference today. In his comments, he stated an unrealistic freeze on personnel and overtime hours, as so imposed by the administration, combined with an unexpected spike in the volume of mail, contributed to the shutdown. Noting the low morale of employees, especially Black workers, and the stonewalling of discussions with senior management, Stokes said that, while the post office would be back up and running soon, the situation was far from over. His superior, postmaster general Lawrence O'Brien, later released a comment on the heavy accumulation of Christmas catalogs and said that workers deliberately caused the closure of the facility in response to the no-overtime order. So, there you have it, folks. Management is blaming the administration and the administration is blaming management, while hundreds of people are giving permission to have their circulars destroyed. Meanwhile, there's still no sign of the man the post office claims broke into the building and ran off with people's prized mail. Anyone who sees the man is encouraged to call the police."

A commercial break cut into the announcement.

Mail was being destroyed? It didn't matter that people had deemed it unimportant. It was still something they were expecting.

Ignoring the comments about being wanted, Henry thought back to all the deliveries he had made so far. While some of them had been less than ideal, so many of them had been happy reunions. He couldn't imagine what would have happened if every one of them had been burned instead of delivered. That girl would never have read the thing that made her laugh so hard, and the man would've kept wondering where his wife was, and Delwyn would have always wondered why Gareth never wrote back.

And . . . he let his thoughts dissipate.

"You won't be destroyed," he said to the letters that lined the wall. "If it's the last thing I do."

That night, he dreamt there was a great big hole in the floor of the receiving platform. Flames were climbing up the sides, and workers were tossing letters in as if to feed a beast they'd never seen. Stan was there too, throwing envelopes into the fire by the handful.

Henry stood on the edge, watching the paper burn while somewhere, far below, words that were written echoed in the fading light. He could hear the prose of long-lost lovers. Wives writing to friends they never saw anymore. Sons writing to the unavailable ears of absent fathers. Smoke started to fill the platform, and Henry couldn't catch his breath.

Every time he took a step back, the hole got bigger, until suddenly it was the size of the whole room and every letter had fallen down into its depths. He was caught, struggling to breathe on the far side of the room, with no way of getting to the door.

Through the smoke, he saw Stan trying to reach for him. Stan was saying something, but Henry couldn't make it out above the roar of the fire.

As he reached out to grab Stan's hand, his foot slipped, and he was falling, and Stan was calling after him, saying, *Henry couldn't save every letter because he couldn't even save himself.*

52

Tuesday, October 25, 1966
3:30 PM

Minneapolis and Fargo passed by without so much as an untoward glance. At least, none Henry noticed. Which may have been due to the fact that he had rushed through every delivery and hadn't made eye contact with another soul. The letters were burning a hole in his heart. He just wanted to be rid of them.

He didn't enter any homes either, though he'd been invited into at least five. Or six.

The roadways of Minneapolis were hard to navigate, with streets going in one direction and avenues another. He got lost three times between East Nineteenth Street and East Twenty-First Street because someone had placed an avenue where it wasn't meant to be and the idea of pulling over to ask for directions made his palms clammy. Instead, he added more miles to the Ford as he drove aimlessly around Mill City, peering at house numbers and street signs until they blurred.

He fought the urge to deliver to the wrong house just to be one letter lighter.

In Fargo, he had one envelope. He took it to the home of an elderly man (a *more* elderly man, that is), who opened the door wearing nothing but an old war helmet—its leather strap torn under the chin. He'd stood to salute with one hand while gripping a well-worn cane with the other. Henry's left hand had gripped his own cane in a mirror image. The letter was from a child—Henry could tell by the writing on the front—and the more elderly man accepted it with tears in his cataract-riddled eyes.

Henry didn't hang around long enough to hear what it said. In hindsight, though, if he'd stayed to swap war stories with the old man in his birthday suit for an extra day, he would've avoided the fat man in the uniform.

914 Co Road #9
Fargo, Illinois

Grandpa,

Dad says you will build a swing with me on Sadturday. I cant wait. I hope the swing takes me so high that I fly.

Love you,

Eli

53

Wednesday, October 26, 1966
7:46 AM

The line at the border dragged. By the time he got to the man with the moustache in the booth, the sun had made a full appearance.

Henry rolled down his window. Moustache man gave a grunt, asking three times where Henry was going, not listening long enough to catch the answer each time and repeating the question. With a final huff of breath that made his facial hair dance, he told Henry to go inside.

"Inside?" Henry asked, unsure if he'd heard correctly.

"Yes, go inside. Someone will speak with you further." With a flick of the hand, Henry was dismissed.

He parked in front of a squat, windowless building the color of oatmeal. There were two glass-paneled front doors. Henry took the one on the left.

Approaching a young woman at a typewriter, he explained that the man with the moustache inside the booth of the fifth lane had sent him inside to speak with someone.

"And who might that be?" she asked, still typing.

"What?"

"Who are you looking to speak with?"

She used only her index fingers to type, and it made the click of the keys rebound around the drab reception area. She still hadn't looked up. Her hair was parted in the middle, and a light sprinkling of dandruff disappeared into her dark curls.

"I was hoping you would tell me." He resisted the urge to tap the floor with his cane.

"You need to go through the other door."

"What?"

With the briefest of glances in his direction, she motioned to the other glass-paneled front door. "Go back outside and go in the *other* door."

The right door would lead him to the exact same spot, he said. He was supposed to go back outside, enter a different identical door, and return to the exact spot in which he was currently standing?

"Yes. The right door is there for people instructed to come inside."

"What's the other door for?"

She pecked at the keys. "What?"

"What's the left door for, if only the right door is right?"

With an audible exhale, she finally made eye contact. "Sir, I can only help people who come through the right door. When you come through the right door, I will be happy to help you."

He exited and entered again.

Without looking up, she spun in her chair and called for an officer standing by a far wall. Tall, with broad shoulders. His chin looked carved from stone.

"Officer Moody, this gentleman was sent in to speak to somebody. Might you be the somebody he should speak to?" She certainly had no trouble looking Officer Moody in the eye.

"I don't think so—" the officer started. And he would have finished if a second, thicker officer hadn't chosen that moment to exit the restroom, fly undone, and join the conversation.

"Whadda we got here, Shirley?" He spoke from the side of his mouth.

"Tony in booth five sent this man in. I was just about to send him on his way."

"Ah. No. If Tony sent him in, we best talk to the old-timer to find out why." The thick one elbowed the tall one, and the tall one sighed.

"This way, sir."

The click-clack of typing hit Henry in the back as he followed the officers into the station.

That was almost two hours ago.

Through the door of the interrogation room, Henry could see the two uniformed officers talking, heads bent close together. The walls were whitewashed, and the only furniture was a metal desk piled high with stacks of paper, an uncomfortable plastic chair that dug into his sides, and a filing cabinet so full the bottom drawer had no hope of ever closing all the way. There were no windows. Two large corkboards covered in photos of those deemed "Most Wanted" lined the wall.

Henry's picture wasn't there. He'd already checked.

The center picture was a man with long greasy hair and more gums than teeth. According to the poster, he was last seen in Minneapolis and believed to have crossed the border into Canada. His hardened eyes pierced straight through the picture.

Henry turned his attention back to the officers. He wished they would hurry up and make a decision. Apparently being a gallant public servant on a mission to give something back to the people without receiving anything in return got you nowhere.

The officers whispered intently. The short one didn't let anything go. He'd already questioned Henry six times, his voice rising with every repeated inquiry. By now, a vein in his forehead throbbed violently. The chiseled one was much calmer. More than once, he'd been forced to slow things down by laying a heavy hand on his partner's shoulder.

"Yes. Yes, I know," Henry heard the tall one say. "But Winston, we need to let him go. He doesn't know anything about the warehouse."

The warehouse.

They kept asking over and over about some warehouse and a man called Pershutoc. And over and over Henry had told them he had no clue what they were talking about. Round and round they danced in a similar circle. Two were sick of it, but one refused to give up easily.

"Goddammit, Mike," Winston hissed, loud enough for Henry to hear. "Those letters came from somewhere, and I'm telling you, they musta been hiding in that damn warehouse. I can feel it in my gut."

"The only thing you feel in your gut is indigestion," Henry muttered.

During one endless stream of questioning earlier, Henry had pretended he knew the man they were looking for. The one with the name he couldn't quite pronounce. Bothering with the calluses on his hands,

Henry had said, in effect, so what if he knew the man? What was it to them?

Joking had been the wrong thing to do. Shorty had exploded, jabbing a finger into Henry's chest, demanding answers that Henry obviously didn't have.

The interrogation had started all over again.

From the hall, Mike sounded exhausted. "They're all postmarked Chicago, Winston. Come on, you know you're grasping at straws. That guy doesn't know who Pershutoc is."

Henry rubbed his knee.

The vein pulsed as Winston refused to let things go. "Then how do you explain all those notes in his pocket? They're codes."

"He wrote them to himself. He admitted he's been a little forgetful—"

"Exactly. What if he's forgetting right now? You honestly think he found the letters in a bag on a side street in Chicago and decided it was his *duty* to deliver them? And that he's on his way to Winnipeg to reunite a Mrs. Sandra Crawford, whom he claims he's never met, with a lost letter?"

Okay. Just a *little* white lie.

Henry couldn't tell them he'd broken into the Chicago Post Office, shoved hundreds of letters into large bags, and taken off with the security guard hot on his heels, could he? Or that his picture actually *was* on a "Most Wanted" poster?

The conversation dragged on. "I want to know what's in that letter and how he knows Pershutoc." By now, Winston wasn't trying to keep his voice down. His anger was as swollen as his belly, filling the now-empty building. "Think about it, Mike. This man is the perfect mule for these guys. Who's going to suspect the old loon is up to anything criminal? He already admitted to knowing—"

"Enough!" Mike exploded. "Winston, that is enough." The thick officer turned purple and opened his mouth to speak, but his partner cut him off. "I'm letting him go." Mike turned to Henry and leaned into the room. "Mr. Walton, you are free to leave. I'm so sorry we kept you here for so long. It was incredibly inappropriate of us."

Winston let out a whimper. "But we need to find Pershutoc."

"We will. But keeping an elderly man captive is not the way we'll find him."

"Have you tried asking his wife?" Henry asked, blood flowing back into his legs as he stood. "In my experience, when a husband flees home for one reason or another, he lets his wife know where he's going. *Tell the boss and you'll never be lost* is my motto."

With that, he left through the right door.

54

Wednesday, October 26, 1966
11:52 AM

It took almost two hours to get to Winnipeg from the border. Shops lined the wide streets, large, flashy billboards attached to their roofs. Signs for Winnipeg Laundry, Hotel McLaren, Coca-Cola, Toronto Dominion Bank, and Red Rose Tea shouted messages from the sky.

Buy me. Sleep here.

Orange trolleys ambled up and down the main streets, their cables squeaking at every stop. Henry got stuck behind one for so long a dull ache thumped behind his eyes.

When he first arrived, he'd stopped at a place called Mac's Milk to look at a map of the city. He'd hoped to find Fennell Street, memorize the fastest route to get there, and leave. But when he unfolded the giant mess of paper, a man behind the counter (whose name tag said *Miles* even though the store was named after Mac) told him in a clipped voice he couldn't look at the map without purchasing it.

Henry now owned a Texaco Touring Atlas for a city he would never visit again that he'd bought off a man who hardly sold any milk at all.

He turned onto Fennell Street and slowed down to count the numbers.

There: 3146 Fennell Street, home to a Mrs. Sandra Crawford.

He stopped in front of the nondescript house and cut the engine. Her letter was resting beside him. Reaching for it, he had the distinct feeling of being watched. He glanced in the rearview mirror in time to see a black cat run across the street and claw its way up the trunk of an oak tree. From the branches, a single crow took off into a bright sky.

Henry left the car cane first and looked around. Her street was quiet, save for the cat. There was a large tree in front of every house, and Henry imagined its blackness flitting from one yard to the next all day long. The tree in front of Sandra's house had thick branches that twisted in on themselves. The lowest one bent like an elbow, the chewed-up rope of an old swing hanging from it.

Motion in the window of the house next door caught his eye. Henry lifted a hand and the curtain flicked shut.

Clutching the letter, he turned back to his destination. The concrete paving stones leading to the front door were crumbling and broken underfoot. He hobbled with caution. The last thing he needed was a broken ankle. Another oak stood like a sentry beside the house, its branches trimmed so they didn't bang on the moss-covered roof each time a gust of wind flew by. It looked disproportionate with so many of its lower boughs sawed off.

Henry reached the front door, ankles intact, and knocked twice.

Nothing.

He knocked again, louder this time. Shifting to the left, he tried to peer through the front window, but thick curtains blocked his view. The fourth knock was equally unsuccessful.

What a waste. After everything he'd been through to get here, Sandra Crawford didn't even have the decency to be home to receive her letter.

As he bent down to slip it under the door, a tap on the shoulder threatened to loosen his bladder.

"Oh." He gripped his cane like a vise and spun around. "You frightened the daylights out of me." His chest heaved.

Her voice was a soft breeze you'd have to think about to notice. "I'm awfully sorry," she said, "only I saw you knocking and thought you would want to know." Her hands moved about when she spoke, as if to make up for the lack of sound.

The nosy neighbor, Henry realized. She was so small, it was as if she took up no space at all. The same couldn't be said about her eyes, though. They took up her whole face, crowding in on a delicate nose, giving her the look of Athena—a Greek goddess of something or other. She stopped waving her hands and clasped them together until her knuckles turned white as she waited for his response.

"Know what?" he asked, his heart rate beginning to slow.

"About Sandra."

Henry looked down at the letter. "I have something for her." He held it out so she could see the name on the front. She took two steps back, as if she shouldn't be there.

"Ah," she breathed. "The thing is, Mr.—"

"Henry."

"The thing is, Henry." She paused her arm midair and let it fall to her side. "Sandra's dead."

It was as if the ground opened beneath him. Henry stumbled, reaching out to grab the porch railing. He dropped his cane and tripped over the top step on the way to retrieve it. His bad knee hit the ground first, followed by the rest of him. Sandra's letter landed in the grass with a flutter. With a groan, he pulled himself to sitting. His trousers were torn, blood beginning to ooze from a gash on his knee. He reached for Elsie's handkerchief, but it wasn't there. Pressing a thumb to the cut, he looked up. "Was she sick?" he asked, smearing blood onto his ruined pant leg. He leaned forward for his cane.

"Cancer," the neighbor whispered, sinking down to the path beside Henry. "She was diagnosed a few months ago. She passed away last night." She wiped at her tears and stood, reaching down to help him up. Gently, afraid his weight would pull her over, he let her lift him to standing.

"There's a son," she said. Her eyes were a pool of sorrow, so deep a man could drown. "Anthony. I could give him the letter."

Henry clutched at it. Failure seeped through him, into his shoes. He felt the weight of his entire mission crash from the sky. Sandra Crawford was dead. He was too late. The realization weighed him down more than he would have expected. His thoughts doubled back on themselves, and he couldn't keep them straight.

An arm steadied him before he even realized he was falling again. She held him just above the elbow, her grip firm. Comforting. Across the street, the black cat leapt down from the tree and pawed at the grass.

"On second thought," she said, louder than before, "why don't you come in for a cup of coffee while we wait for Anthony to get back?" Her smile was a slow stretch.

Henry nodded and followed her next door.

55

Wednesday, October 26, 1966
12:03 PM

While his host busied herself in the kitchen, Henry placed Sandra's letter on a small side table beside the sofa. The white envelope contrasted with the dark wood, and it looked out of place.

Mugs clanked as they were removed from a cupboard. A spoon tinkled brightly against a sugar jar. One scoop, he told her when she called out to ask. Moving four decorative (and useless) floral pillows out of the way, he settled onto the sofa.

There was a picture on the wall of the woman and an older man. He was half hidden in the shadows, as if the photographer had told him to take a step back and disappear. In the photo, her smile didn't quite reach her wide eyes.

A clock on the mantel ticked softly, reminding Henry of his time with . . . what was her name?

"Here we are." Her voice was low. She placed a steaming mug on a yellowed doily, cutting through his broken memory. "One sugar and—" She was interrupted by a series of loud bangs above their heads. Henry moved to stand, but she signaled for him to stay sitting. It was just her husband, she explained, taking a seat in the armchair opposite.

The banging continued.

Henry wrapped his hands around the mug and inhaled the rich, earthy scent. They sipped for a moment in unison, and he watched her from behind his mug. She was graceful, the hold on her mug delicate, the pout of her lips downy.

"Did you know her well?" Henry asked. "Sandra?"

A nod at first. A small dip of the head in answer. And then: "Yes, I suppose kids these days would call her my best friend. At least, she was the closest thing to a friend I've ever had. We've lived next door for a decade. We didn't do Christmas together, nothing as intimate as that, but we swapped sugar, loaned eggs, traded tips on how to keep the monarda and the roses alive during the frost." She paused, and so did the banging. "We made soup if the other was ill, whispered gossip over the fence while we sheared and pruned. Richard," she said with a nod at the ceiling, "used to joke that we were sisters separated by a white picket fence. 'Sandy and Maeve together till the grave,' he would sing." She gasped, realizing what she'd said. Her eyes threatened to overflow.

As if on cue at the mention of his name, a third string of crashes came raining down. A door slammed. Henry flinched.

She murmured an apology. "Richard has trouble holding on to anything with a firm grip. And the fact that he's angry with me today *apparently* gives him the allowance to slam every door he encounters."

"Angry?"

Her frown was slight, muted. "He thinks I should get over my grief and get back to work." She stared at the ceiling like it was a living thing, compressing the breath from her lungs.

Henry shifted on the sofa, lost for words. "Didn't she just pass," he said finally, "last night?" His voice had taken on a strained texture.

She met his gaze, and he could taste her sorrow.

"I wanted to go to the hospital." Her voice was barely audible above the noise from overhead. "To be with her at the end. But Richard said it wasn't appropriate for me to be underfoot when the family had so much to deal with. That and he wasn't about to let his wife enter one of those godforsaken buildings while he still had breath in his damned lungs." She'd been waiting by the window ever since, she said.

And then Henry had turned up, knocking on her dead neighbor's door.

Henry cleared his throat and set down the half-empty mug. He wanted to unpack her words and make sense of them.

"Why," he ventured, "would God forsake a hospital?"

Her mouth formed an O to match her eyes. He knew she hadn't expected him to linger on that part of the story. Her best friend had passed away, and she hadn't been offered a chance to say goodbye. That was more important. But what she'd said had sparked something in the back of Henry's mind, and he needed to explore where it took him.

He leaned back against a pillow.

"Did you fight?" she asked. She didn't elaborate.

His nod was slow to come. The first war, he explained, after searching the recesses of his mind for the full story. He'd been a messenger, responsible for running letters between two camps. He had his route perfected by August of '18: a ninety-degree angle between the two locations. He would slip in and out unnoticed, bringing messages scribbled on bits of paper, map corners, and one time, the torn uniform of a fallen soldier. Back and forth he would go, every few days, carrying words like gold.

Until the day he cut a mile off his route.

"I was too complacent, too rushed. I cut a new path and paid the price." He tapped his knee, where shrapnel was still lodged all these decades later. "In my experience, nothing good has ever come from war." He closed his eyes, the smell of long-ago mud filling his nostrils, the shooting pain, the crushing feeling of failure. When he finally came back to the present, she was waiting, eyes wide, lips tight.

He rubbed at his knee, wishing they could open a window for fresh air.

"Richard," she began, "tried for years to get enlisted. Too young, they said. Too damaged." The damage, Henry soon found out, was to his lungs from a bout of tuberculosis at the age of five. "And after D-Day, when he still hadn't been asked to join, he'd all but given up. Until a corporal saw him one day and said he was needed to keep the Fritzes at bay in Belgium. They weren't retreating fast enough—"

It was a few bang-filled moments before she told him about Ardennes.

But Henry knew about Ardennes.

"He never expected to see battle. They told him he wouldn't. The war was over, everyone said." The banging stopped, and she cocked her head toward the ceiling, listening. "Of course, everyone was wrong." The most inexperienced men had been positioned in Ardennes, along the borders of France and Luxembourg. Tired from travel and untrained, they were ill prepared to hold off the invasion.

"He was shot," she said softly, "twice. Once in the leg and once in the torso—straight in the side of a decades-damaged lung. His regiment dragged him into a cave and tried their best to bandage him." Henry could picture the scene. "And when it was clear the attack was far from finished, they said they had to leave." She paused, gulping for air like currency. "He'd been there for days, bleeding out, starving to death, and struggling to breathe, when they finally came back. By then, reinforcements had arrived, and they were able to get him to a makeshift hospital in Bastogne . . . It was worse than the cave, he said once. To be so surrounded by death. He hasn't been back since. To a hospital, that is."

Henry's ears were ringing, his mind so full of memories it was as if he could reach out and grab them.

William.

"My son was there," he said after a heavy pause. "At Ardennes."

"Did he come home?" she asked tenderly. Outside the window the cat ran from tree to tree, trying to find its place.

Henry shook his head. William had always wanted to fight. He used to touch Henry's knee just to feel close to battle. *I'll get revenge for you one day,* he would say, with a grin that tore his face in two. Henry understood the desire to defend your country, to fight for justice. He knew, when America entered the war, that William would be first in line to enlist. He knew they would take his beautiful son, hand him a gun, and send him wide-eyed into battle.

Henry's mouth filled with bile.

How could a father forget his son was gone? It wasn't until she handed him a handkerchief that he realized he was crying. He let out a sob and hung his head, wishing he had a note to remind him of his life. He needed words to fill in all the missing pieces. Elsie wasn't visiting William. Not in person, at least. They were already together—fragments of his broken mind, waiting for him to join them.

He felt like a shadow of his former self, as if chunks had been cut off and discarded along the way. In the back of his mind, he'd always felt the letters he wrote his son would go unanswered. Now he remembered why.

Outside, a car door closed. With a final dab, he handed her back the handkerchief and rubbed at his knee. "Is that her son?"

She nodded. "Yes, that should be Anthony, home from the hospital."

"I hope I'm bringing good news. I need to be bringing some good news."

She helped him stand and linked her arm through his. "Let's go see, shall we?"

3146 Fennell Street
Winnipeg, Manitoba

Dear Mrs. Sandra Crawford,

Elizabeth would like to pass on her sincere gratitude for your letter. She reads every piece of correspondence and oh, how she loved what you wrote. I haven't heard her laugh like that in quite some time.

While Elizabeth won't be passing through Winnipeg anytime soon, she has signed the accompanying photograph and hopes you will accept it as a consolation prize.

She also sends her deepest sympathy. She knows firsthand how dreadful injuries and illnesses can be and sends her well wishes your way.

Be well,

Delilah Rose

Personal Assistant to Ms. Elizabeth Taylor and family

56

Wednesday, October 26, 1966
2:05 PM

He had a car. Technically speaking, it belonged to a friend of his mom's, the tank was empty, and inside was a mess, but it would do.

Roger had started to clear the mess off the back seat and out of the footwell, but his mom had *tsk*ed and told him to stop delaying things.

"Who cares if there are a few candy wrappers on the floor, Rog? It's a free car," she'd said.

Ignoring the sorry state of his transportation, Roger threw clothes into a backpack in typical teenage fashion and forced his growing feet into too-small shoes. He didn't want his mom to know he already needed a new pair. Besides, shoes weren't very important in the car. He could drive barefoot if he needed to. That wasn't illegal, was it?

"What else?" Roger asked the vacant room. He walked around checking everything off his list. "Clothes, tick. Toothbrush, tick. Tiny shoes, tick."

He grabbed the Batman marble from the top of the jar and shoved it into the bag in an attempt to borrow some of the superhero's bravery.

Lifting his shoulders, he did a final scan of the room. When he was satisfied he had everything he would need on the short trip, he threw his backpack over one shoulder. In the kitchen, he left a note for his mom and grabbed the map they'd found in the basement the night before. She'd dog-eared each page he would need.

Swallowing a fistful of apprehension, Roger folded the map, tucked it into his back pocket alongside the envelope his mom had rescued from the trash, with its annoyingly perfect writing, and grabbed the keys.

The little mirror ball his mom had given him hung from the rearview mirror. It spun as he made a left turn. The Texaco star rose high into the sky, and he pulled up to the pump. The attendant was only a year or two older than him and clearly did not plan on holding the position for very long.

"Go in and pay before I pump," the attendant sneered, smacking at a wad of gum.

"Roger that," Roger said with a laugh. The joke went over the attendant's head. Inside the small station, another young man hid behind a magazine. The cover made Roger blush. He cleared his throat. "Pump two, please. Regular."

The magazine lowered. The cashier rang in the gasoline without saying a word before returning to his reading. If you could call it reading. Roger was about to ask what was so engrossing when a poster on the wall caught his eye.

"Most wanted. In Chicago? How exciting." He looked at the image of the clean-shaven man and wondered what it was that made him so wanted. "Wish I was."

The cashier never reappeared from behind the magazine, and with hundreds of miles to go, Roger didn't want to waste time trying to elicit a response. He glanced once more at the poster before heading out the door.

57

Wednesday, October 26, 1966
6:13 PM

Henry was lost. And broken.

Black smoke swirled around the engine. Just outside a place called Elk Point and on his way to Sioux City by way of Sioux Falls, the Ford had decided she needed a break.

"Damn pile of—" His mild curse was drowned out by the reverberating sound of skull on metal. Henry inched his way out from under the hood. Rubbing the back of his head, he tried to get his bearings.

He was on Route 45. Or was it 48?

Kicking up dirt and stones, he cut a path back and forth in front of the car. The setting sun was unseasonably warm. Sweat traced its way down his temple. Endless fields filled his vision, stretching out on either side of the deserted road. When the car had started shuddering, Henry had turned off the interstate onto a little dirt road and continued until it had hopped to a complete stop. Now he wished he'd stayed on the main road. At least there had been a hint of civilization there. Someone would have passed by eventually on their way to . . . Where was he again?

Henry forced the air from his lungs and wiped his palms. Leaving the hood open, he climbed back into the car and grabbed the bag of remaining letters. They would hold the key to his destination.

Sioux City. Kansas City. Hannibal. Springfield.

Okay. He was headed south.

Four cities. A handful of letters left. A seed of self-pity was just starting to lodge itself into his mind when something caught his eye.

Picking up the letter for Hannibal, he held it close. Something was stuck to the back. Henry tore another envelope away. This one had a Chicago address.

"What the . . . ?" he asked the empty road.

The presidential seal on the back of this envelope had flicked up at some point, sticking to another letter. When Henry had organized all the mail for Chicago, he'd missed this one.

He ran a thumb over the embossed gold seal, an eagle surrounded by stars, pressing it back into place.

Rev. Martin Luther King, the Junior

210 Lake Street, Chicago, Illinois 60606

He could have delivered this letter first, he realized. Lake Street wasn't far from that hotel he'd stayed in. Sherman something. He could have walked it over and handed it to the expectant reverend on the very day he'd set off on his journey. Henry rolled the words around in his mouth, trying them on. There was something familiar about the name, but he couldn't place it.

He was just piecing together the fact that he had one more letter to deliver when he got home when the squeal of tires on gravel filled the air.

A truck was approaching. Fast. Henry leapt from the car to the cry of his knee and flung his hands overhead. "Hey!" he cried. "Stop!"

Stones flew, and a cloud of dust encircled Henry as the truck came to a screeching halt a few yards from his outstretched palms. He swallowed his stomach and leaned against the side of the Ford. Two large boots attached to denim-clad legs stepped down from the lifted cab.

"Got yerself in a bit of trouble, son?" The man, whose weathered copper skin was lined from decades of working under a midday sun, spit a wad of saliva on the gravel and stretched out a dirty hand.

Henry flinched slightly before returning the gesture. "The car won't start." He watched the man disappear under the hood and placed the president's letter on the passenger seat. "I'm Henry."

"Hank Bourbon. And before you ask, no, I can't stand the stuff." Hank's voice mixed with the smoke and took on a hazy quality. "Right, then, Henry. Looks like your fuel filter is clogged."

"Oh. I don't know what that means. Can you fix it?" He didn't know anything about cars, or where he was, or what to do now. Thoughts jumbled around in his head, each one louder than the last.

Without a word, Hank reached down, removed the small metal cylinder, cleaned it with a rag from his back pocket, and wriggled it back into place. "Give 'er a go."

Henry climbed into the front seat. The car started on the first turn.

Hank let out a series of whoops and came around to the driver's side window. "Whaddya know, it really was the fuel filter."

Henry said, "I owe you one."

"Tell yeh what, there's a little bar a few miles back." Hank nodded in the opposite direction Henry was headed. "I could really use a nice cold beverage right about now."

Henry stared down the road in front of him, his mind working to determine how much he really owed the man, how far out of the way this bar was, and how much cheaper buying a beer for a stranger was than having to pay a visit to the mechanic.

"Lead the way."

Rev. Martin Luther King, the Junior
210 Lake Street, Chicago, Illinois 60606

Dear Dr. King,

I am writing to you on behalf of the president.

As you know, he has appreciated your generous comments about his address to the Congress and the nation on the need for voting rights legislation. President Johnson sincerely believes the mood of the country is changing—and now is the time to act.

We will be enacting the Great Society domestic agenda. Through the Great Society agenda, we will address racial injustice once and for all and introduce a voting act that gives ALL citizens the right to register and vote.

To do so, we need your help.

Only once the president is sure of your support, will he put forward the Great Society agenda and the Voting Rights Act. As I'm sure you can understand, he cannot implement either until he knows you're on his side. It's time to move toward our goal of universal suffrage, together.

We will await your answer. The next step lies with you.

Sincerely,

W. Marvin Watson, advisor to President Lyndon B. Johnson

58

Wednesday, October 26, 1966
6:47 PM

Half the roof was missing, and the whole building seemed more suited to a gas station than a pub. But tucked around back, in a place you'd have to know about to find, was a small wooden bar with two wobbly stools standing almost upright on a dirt floor.

"Charlie," Hank called as they rounded the corner. "Two pints, my good man." He settled onto a stool and motioned for Henry to do the same. Henry brushed dirt off the seat and perched on the edge of the torn cushion. Beer sloshed over the rim as the largest man Henry had ever seen set a glass down in front of each of them. The barman's forearms were bigger than Henry's thighs, and his neck was as thick as his head, creating a seamless line from ear to shoulder.

Hank raised his glass. "To old cars and new friends. Where were you headed?"

Henry took a sip of foam. "I'm not entirely sure." He cupped his hands around the cool glass. Finding the extra letter for Chicago had muddled his thoughts. "If I remember correctly, I'm going to Sioux City, Kansas City, Hannibal, and Springfield. Then Chicago." Henry ticked the destinations off on his fingers.

"Whoa, pretty specific."

"I'm delivering letters."

"Like a mailman?" Hank rolled his glass between his hands.

"Yeah, like a mailman." Henry gave him the abridged version of his story, skipping over the parts he couldn't fully remember.

"Pretty noble."

"What is?"

"You. Delivering all these letters. It's noble."

"No, no, it's—"

Hank interrupted. "It is. Trust me. These letters . . . they're people's lives, you know. And without you, who knows how long it would have been before they made it to their destination." He'd waited years for a letter once, he continued. It was from a man he went to school with. They'd been best pals, always over at each other's house, trading baseball cards and whispering about the prettiest girl in the class. "He had the loudest laugh you ever heard. Like a banshee. People used to turn in the street when they heard Carl laugh. He clapped a hand over his mouth every time, as if he never expected that much life to erupt from him." After school, while Hank got work at the local mechanic's shop, Carl had gone on to New York City to be a banker. "He always wanted to be on Wall Street. His parents lost everything in the crash, and he was determined to never let that happen again. You could see dollar signs in Carl's eyes, even when he was young." They wrote at first, letters traded between small Elk Point and the Big Apple. Hank got married; Carl bought an apartment overlooking the park. Every month, for five years, they wrote to one another, until one day Carl stopped writing. "Months went by," Hank said, spinning the now-empty glass faster and faster, "and I never heard from him. I kept writing. Figured he was busy being a high-powered banker in the big city and all . . . but . . . he wasn't busy. He was dead."

Henry felt dizzy.

Carl had swallowed a shotgun at the start of the recession in '57, Hank explained. And he penned a letter to his best friend before picking up the gun.

"It was postmarked July '57, but I didn't get it until Christmas three years later." Hank dropped his head into his hands. "The postwar mail was clogging up all the post offices, they told me. And some things were bound to slip through the cracks."

It was true.

The uptick in mail after the war had sent every postal facility across the country into a tailspin. So many people were sending letters, ordering parcels, wanting catalogs. There wasn't enough space for it all, and there weren't enough workers to deal with the overflow. The US Postal Service had been failing for decades, Stan had told Henry. It was why they had implemented the Zone Improvement Plan: to help organize the overflow of mail each facility was dealing with.

"So"—Hank placed a hand on his chest—"what you're doing isn't just noble, Henry. It's brave."

They sat for a moment, in the little pit stop bar, each lost in his own thoughts. Hank's words had summed up exactly how Henry was feeling. It was as if he were carrying around tiny capsules of life, sealed up in envelopes that were sometimes white and sometimes cream and even sometimes marked with a very official stamp.

Henry thought about Carl and the loneliness that could drift into a man's life like a slow-building wave.

He couldn't remember what year Elsie had died—it felt like yesterday—but he knew that if he was asked to pinpoint exactly when his life had changed, it had been that moment. One day his life was full, and the next it was completely different. They'd had to adjust after William's death, of course they had, but the loss of a son in a war held a mix of sorrow and pride. William had been struck down in battle, fighting for the betterment of the world. And Henry and Elsie found themselves, like so many other mothers and fathers of the time, putting together the broken pieces of life after war.

When Elsie died, it was different.

His whole world was gone in an instant. Everything he had left was shattered. So he understood, deep down, the feelings that could make a man write a letter and reach for the end with both hands.

After Elsie was gone, he didn't feel the fog descending. It crept in slowly, steadily, over the years, so quietly he wrote it off as part of the aging process anytime someone sent a concerned look in his direction. "Just getting old," he would laugh, "don't mind me."

Everything changed the day he forgot Elsie's name. It was there, on the tip of his tongue, but no matter how many times he tried to form the word, it got stuck. It was as if his brain were filled with cobwebs and he couldn't find what he was looking for.

He knew then that it was more than aging, that something was truly wrong. Oh, how it made him angry. He despised the pitying glances, the offers of help. The crushing feeling of being unable to grasp words and memories—and everyone getting up in arms over silly things, like when he forgot to put pants on. (It happened *one* time, and that batty old woman didn't need to start crying. It wasn't like she was going to go blind seeing a couple of spindly white legs walking down the street. He would have liked to give her a smack with his cane, but no one would let him, everyone saying it was time for him to go home and he didn't need to be outdoors in his underwear.)

Nothing made you feel more insignificant than a constant need for help.

From then on, he wrote notes when he was lucid and read them when he wasn't. He scribbled Elsie's name on paper all over the house, etching her existence into his mind. He wrote names on the backs of pictures and placed labels on items in the fridge. He caught himself forgetting and tried everything he could to remember. And it worked, mostly. He had made it through each uneventful day with a little more fog and a few more notes.

Until the day the post office closed.

"I should go." Hank slid off his stool. "Thank you for the beer, Henry."

Henry tucked enough money to cover the cost under his empty glass. "Thank you for the . . . that thing you fixed." Above them, through a hole in the makeshift roof of the makeshift bar, the stars turned on.

"Ah, it was nothing. I'm glad I could help."

They made their way in the dark to the front of the building. Only two cars were left. Henry turned to Hank and reached out a hand the moment Hank leaned in for a hug, and they were caught in an awkward embrace. Hank's laugh rolled through the night air as he embraced Henry. "Good luck, mailman. I'll be rooting for you."

Henry watched as Hank climbed back into his truck, a hand raised in farewell. Climbing into the Ford, he looked at the small stack of letters. He rolled Hank's comments around in his mind, searching for a permanent home for them. *Brave. Noble.* Words so vast they could swallow you whole.

Tucking them away, he turned the key.

July 8, 1957

Hank,

I don't know who else to write to. It's like I'm drowning inside and everything is doing its best to tear me apart while I do my best to stay together.

Except I'm not together. I'm broken in ways I don't have words for. All that hope? Gone. All those dreams? Dashed away like sewage down the city's drain.

I know, of course, none of this will make sense to you. I haven't opened up to a single soul about the thoughts that run through my mind on an endless loop. They keep me awake day and night. And we both know no sane person stays up all night.

I'm falling.

No matter how hard I try to stand, I can't do this on my own. Everything I've lost. All the pain I've caused, it's tearing me in half.

I need someone to catch me, though I fear no one will get here in time to save me.

Goodbye, my friend. May you never doubt how much you meant to me.

Carl

59

Wednesday, October 26, 1966

9:40 PM

Stan answered the phone on the third ring. He could hear Flora upstairs, doing her nightly beauty routine. She would be wiping off her brows and rubbing cream into her hands in slow circles.

"Mmm . . . hello?" Stan said, twisting the cord around his finger. It was rare to get a call so late.

"Stan? Stan is that you?" A fit of coughing filled the phone, and Stan strained to hear who was on the other end.

He repeated his greeting.

A sputtering sound, closely followed by "Stan, it's me."

Stan untwisted his fingers and switched the receiver to his other ear. "Henry? Henry, where are you?"

Henry's words came in a rush, as if he couldn't get them out fast enough. "Are you alone? Can you talk?"

Stan leaned an ear toward the stairs. Flora would be combing her wig by now, a chore that took at least a quarter of an hour. "Mmm," he said, his voice a whisper, "I'm alone."

He listened as Henry told him about the broken-down car and the pit stop and the makeshift bar and the beer with the stranger who had helped him.

"And now the car won't start," Henry said. "I tried the door of the pit stop, but it's locked. I did manage to find a blanket under the bar around back. And this telephone hanging in a booth on the side of the building."

"Are you in Chicago? I can come get you." Stan felt like an anxious father.

"No, no. I'm in Dakota, I think."

"Dakota? North or South?"

"Is there more than one? I made it through the border and headed south before the car broke down."

Stan couldn't keep up. "Okaaaay," he said, pushing the word through clenched teeth. "Is there anyone around to help?"

"No. Hank is gone now. I climbed in the Ford to leave after him, but the engine won't tick over."

Stan's voice was hushed. "Henry, you aren't as young as you think you are. Flora was right, I never should have let you do this. You can't . . . breaking into the post office to deliver letters in Chicago was one thing, but Dakota? And the Canadian border? What are you thinking?" He hadn't meant to say that last bit. It slipped through unfiltered.

"I'm *thinking*"—Henry spat the word—"that I only have a handful of letters left to deliver."

Above him, Flora's footsteps moved from one room to another. He didn't have long. "Henry, you're on the news. You've been on every news channel from Chicago to Wichita. And there are posters . . ." Stan didn't elaborate.

Henry knew about the posters, he said. He'd had some strange sideways glances before being shown the poster on television by a young gas station attendant and questioned. "I hightailed it out of there, of course," he said with a chuckle.

Stan squeezed the bridge of his nose and switched ears. A sigh escaped his lips.

"I've got a beard now," Henry said. "So the posters only bear a slight resemblance. And so far, no one in this state has recognized me."

"You don't understand." Worry attached itself to Stan's words. "A border officer called in a tip this morning from just south of Winnipeg. Said he'd had you detained because he knew there was something fishy about you. Waxed on about how his partner had been too soft and let you go. The last thing he said was that you were headed south."

"Ha. That thick little officer thought I was part of some . . . I can't remember . . . some crime operation. The perfect mule, he called me," Henry preened. "Anyways, a lot has happened since then . . ." He went on to explain, in a scattered, roundabout way, about the woman in Winnipeg and the letter that was too late.

Stan had a hard time believing so much had happened in a single day for Henry when he spent most of his time watching baseball. He could imagine Flo using that as an example of why he needed a new hobby. When he spoke again, his voice was strained. "We're worried about you. We've been talking, Flo and I, and we think it's time to—"

Henry cut him off. He didn't need a lecture, he said. He had a job to do. A very important job that Stan knew nothing about. "It's people's lives," he said over and over.

People's *lives*.

Stan was concerned about only one particular life—that of an elderly, not always lucid friend. But he couldn't say that out loud. They went around in circles before Henry hung up, saying he needed to prepare the car for the night and that he would use his bag as a pillow and it was a good thing he'd brought a sweater because the temperature had dropped right down and there was a nip to the air that hadn't been there during the day.

Nothing Stan said was getting through. "Call anytime," he urged. "I'm here if you need me."

Flora came downstairs as he hung up the phone.

"Who was that?" If she'd had eyebrows, one of them would have been raised in his direction.

Stan hesitated and scrubbed a hand across his face. "Henry."

Flora nodded. "I'll put a pot of herbal tea on, and you can get all that worry off your chest."

Stan sank into the chair and told his wife everything.

60

Wednesday, October 26, 1966
9:55 PM

Flora listened while Stan spoke.

At first, his words came out jumbled and unorganized. Slowly, they straightened out. When he was done, Flora rose and left the kitchen. In the front room, she opened the small top drawer of the bureau. She reached for her diary and took it back to the table. Stan was still worrying in the same spot she'd left him.

"I'm going to write it down," she said, pushing her mug out of the way. She turned to a new page.

"Why?"

"Because he's going to need to remember this. Everything he told you. Stan." She looked across the table at her husband and saw the invisible anxieties that lined his skin. "By tomorrow, he may not remember today. And while he can still function out there on his own, we both know his memory is getting worse. I swear, somedays he eats ten times because he's forgotten he had a meal the hour before." Her messy script filled the page.

Stan finished her cold tea in a single gulp.

"I promise you," Flora said, "one day Henry Walton is going to need us to remind him that he took something into his own hands and went out blazing to see it finished till the end. He'll need us to remind him that he *lived*."

61

Wednesday, October 26, 1966
10:12 PM

Henry crawled into the Ford and slammed the door shut. He clicked the lock to be safe, though there wasn't another soul around. Pushing the seat back, he crushed the bag under his head and leaned back.

It was just like Stan to think he couldn't do this. Stan had been worried about the plan since before it was even solidified, and Henry should have known he'd be questioning him every step of the way. It made him want to shout. The hand-holding. The coddling. The silence when he couldn't answer a question or find a word or remember anything from his life with any true clarity.

What did he need a clear mind for anyway? He'd made it this far on his own. He didn't need anyone else's assistance.

Wind whipped across the windshield, rumbling the glass. Reaching behind him, Henry pulled the warm wool sweater from the bag. It was soft against his hands. Spreading it out, he slipped an arm through the sleeve. Something cool fell out, landing in his lap.

The compass Elsie had given him.

Carved into the worn brass were four scrolls creating a square, framed by delicate florals. Henry clicked the knob to reveal the intricate compass face. The letter for each direction was printed in a bold font, and the arrow was inlaid with a smaller arrow coated in silver. He circled the face with his thumb in the moonlight. His father had owned a similar compass when Henry was growing up, and Elsie had found this one at a little market stall on a Saturday afternoon. She'd hidden it in the back of the closet until their tenth anniversary.

Henry held the compass up and watched the arrow twist. Southwest.

He tried to imagine how many miles he had left to go, but the distance was nebulous, hazy. There were so many unknowns that it made his muscles tense. What if something went wrong? Something bigger than being detained between countries or having the car break down?

Everything felt bigger, more expansive, the more letters he delivered. As his pile got smaller, his view of the world stretched in all directions.

A spinning compass that never stopped.

Clutching his anniversary gift like a lifeline, Henry settled back and closed his eyes. Outside, the wind swept the night away.

62

Thursday, October 27, 1966
8:14 AM

Fletcher was late.

Stokes surveyed the receiving platform, jaw clenched. Letters were everywhere, stacked like mini mountains along every wall. Each one was a metaphorical slap in the face. Stokes resisted the urge to tear them up and stamp them into oblivion. Without a care for where he placed his feet, he roamed the room, circling his prey. He was on lap number three when the person he'd rather fire than rely on crashed through the doorway.

Stokes swallowed his acrid rage. "Where the hell have you been?"

Fletcher knocked over a stack as he came into the room. "Sorry, sir." He bent to organize the mess. "I was helping Aldo and Denny load a van with magazines. There's something you should—"

Stokes tuned him out and knocked over a pile. How could a tiny piece of correspondence make him feel so small? Every single envelope felt like a personal attack against him. He looked around, and all he saw staring back at him was failure. That stack over there? It was his useless workforce who had never done an honest day's work. That one? It was the separate bedrooms he had with his wife. This pile was the kids who refused to speak to him. And this one was the rep of the colored union who wouldn't leave him alone. Pile by pile, row by row, they spelled out the many failings of Reginald Stokes.

He wanted them gone.

"Are you ready to go?" he asked, fiddling with the cuffs of his dress shirt.

"About that, sir. Like I was saying, there's something you should know."

"I already know you're going to make the car smell like a deli with your Reuben."

Fletcher scratched his cheek. "That's not what I was going to say. It's about the magazines."

"I know, I need to order more. Don't tell Brenda." Stokes slapped his leg. "She'll never shut up if I contribute to the shutdown."

Fletcher shook his head, but Stokes didn't have time to listen to his complaints. They had a job to do. He squared his shoulders and turned to go.

63

Thursday, October 27, 1966
8:21 AM

Vincent Fletcher had one job: protect the building.

He wasn't asked to solve problems or even, really, to think very hard at all. He walked the halls at night, checked that the doors were locked tight, and spent most of his time daydreaming about the life he could have had if he'd had enough courage to follow his dreams. He showed up, protected the building, and left. Each and every day he did the bare minimum and not an inch more.

"Sir," he said, tugging on his earlobe and looking over Stokes's right shoulder. "Don't you think it's surprising how many magazines we've been able to dispose of?"

"Surprising?" Stokes repeated. "Sure. But in a good way. The same way I was surprised you found out what neighborhood Walton lived in just by visiting a few shops."

It had been more than a few shops. Fletcher had gone from store to store for what felt like days, asking about a man with a cane and showing the grocery list.

When he'd finally found the right place, the shopkeeper had doubled over with laughter at the crossed-out *carrots*. Fletcher didn't understand how vegetables could be so funny, but to each their own.

"But the number, sir. It's a lot, don't you think?" He needed Stokes to pay attention to the destruction. At night, he dreamt the whole post office was on fire, with letters going up in flames, and he was stuck behind a glass wall unable to stop the inferno. He'd started drinking warm milk before bed, a tip his mother had gotten somewhere, but it wasn't helping.

Stokes picked up a letter.

Fletcher could just make out the name on the front: Violet Blume; lived in Dubuque. Sliding his finger under the lip, Stokes ripped it open.

Fletcher cringed.

"Violet is invited to her nephew's fourth birthday," Stokes said with a snort, "and her sister is really hoping they can put the Easter drama behind them. For Owen's sake, after all."

Fletcher held his breath, already knowing the Easter drama would continue because Violet would never get the invite. He pictured chimneys of smoke and all the ash left behind and clenched his fists to stop from crumbling.

Stokes moved toward the door. "I'm glad it's a lot. It's all a lot. And before I can focus on this"—he pointed at the overflowing conveyor belt—"I need to find Walton. We can't let him do a better job at delivering mail than us. Let's go."

It was a mad idea.

Completely far-fetched and utterly impossible. But maybe it was worth a try? The sooner they found Walton, the sooner they could sort this mess out. Turning their backs on millions of letters, Stokes and Fletcher set out to find a single one.

17501 Cloverview Drive
Tinley Park, IL

Mother,

What in the world have you done? Doctor Stewart called and said my first scheduled ECT treatment will take place on November 14th at approximately 3:30pm.

Do you know what ECT stands for?

ELECTROCONVULSIVE THERAPY. Shock therapy! Or, more specifically, 70 volts for a total of 6 seconds, twice a week. To the brain.

I cannot fathom why you would write to my doctor asking for a treatment that will help me "be more of a man," according to him. I could hear his nurse sniggering in the background!

I don't need any treatment. I'm fine. Everything is fine. Please, for the love of God, stop meddling.

Vince

P.S. Can I please come over on Sunday to do my washing? Perhaps you could make a roast? That would be nice.

64

Thursday, October 27, 1966
8:22 AM

The bus jostled its way down empty streets, stopping and starting again every few miles. Loud and cramped, Henry felt himself lift off the seat with every pothole they barreled over. A rather large woman hogged most of the seat. She smelled of toffee, and Henry had to resist the urge to ask if she had one to spare while he squeezed himself into the window to give her more space.

He'd been on board for twenty minutes and they'd already made several stops. Charlie had estimated the library was forty minutes away by bus, though Henry found it hard to believe a burly barman knew exactly how far away the library was from his pit stop. He had, at least, dropped Henry off at the stop that morning before opening his shop.

Eyes fixed out the window, Henry watched the landscape pass by in a blur. Rolling hills spilled across the horizon. A swallow swooped through the thick clouds, twisting and turning. It was a while before he realized his nose was no longer filled with the scent of toffee and he had some extra room beside him.

His new seatmate peered past him out the window. "Looks like rain."

"Pardon me?"

"Rain," she said, leaning back in her seat. "And I think we need it. Don't you?"

"I honestly couldn't say," he replied, eyeing the bulging clouds as the swallow dipped lower. "I haven't a clue when you last got rain here, so I can't say for certain whether it's been too long or not long enough between showers."

Her laugh was a wind chime, loud and clear.

"Fair enough." Her eyes were the color of cornflowers, and Henry could imagine how easily a young man might get lost in them. The way Elsie's eyes had captured him with flecks of green and gold . . . He blinked away the memory in time to register her question. "Where are you from?"

"Chicago." He didn't elaborate.

"Oh lovely. I've never been, but I've heard such wonderful things about the Shubert. I've lived here my whole life. Bought a house recently; my husband's been renovating it. I've never had to make so many decisions in my life. What brings you to Elk Point?"

What was an Elk Point? It wasn't something he'd heard before. Though perhaps it was the name of the bus depot. He hadn't stopped to read the faded print on the side of the bus when he'd climbed on. Henry racked his brain. He wanted to keep talking to Cornflower, and that wouldn't happen if she thought he was a senile old man.

"The little town we're headed to . . ." she added kindly, trailing off to let it process.

"Ah, Elk Point. Yes. Well, you see, my car broke down, so I'm on my way to the library."

"To take out a book on mechanics, I presume?"

"Oh, no. I left the car in the capable hands of a barman named Charlie. I'm headed to the library for some research. I'm down this way delivering letters, and there's something I need to confirm."

"Letters? How wonderful. I just received a letter in the mail from my sister telling me about her new sheep. She lives on a farm. I'm posting a response—including a pattern for a new wool dress—back this afternoon." She tapped the handbag on her lap.

The bus rumbled to a stop at the same time the sky cracked overhead.

She winked at him, though he didn't know why. "What research are you doing at the library?" she asked.

"I need to look something up," Henry said. "About someone famous."

"Oh! A celebrity," she squealed, clapping her hands. The chunky bangles on her wrist clacked together. "Who is it?" The twinkle in her eye had doubled at the mention of fame.

"No one terribly exciting, I'm afraid." The bus was slowing down, and Henry didn't want to miss his stop. How many had there been since she had started talking to him about the weather?

"Oh, go on, try me."

"Well . . . it's . . . I need to know more about . . ." He stopped. Who was he going to research again? "Oh golly," he sputtered. "I can't remember."

Her laugh was quieter this time. Henry's shoulders hunched as the first drops of rain splashed the window.

"I'm sorry," she said softly. "I get overly excited about anyone famous. I saw the local weatherman in the grocer the other day and nearly fainted from enthusiasm." Creases formed at the corner of her eyes. "This is you," she said.

"I beg your pardon?"

She waved. "This is your stop. The library." The doors started to close as the driver geared up, eager to keep moving along his route.

"Wait," Henry cried, smashing his knee on the seat in front of him and dropping his cane. It clattered to the floor as he struggled to stand. "I need to get off." Beside him, a woman with bright eyes—the color of a flower Elsie used to grow—slid out of her seat to lend a hand.

Henry climbed down the steps and watched the bus pull away. He turned to the building behind him.

Why was he at the library?

1409 E Old Hickory St
Sioux Falls, SD

Dear Marguerite,

We've almost finished the house. You know Minnie asked us not to change anything when we bought it off her, but I can't stand living upstairs anymore. We've kept the barbershop and pool room, and Don will continue to work from there. The back part of the house has been renovated into a living room, den, and kitchen. We got rid of the office and the restaurant, finally.

It's splendid! I've got enough room to have a whole assembly-line of pie makers in the kitchen with me now. In the summer, Don built a patio on the side of the garage, and we ate most of our meals out there in the sun. I cannot express how much I enjoy spending quality time out there. Next, we're going to cover the whole house with insul-brick. But that's a '67 problem, Don says.

Now, I've included a pattern for that Jiffy Dress. You only need two pieces, so even you should be able to handle it. A little contrast collar would be nice. Or a bow. Do let me know how it turns out.

All my love,

Doris

65

Thursday, October 27, 1966
9:23 AM

Three-quarters of an hour later, Henry was still clueless. So far, he'd walked up and down each aisle almost fifty times and picked up too many books to count, scanning the covers before placing them back on the shelf without cracking the spine. The woman behind the desk had started shooting him a narrow glare every time he picked up a book.

He hovered among the rows of nonfiction, out of sight.

Picking up a biography about Anne Jackson, he flipped through the pages. Facts about her life jumped out as he skimmed. A new Obie award. *Summer and Smoke*. Eli Wallach. Sentence after sentence about life in the spotlight. Henry was wondering whether *The Tiger* was actually about a tiger when a voice made him jump.

"Excuse me. Can I help you?"

He slammed the book closed. It was the woman from the front desk. Up close, Henry could see she was younger than the shapeless brown dress and burnt-orange lipstick made her appear from afar. She looked him over head to toe, lingering on the tear in his trousers. A scab had formed over the small cut, and he resisted the urge to itch it.

"No. Thank you," he said, returning the biography to the wrong shelf.

He moved away, blinking at the shelf markers on the end of each row, trying to find somewhere safe to land. Passing a young man at a table, head bent over a thick textbook, Henry slid into a new aisle and resumed his browsing. *One Flew Over the Cuckoo's Nest* jumped out at him. He remembered the cuckoo clock in the Welsh woman's basement. A few shelves down was a cream-colored novel with bold black font. *Why Can't We Wait?* Henry stared at the skinny spine.

The librarian tapped her foot, making Henry jolt. Had she followed him? He tapped his forehead.

And something clicked, sliding into place in his mind, moving from gray matter to cognition in the span of a millisecond.

"Oh," he cried, filling the quiet room with his outburst. The fog lifted and the letter to Martin Luther King Junior filled his mind. He moved to a magazine rack by the door, ignoring how closely she kept to his side. Skimming the shelves, he found what he was looking for: a *LIFE* magazine from '65 featuring an article about the colored march and the demonstrations that had started spanning the country. Dr. King was on the cover.

Flipping to the article, Henry read every word.

The librarian finally slipped away, seemingly relieved that he was acting like a true library patron, and he worked to commit the article to memory.

An hour later, when he stepped from the building, the clouds had lifted. A bright sky greeted him as he stepped over a puddle and crossed to the bus stop.

It was time to get back to the Ford. He had a mission to complete.

66

Thursday, October 27, 1966
4:50 PM

"I've called you a tow truck." Charlie stood behind the bar, wiping clean glasses with a dirty rag. "I can't get her to start."

"Right. Okay." Henry rubbed his neck. He thought about asking for a drink but changed his mind. He needed to stay sharp. Charlie had been working on the car when Henry returned from the library, so Henry had spent most of the day staring into space from the barstool, his minding racing with thoughts of a famous activist and a letter from the president.

His toes ached from having to walk back from the bus stop on his own. It had been farther than he'd thought, and every inch of him groaned for the comfort of his Ford.

"Should be here any minute." Charlie replaced the last glass, streaks marking its clear surface, and tossed the rag over his shoulder. "I'd tow you over there myself, but . . ." He gestured to the makeshift bar and pit stop building.

The operation was a one-man job.

Henry assured him it was okay. He would wait for the tow truck driver. "When did you open the pit stop?" he asked, trying to pass the time.

"Oh, 1893 or '94. My grandfather was a blacksmith. He lugged an anvil to the crossroads, and every day he would walk a mile with a stool and a sledge and wait for work. By the end of his first year, people all over the county knew where to find him. Best blacksmith in the state, they reckoned." He'd built a small outbuilding after a few years,

Charlie continued, and eventually moved the family into a small set of rooms in the back. "We lost those rooms in a fire when I was a boy. After my dad took over the shop." The back of the building still showed remnants of the disaster, black soot creeping from window to roof. Charlie pointed the marks out.

"Is that when you added the bar?"

"Nah, I added this beauty"—he rapped his knuckles on the bar—"in '59. They sent me home from Nam, and the pit stop was boarded up when I returned. Graffiti painted on the shutters and cobwebs stretching across every surface." Charlie pulled the rag off his shoulder and wiped at a nonexistent spill. "Anyways . . ." He cleared his throat. "It took me a while to fix it back up. Pull down all the shutters, turn it into a functioning garage. The boys used to come by on a Friday night, trading stories from the jungle. I built the bar then, so we had somewhere to escape the demons. Somewhere a little hidden, ya know."

Henry did.

Though his demons were of a slightly different breed. He ran a hand along the roughhewn wood and pictured men carrying invisible loads sitting at its edge. Each place—every hidden bar and middle-of-nowhere shop—told a story.

Charlie continued. "I wanted to travel, when I was a young boy. After the rooms burned down, I thought we could sell the place and move on. But then my grandfather died, and the war happened for my father. And then for me. When I got back, here was this ancient shop with a hundred stories to tell—of injured horses and weary travelers and new technology advancements every year—and I was the only one alive to tell them. With my country served, I felt it was about time to do my duty for my family. So . . . I stayed."

"Do you still want to?" Henry asked, leaning in. "Travel?"

"Nah. Some dreams die the minute you reach for a different set of keys. And I figure that's okay."

Henry nodded. It was. Okay to change course, that is. Take a different path and leave old pieces of yourself behind.

From the front of the building, tires came to a halt on the gravel. "That'll be your tow." Charlie tossed the rag onto the counter, and Henry slid off the stool to follow.

"Henry?" A wad of chewing tobacco shot from the window, chasing the question through the air.

"That's me." Henry watched a man swing down from the cab, denim rolled up against heavy work boots.

"Which'un's yers?" His voice scraped.

Henry cleared his throat instinctively, pointing to the Ford.

It took half an hour for the man to rig the car to his truck, Henry itching to climb into the cab while he waited. To rest his bones and his ears. Because Blue Collar Bill, as he'd mentally started calling the tow truck driver, had yet to stop talking.

"Prettiest thing you ever did see, in that yellow dress." The Ford swayed as Blue Collar Bill shifted the gears back and forth. "Reminds me of them buttercups. You know, those little flowers that pop up in spring."

Henry nodded absently, watching the road. He'd stopped listening a dozen minutes ago.

It didn't matter. Blue Collar Bill didn't need an audience to continue. "Last year we went to—"

Henry tuned him out again.

In the distance, bales of hay dotted the landscape in morse code. A bird landed on one only to flit immediately to another. Behind Henry, an engine roared to life. Bill was back behind the wheel of his tow truck.

"She's ready to go." He leaned out the window. "Ain't goin' nowhere the way I've strapped her down."

Henry made to climb in beside him, tucking his cane under his arm.

"No can do, my friend. No civvies allowed in the truck."

Henry frowned.

"Rules are rules. You can pick the pretty little thing up at Old Mill Oil and Gas up on Route 50."

Henry wondered if he meant the car or the girl, but he never got the chance to ask. Before he could even inquire about the direction of Route 50, the tow truck was flying out of the parking lot, his Ford swaying as it disappeared.

Leaving Henry, his bag, and a handful of undelivered letters stranded.

In the pit stop, Charlie had his head bent under the hood of an old truck, dirty rag draped once more over his large shoulder. Henry watched as Charlie reached out blindly for a wrench, engrossed in the fix.

He'd taken enough of the barman's time already.

Pulling the compass from his pocket, he watched the arrow spin. The north it indicated wasn't the north he'd expected. He gave it a shake and held it up again. Same result. He tried to think back to the way he had come, from Sioux Falls. He remembered a town starting with *B* and another called Junction City, situated, naturally, at a junction. Henry closed his eyes and tried to picture the crossroads but drew a blank. The map he'd been using stopped at Sioux Falls, and he'd planned on buying another in Sioux City, making the land between where he was and where he was going foreign.

Hazarding a guess that by saying "up on Route 50," Blue Collar Bill had meant north, Henry checked the compass one last time before slinging it into the bag and setting off.

67

Thursday, October 27, 1966
6:16 PM

Roger drove into the sunset.

He could feel the blood coursing through his veins, a river of trepidation running up and down each limb. His goal was to drive through the night for as long as he could before finding a rest stop.

What he really wanted to do was slow down. Hit the brakes. Turn around.

The envelope with his father's address rested on the dash. It slid from side to side with every turn Roger made. Fitting, he thought, to have a letter from his father act as slippery as the man himself.

A red car passed going the opposite direction. "That brings the total to seventeen red, forty black, twenty-nine blue, a beige one I wouldn't class as white, and two orange, one brighter than the other." He tapped the steering wheel. "The second red one was probably my favorite. It really popped."

He wondered what color car his dad had and immediately regretted the thought. Knowing things about his dad wouldn't change anything. Not even if he had a cherry-red Mustang.

"I wish I could delay this trip." He passed by a pit stop on the side of the road and pressed his foot down. The sooner he arrived, the sooner he could leave.

68

Thursday, October 27, 1966
6:26 PM

Cars whizzed past him on the road, flinging up dirt that flirted with the air. Henry passed a dozen fields as a glow inched its way across the sky. He knew darkness would fall quickly, but between his bag and the cane, he couldn't walk any faster. Every few minutes he had to stop and hoist up the bag that had decided it would rather slip to the ground than stay put upon his shoulder.

Step step, hoist. Step, step, hoist.

When Henry finally stopped, the first stars were waking up and the blisters on his feet were howling, the skin cracked and painful. Moving away from the road, he sank down to the tune of two loud cracks.

So much for making it to Old Mill Oil and Gas before nightfall.

Henry laid the bag on his lap and rested his elbows on its side, sinking slowly into the soft material. Exhaustion coursed through his veins, connecting one aching limb to the next through decades-old muscle and fascia.

He hung his head.

The back seat of a Ford wasn't the most comfortable bed, but at least it was better than a desolate field on the side of a road in the middle of nowhere. Above him, more and more stars flickered, as if to say he wasn't alone.

Because he wasn't. Headlights cut around the bend at an alarming rate, and Henry had just enough time to pull one good leg and one bad leg into his chest before a car raced past, more on the shoulder than the road.

Brake lights flashed a hundred yards from Henry's pretzeled form. The sudden reversing of tires threw gravel into the air.

He pulled himself up to standing with his cane, wobbling from the sudden movement.

The car came to a stop a few feet from where he stood. The passenger window of a Datsun rolled down in a jittery dance, as if the hand rolling it down was too far away to maneuver it properly. Henry squinted into the dim interior of the car. The only thing he could make out was a small mirror ball hanging from the rearview mirror, still twisting from the sudden motion.

"Sir!" Falling out of the driver's door was a young man—a teenager, really, barely out of school, if at all. He scrambled around the front of the car, pulling up short at Henry's expression. "I'm sorry, sir. I didn't see you there."

"Oh." Henry reached overhead, cane sticking out at a ninety-degree angle. "That's all right." His bag sagged against his shin.

"What are you doing?"

Henry bent at the waist to reach for his toes. They were a long way away. "Stretching."

"Oh." A stifled laugh. "No, I mean, what are you doing sitting on the edge of the road?"

"I was hardly on the edge of the road," Henry said. The kid cocked an eyebrow. "I was taking a break. My car broke down and the tow truck driver refused to let me hitch a ride, so here I am." Another car whizzed past them, headlights cutting a path in the darkness. In the teenager's car, the mirror ball caught the light and flung it around them.

Henry didn't know how much farther Route 50 was, but he knew standing around explaining himself to the person who had almost run him over wouldn't help him get there any faster. "Anyways. I best keep going to . . ." Where? He tossed the bag over his shoulder with a wince.

The kid hopped from one foot to the other, like a child who needed to relieve himself. "I can drive you."

Henry blinked. "I beg your pardon?"

"I can drive you." He hopped again. "I'm off to say a few choice words to my dad, who I haven't seen since I was ten." He flashed his teeth. "So I can drive you to get your car on my way."

Henry didn't know what to say.

The stars were brighter, and the car looked green. Or maybe it was black with a tinge of green. The mirror ball had stopped spinning. "Okay." He nodded. "If you could drop me off at Old Mill Oil and Gas, that would be great."

"You betcha." The kid slid the bag from Henry's shoulder, doing a double take that Henry didn't understand. Without a word, Henry climbed into the passenger seat. If, that is, you could call it a seat. It was covered in debris: candy wrappers, old juice containers, three paperbacks, a hammer, two ragged shirts, a bottle opener, and a bright-yellow marble. Henry gingerly pushed the pile to the floor and climbed in. He took the bag from the kid and held it in his lap. The door slammed shut beside him, locking him in. Henry wished he were anywhere else.

The pit stop, the border, that lovely Welsh woman's house. Home.

The kid shifted into gear and put his foot down. Hard. Henry caught himself on the dash with one hand and the seat with the other.

"Roger," the driver said, accelerating faster. "My name is Roger. But you can call me Rog. Everyone calls me Rog, even the people I don't like, who say it with a sneer as if to upset me. Like Jerry. But nothing really upsets me. My mom always taught me to look on the bright side, so even when people are saying mean things to my face and behind my back, I just let it roll off me. There isn't enough time in life to get upset over the small things. Is there, Mr. . . ."

Henry clutched his cane. "Henry," he said.

Roger turned the radio up and tapped the steering wheel in tune with the song. He took the bends at breakneck speed, shifting down and up in a fluid motion. Henry's stomach churned. When had he last eaten?

Eight songs passed, and Henry was beginning to wonder if Roger knew where the service station actually was. It couldn't be this far.

Was he being kidnapped? It was possible. Teenagers had been known to have bursts of anger that were uncontrollable and do unexpected things.

When William was a teenager, he had tried to run away. *Tried* because he had been walking down the street, bag slung over his squared shoulders, when Elsie pulled up beside him on her way to the store. She'd rolled down the window, asked their son if he needed a ride to a friend's, and put an unknowing stop to his plan. William had been so embarrassed that he'd picked up a stone from the side of the road and thrown it as hard as he could, telling his mother to leave him alone. The stone went through a neighbor's front window, and William had worked all summer to pay it off. He'd never tried to run away again.

After a few more miles and another song, a sign up ahead blinked. *Old Oil and Gas*. The lights for *Mill* were burnt out.

Roger twisted into the parking lot under the haphazard sign and skidded to a stop. "Right, then." He turned the radio down. "See your car?"

Henry peered through the smudged windshield at the fenced lot, surveying each vehicle. Their colors washed away in the night, but he could make out the make and model of each. Alfa Romeo. Chevy truck. Suzuki Fronte. There was even a Holden HD in the corner.

"It should be here," Henry whispered. Untangling himself, he exited the car for a closer look. There were nine cars in the lot, and he scanned them each twice. Three times. The Ford should be among them. But it wasn't. There wasn't a blue Ford (or any Ford, for that matter) in sight.

A hand on his shoulder made Henry startle. "Where's yours, sir?"

"Gone." Henry flicked dirt up with the end of his cane, shoulders drooping toward the earth.

"Like, gone, gone?"

Henry couldn't answer. A sharp pain pierced his side and his vison blurred. Desperate for breath, he inhaled through his nose in short, rapid bursts. Roger steered him to the passenger seat and gently took the cane from his hands.

Thoughts leapt around Henry's mind like a pinball. What was he doing? He wasn't a man on a mission. He was an aging fool slowly losing his mind.

"We should call the cops," Roger said, bouncing on the balls of his feet. "My uncle Ross had a bike stolen once, and they—"

Henry cut him off. "No. No cops."

"But, sir, we need to get the authorities involved. They'll know what to do. We can't just have tow truck drivers stealing cars all around town. Oh no, that won't do at all."

"Kid." Henry shook his head. "Can you stop talking so I can think?"

Roger obliged, lips squeezed together. He blinked rapidly as if it pained him to be silent. Henry stared at the row of unrecognizable cars again.

"The old girl was busted," he said with a huff. "No point trying to get her back. I have everything I need with me." Henry nodded at the bag sitting in the footwell, glad he had grabbed the letters before Blue Collar Bill took off with the Ford.

He rubbed his eyes and took a deep, shuddering breath. "Do you know where I can find a bus stop?"

"A bus stop?"

"Yes. Isn't that what they're called?" Had he said the wrong thing? "There's usually a sign by the road and a bench. Then a bus comes along and picks you up."

It would take him a lot longer to finish his mission by bus, but he would make it work. There were no other options.

The kid looked at his watch with a frown. "I don't think there are any more buses running on this route. It's after seven."

Great. Now Henry would need to spend the night sleeping under a bus bench. He never should have let that man tow his car. Surely with a little more time, Charlie could have fixed it.

"Look. Why don't we go grab some food, and then we can figure out what to do."

Henry looked at the kid properly for the first time, under a half-glowing sign.

Freckles dotted his nose, giving him the dewy look of someone caught between adolescence and adulthood. His cheeks were pocked from acne. Thick, unruly brows twitched on a large forehead above eyes that were almost too close together. Henry could practically feel the energy radiating off him, wound up and ready to be set loose.

His stomach grumbled in response. "Okay. Let's grab a bite to eat."

69

Thursday, October 27, 1966
7:21 PM

Roger snuck a glance at his passenger. The man didn't move a muscle. He sat, ramrod straight, clutching a wooden cane, staring out the window.

Bad luck for his car to get stolen. Roger didn't really know what to do with him. After food, he'd try to find a place for Henry to stay, close to a bus stop. The delay made him want to whoop, but he worried he'd scare the man half to death. That's what his mom said every time he whooped: *You scared the living daylights out of me, Rog!*

He looked at Henry again. "What do you want to eat?"

"I'm not picky," Henry said. Though it did sound like he muttered something about carrots under his breath. Did that mean he wanted a prime rib with all the sides?

"Let's see what comes up first." Roger shifted in his seat. "We're bound to pass a diner at some point. The last diner I went to served something called Al's Ultimate Burger. I should have ordered that instead of a plain burger. It was so dry. How do you like your hamburger?"

Henry grunted. "I don't know."

"Oh. Okay. Well, if you get a burger when we stop for food, I recommend pausing to consider all the options. The waitress came over too fast, and I didn't have time to think about everything before making a decision. Plus she tapped her pencil in the same way my teacher does when she's waiting for an answer. That's only if I haven't already been sent to the back of the room to make a radio, though."

He shot Henry a wink. The old man leaned away from him.

"I'm just saying," he carried on. "Options are good."

"I don't think I like having options."

Roger spotted a neon sign advertising food twenty-four-seven up ahead. "Okay. We can go to the first place we see." He nodded at the diner on their right. "If you'd rather not have to choose."

"Yes," Henry said, voice small. "I think the first choice will do."

Roger's smile grew. He could appreciate a man who spoke honestly.

"The first choice it is." Roger cut the engine and hopped from the car. Henry took a little more time, refusing help. Roger stuck close by his side as they made their way to the front door.

It would be nice to have someone to talk to, if only for an hour or so.

70

Thursday, October 27, 1966

7:40 PM

Men came and went from the house in a steady stream. So far, all of them had been Black and none of them had been pushing ninety with a cane.

Stokes's head throbbed. How long would they have to wait for Walton?

In the car beside him, Fletcher chomped on a piece of Bazooka and picked at his cuticles. Cool air began to creep into the Riviera. The nights were getting colder as each day passed.

"This is useless," Stokes grumbled, flicking the butt of his cigarette on the pavement and lighting another. The faded bricks and endless strands of dying ivy were getting on his nerves. "It's either not the right place or not the right plan."

Fletcher stayed silent, eyes glued to the front door as if he could force it open by will alone. Nails fully attended to and clearly not in a rush for any action to happen, he folded his arms behind his head and settled in deeper.

Stokes exhaled into the car. Fletcher coughed on the smoke.

Reclining his seat, Stokes placed his hat over his eyes. "Keep watch and do something useful for a change," he said, his voice softened only by the thickness of the wool.

71

Thursday, October 27, 1966
7:56 PM

The security guard leaned away from his boss. He wished he could flush the overwhelming sense of anxiety from the car. If there was anything Vincent Fletcher knew for certain, it was that patience was a virtue. Nothing good ever came from rushing into one thing and out of the next. If they wanted to find the Reverend Martin Luther King Junior, they were going to have to wait. If they wanted to meet up with the elderly man who'd broken into the post office and made off with hundreds of letters, they were going to have to wait.

Much of life was waiting. What mattered most was the mindset you kept during the in-between times.

Right now, Fletcher wasn't sitting outside a building with peeling shutters picking at his fingers and trying to suck some flavor out of the same piece of gum he'd popped into his mouth an hour ago. He was flying a plane. A little two-seater, with a beautiful woman in the back. Soaring over mountains and skimming the tops of rivers while she squealed and grabbed at his broad shoulders. His hands gripped the column while she exclaimed at every sight.

They passed over jungles he'd only read about and circled pyramids rising from the sand. They waved to the Eiffel Tower, imagining fresh-baked bread and endless glasses of cabernet.

It was peaceful up there in the sky, with no one to tell him he was doing a bad job or that he should speak up or when was he going to lose the extra weight he carried around?

Stokes let out a loud snore, and Fletcher fell from the sky to the passenger seat. He rubbed at his eyes and reached for the radio dial.

"—it appears fanfare for an elderly man who broke into the Chicago Post Office is growing." The clipped voice of an announcer filled the car. "When wanted posters for Mr. Walton were first spotted in and around the city, people assumed he was deranged and dangerous. In fact, a tip from the US-Canadian border confirms that Walton did indeed spend time detained at the border. But as more facts begin to come to light, the public is asking itself: Who is at fault here, Henry Walton or the post office?"

Fletcher glanced at Stokes, relieved to see his superior was sleeping too deeply to hear the news. Reducing the volume, he continued to listen.

"So far, six individuals have called in with stories of Walton, each one letting us know he's delivered a letter straight to their door. A Mrs. Delwyn Davies claims Walton spent several nights at her house before setting off to deliver more letters to unsuspecting recipients. As information on the so-called thief spreads, public opinion appears to be shifting . . ."

Fletcher turned the radio off and swallowed his gum. Support for Walton would not help their cause. He turned his attention back to the house and waited, patiently, for something to happen.

72

Thursday, October 27, 1966
8:01 PM

A smear of dirt on the bottom of his glass stared him in the face every time Henry took a sip, becoming more prominent the emptier his glass became. It was too late to say anything, and he didn't check whether the dirt was on the inside or the outside of the glass. The answer wasn't something he wanted to know.

"Plain burger, side salad?" A waitress appeared from thin air, brandishing their dinner.

"Dressing on the side?" the kid confirmed before accepting the meal. He'd ended up ordering the plain burger after a long conversation with the waitress about all the options: Did the chef have a special sauce? What was her personal favorite? Was it possible to get the sauce on the side? No? What about salad with the dressing on the side?

Roger leaned across the small table to grab an almost-empty bottle of Heinz while the waitress stooped to place a steaming bowl of chili in front of Henry. He reached for the two-in-one salt and pepper and sprinkled the seasoning on generously. Roger shook the ketchup with a heavy hand before resigning himself to banging it on the side of the table.

Chili sloshed over the side of Henry's bowl.

Henry turned away from the great tomato sauce heist and watched the waitress flit from table to table in the busy diner. She moved with an awkward grace, taking orders and clearing plates. Sleek black vinyl benches framed wobbly metal tables along a wall of greasy windows. There was something comforting about a place where grease latched itself to every surface. It transported him back to his youth, and he had a sudden flashback of Don Monroe, Dave Watford, and Sam Smith all piled into a corner booth with its torn persimmon vinyl, catcalling girls as they walked past. Sam used to claim rights over the jukebox every Saturday night. If a pretty girl requested a song, the price to hear it was a kiss. Sam got quite a few kisses in those days, as Billie Holiday serenaded and Bing Crosby crooned. Henry hadn't joined in, preferring instead to be the quiet one in the corner, watching everything, taking it all in. Between songs, when the low hum of the diner was the only sound in the world, Henry felt complete. He relished the stillness, the moving forward of time without any need to speed it up or showboat or fill every crevice of space with noise.

They'd called him "Hardly Talks Henry" back then, always pulling him into the middle of their boisterous world.

By the bar, hungry occupants perched on upholstered stools. A lineup of diners waiting for a table had started to form by the door. Henry felt their vulture-like gazes on the back of his neck as he regarded his meal.

She hadn't left him a spoon.

It would take too long to get her attention, ask for appropriate cutlery, and wait while she walked past the growing line to deposit the only piece of equipment needed to eat what he had ordered. He would have to make do.

"Is your chili funny, sir?" Roger asked around a mouthful of burger.

"Huh?" Henry took another forkful and looked up.

"You were just laughing at your food."

He swallowed a bite. "I was laughing at the fork."

"The fork?" Roger added two small dabs of dressing to his salad and began tossing it around his plate. It made him look older than the years he'd actually lived.

Henry explained. "Years ago, when we moved into our first home . . . or maybe it was the second? My wife, Elsie, made a pot of soup for us to have while we unpacked. I think it was soup." Henry shook his head and met Roger's gaze. "She makes the best soup, my Elsie, always tossing in the most unlikely ingredients to create a delicious concoction." That much Henry knew to be true. "Problem was, we couldn't find any spoons. We looked through every kitchen and dining room box, and you'd never believe it, but there wasn't a damn spoon in sight. We ended up eating the noodles with a fork before slurping the broth out of the bowl, sitting on the floor." He paused. Elsie's pealing laughter had filled the house, days later, when she found the spoons. "They turned out to be in a box filled with curling irons and hosiery." He ate another bite and added another dash of salt and pepper. For years after that, he'd joked about forks whenever Elsie served a meal in a bowl. He gave her a brand-new set of spoons for their anniversary one year, all tied up with ribbon and a large grin. She'd taken one out of the packet and smacked him across the cheek with it before falling, her joy hitting the ceiling, onto the couch in his arms.

The memory wrapped itself around him like a big warm blanket as he finished the chili. He might not be able to recall all the specifics, but he would never forget how something made him feel.

Wiping the fork with his napkin, he pocketed it with a wink. "A gift for Elsie," Henry explained. "A little something to say sorry for being away so long."

Something niggled at the back of his mind, but Henry brushed it away.

"I've been meaning to ask, sir," Roger said, pushing his empty plate to the side of the table, "about this mission you're on?"

"Letters," Henry said. "I'm delivering letters. Only a few more to go, but they're important, you see. Very important. Maybe life-or-death." Roger cocked an eyebrow. "Or not death, but . . . national security. I need to make sure they get to the right place."

"Roger that," the kid laughed. Henry chuckled. Wouldn't it be funny if the boy's name was Roger?

He swallowed the rest of his water and ignored the smear one last time.

73

Thursday, October 27, 1966
8:21 PM

Roger listened as Henry talked about his mission. He could appreciate the man's passion, though he really wished the letter from his dad had never been delivered. It would have been so much better if it had been lost at the post office.

The thought of the journey ahead, to visit someone he actively tried to forget about every day, made his mouth dry.

If only he could delay things a little longer.

Across from him, Henry asked a question for the third time. Roger answered it again, working to keep his face straight.

The man must be exhausted after walking all that way, only to find his car had been stolen by someone he should have been able to trust. For the first time, Roger noticed how small the man seemed, hunched over the edge of the table, staring at a mark on the bottom of his glass.

It said a lot about the man that he didn't demand a new drink.

A thought began to take root in the back of Roger's mind. What kind of person would he be if he abandoned an elderly man on the side of the road with only a cane to keep him company?

No. Roger couldn't do that. He would help Henry deliver these letters no matter how long it took.

"I'd be glad to drive you for the remainder of your mission," he said. "Where are we headed? I can take you anywhere you need to go; it's no problem whatsoever. My mom always says it's good to help others when we can. That's why she volunteers at the soup kitchen even though she works two jobs."

Henry rubbed his eyebrow. "Chicago, by way of a few other places. But seriously . . . uh . . . kid."

"Oh, it's no trouble at all." Roger tapped out a tune on the table. "Seriously, zero trouble. And you can definitely call me kid, that's no trouble either, but if you did want to use my name, it's Roger. I was named after Ginger Rogers. Mom wanted a girl to call Ginger, but she got me, so instead here I am. Roger."

"Who did you say you're visiting again?" Henry asked.

"My dad. But, honestly, he can wait." Roger didn't add that making his dad wait for his arrival filled him with unexpected glee. He pictured a man he didn't recognize pacing in front of a window, wondering when he would be there. The same way his mom had paced for weeks after his dad left in the first place.

"Does he live in Chicago?"

"No, sir. I'm headed to the Badlands. But I'd be glad to go back to Chicago instead." More than glad, but he kept that to himself. "I swear I can take you the rest of the way."

Roger bit his lip. His fingers shook slightly as he finished the made-up tune. He really needed Henry to say yes.

Henry smoothed a hand down the front of his wrinkled shirt. "Okay," he said after a long pause. "Let's finish this together."

74

Thursday, October 27, 1966
9:45 PM

The moon, almost full, lit their way. The faint double line cutting the road in half appeared like a dream, fading in and out as they pushed forward, so that for long stretches of time you didn't know if you were on the proper side of the road or drifting into absent traffic.

Henry assumed the kid knew where they were. He certainly didn't.

Their words had dried up after a quick stop in Sioux City; conversation of school and Datsuns and directions to Kansas City had all been exhausted. Now Roger's constant thumb drumming was the only noise that filled the car. The irregular beat made Henry's skin feel tight, clammy.

"Do you mind?" He flipped on the radio without waiting for a response.

Fiddling with the dial, he found a station that wasn't static. The kid started bopping along, though Henry wasn't sure he would've called what they were listening to music. The voice coming from the radio was angry, slurred.

How could Roger like this?

Things had certainly changed since Henry was a teenager. Back then, music had soul. The first time he'd taken Elsie to a club . . . blues, or maybe jazz . . . her eyes had been wet, her cheeks the color of ripe cherries, and he'd thought with a pang that she'd been frightened of all the men and the scream of trumpets. Gripping her hand, Henry had turned to the door so they could make a quick escape, but a delicate hand on his arm had stopped him. She loved it, she yelled above the noise, long hair spilling down her back. She'd never felt so free.

They'd danced, in the crush of other bodies, into the small hours of the morning before heading home to make music of their own.

The half-formed vision and a lingering feeling of peace blurred, mixing with the fading message that they were no longer talking about his generation.

"Who was that?" Henry asked, turning the volume down.

"The Who."

Henry sighed. "Yes, *who* was that?"

The kid shot him a grin. "No, sir. What I mean is, that's what the band is called. The Who." It was the most ridiculous name for a band Henry had ever heard, and he said so.

"I suppose," Roger agreed, "but I think it's more of an ironic joke, sir." He followed the curve of the road. "Do you ever sit and think about that word? Who? It's so big for something so small. It's a subjective pronoun—the doer of the action—but it's also the person, the clause. The sum of someone. Who they are, who they want to be." He glanced at Henry, "I think that's why it's ironic as a band name. It's a declaration and an interrogation wrapped up in three little letters."

Henry rolled the word around in his mouth.

Roger continued. "I don't know who my dad is. Does that mean I don't know who I am? I'm not sure. My mom says I've never had a male role model, and because of that, she thinks I can't fully step into myself as a man. That's why I'm going to see him, I guess. To please my mom, sure. But also, maybe, to fill in the cracks of myself everyone else can see."

"Do you feel them? The cracks?"

"Oh." Roger paused. "I've never talked about it with anyone. I suppose, sometimes, though not in a way that makes sense." His leg bounced faster. "If I'm honest, I feel unfinished. Like someone started to make me and then got distracted and I've never quite known how to fill in the gaps on my own. But I guess I don't agree that meeting someone who walked out when I was young will help at all. I don't think meeting my dad will make my life different in any way." He gripped the wheel. "I don't have friends. Not since Pete moved away. I'm not like anyone else my age, and they make sure I know it. Oh yes. They make sure. My mom says I just need to find my people . . . that one day I'll meet someone who makes me feel like there's a reason I exist."

Henry looked at the kid in the moonlight.

Since Elsie died, there were days he didn't know who he was either, and the reminder created an unsettling sensation in his stomach. He opened his mouth to speak, but nothing came out. What was there to say?

"You Can't Hurry Love" came on, and Roger turned the volume up, thumbs once again following along to the beat. Henry settled back and tried to relax.

Nothing could go wrong now that there were two of them. Right? Even if they were just a couple of cracked, unfinished wisps of life.

The dream was a memory, soft and warm. A faint glimmer around the edges of his subconscious.

They were on a small patch of grass beside the river, under a weeping willow; their favorite place to lounge in the heat, before he'd been sent to the front. Elsie was sitting with her legs tucked underneath her, and Henry's head rested in her lap. He pulled her wrist close, inhaling the mix of sweat and sun on her skin.

"You smell of plums and lavender," he whispered, kissing the back of her hand and turning it over. "Oh my. What have we here?" He held it up to study the lines cutting ridges across her palm. She tried to tug herself free, and Henry tightened his grip playfully. "Let's see what kind of life you'll lead." His fingers were feathers across her skin. "This line says you'll marry the most handsome man in town and grow old alongside him."

"Oh, does it?" Elsie leaned over Henry to study the palm he was holding. "I suppose I'd better go introduce myself to Sal Shipman, if I'm to be his wife?"

He smacked her knee gently, and she doubled over in glee.

"And look here," he said, continuing the amateur palmistry, "you're going to have a dozen babies! Eight boys and four girls. And you'll sew all their clothes and help them with their schoolwork. At night we'll sit around an oak table, legs carved with their initials, while we share stories of our day." He let go of her hand and gazed up at her. The sun made her hair glow like tender flames. "How does that life sound, my love?"

"Twelve babies?" She pushed him away. "You'll be lucky if you get me to have just the one, Mr. Walton." She stood and brushed the grass from her dress, stray blades clinging to the hem.

Henry climbed to his feet beside her and pulled her into his arms. "We'll have as many or as few children as you want. All I ever need is you."

She responded with a kiss.

July 28, 1918
501 Dearborn Way
Chicago, Ill.

My darling Elsie,

The rain is endless here, a lashing from the heavens intent on making humanity grow up. Man up. Get up. If your legs are blown off, how is one supposed to get up? I wonder.

My mind is blank more often than it's full these days. A loop of your face, your laugh, my mom. Over and over. My ladies waiting for me to return. Please let me know how she is. The last fall she had was a scare for everyone. You'll keep checking on her, won't you?

I long for the day I can eat her cherry pie again. I'd say I'm missing your food too, but you'd know that to be a lie, my darling. It's no wonder everyone thinks you're so thin. Ha.

I have a new route now. It's longer than before, and more visible to the enemy. I need to move fast and stay low. Like that time I had to race Sal Shipman for a bar of Hershey's. Oh my. What I wouldn't give for a square of that chocolate right now. I can't wait to be home with you, my love. I'll write again tomorrow, after I dream of me, and you, and endless sweets instead of rain.

Love you forever and always,

Henry

75

Thursday, October 27, 1966

10:17 PM

A car passed, heading in the opposite direction, and Roger added it to the tally. Beside him, Henry mumbled incoherent words in his sleep. Roger wanted to answer, to have a two-way conversation, but that would be strange given the fact that his companion was unconscious.

Perhaps if Henry were to wake up . . . "Henry!"

The old man woke with a start, smashing his head on the window. "Wh-what?" He looked around wildly.

Roger twisted in his seat to make sure Henry wasn't concussed. Did men his age have fragile skulls? "It's me, Rog," Roger explained slowly. "Did you forget who I am?"

Henry sat straighter. "I never forget anything. What happened?"

"Sorry, thought I saw something in the road. A mole or something." A blush crept up his neck at the lie. He ignored the sensation.

"They can remain undetected, you know." Henry settled back into the seat. "Or maybe it's badgers who can do that."

"Oh, it's definitely moles." Roger checked his rearview mirror. "I learned in school that they spend their lives underground. Did you know that? They dig huge tunnel systems under our feet. Have you ever thought of them? Burrowing underneath us, out of sight? I haven't, really, until now. But now that you've brought it up, I think it's fascinating they do it all mostly blind. A bit like you going on this mission." He chuckled and twiddled his fingers on the wheel.

"What do you mean?"

"Well, just that you're trusting your instincts. Facing challenges as they come. You can't see what's ahead of you, but still, you continue."

He felt Henry staring at him. Maybe it was insulting to compare the man's journey to a member of the order Eulipotyphla. He should apologize.

Henry gripped his cane. "I think someone once told me they symbolize self-exploration. Or maybe it's self-discovery. Or maybe I'm wrong. I don't know . . . I can't quite grasp the facts. Perhaps that's what I'm doing. A bit of self-discovery. Still learning, even at my age."

Roger wanted to ask what he'd learned. What traits had come into sharp focus as he went door to door. He wondered what he would discover about himself on his way to the Badlands. More about his life, sure, but maybe something deeper too. Things that would make his brain generate new neurons. He'd tried to talk to Mr. Tucker about that once, how experiences could form new neural connections, but his science teacher had barked that he was disrupting the class with nonsense.

Roger licked his lips. "Can you drive?" he asked, suddenly in need of a break.

Henry replied that he could, and Roger stopped the car for them to switch seats. He traced the stars in the night sky, heading back the way he'd come. The thought of returning home made him feel lighter. Less lonely. The realization felt like a discovery. A new pathway in his complicated mind.

Henry climbed behind the wheel and readjusted the mirror. "Where are we?"

The mirror ball danced.

Roger put his feet up on the dash, tapping the soles of his shoes to the tune of the song stuck in his head. "Halfway to Kansas City."

"What do you need in Kansas City?"

What a confusing question. Roger didn't need anything in Kansas City. Henry must have a concussion. Could you drive with a concussion? They were about to find out.

"It's the address of the next letter, sir. Don't you remember?"

Another grunt. "Of course I remember."

"Great. That's great. Not that I was worried. No, not at all. Just, you know, wondering."

Henry pulled back onto the road as Roger tapped faster and peppered the man with questions and tried to remember the last time he'd felt so free.

76

Friday, October 28, 1966
12:02 AM

They passed Kansas City Union Station as the clock ticked over to a new day. Streetlights shimmered in the dark like tall sentinels guiding their way. Beside Henry, the kid snored softly, finally quiet and asleep. No one was on Washington Street as he crawled through the silent city, slowing to read each sign he passed.

At Jefferson, Henry turned left.

The letter was tucked beneath his leg. He felt an irrational need to keep them as close to him as possible, and so, an hour before when he'd stopped to relieve himself on the side of the dark road, he had found the next delivery and clutched it tight. The address was for a row house on Thirty-Eighth, and he slowed to a stop in front. Even the air seemed to hold its breath as he opened the car door and stepped out.

The sound of his cane on the pavement echoed through the still night. With the creak of a rusty hinge, Henry opened the stiff letter slot and slipped it through. It landed with a whoosh on the rug inside. Unknown words arriving at the start of a new day.

The door swung open and Henry stumbled backward.

"Oh!" He dropped his cane.

"What are you doing?" The voice was a snarl, cracking across his face. A shadow stood in the darkness. "Why the hell are you on my property?"

"A letter," Henry said. "I didn't want to knock . . . it's late . . ."

"I don't want your letter." The man kicked at the mail, tearing the envelope as he scraped it out onto the front step. He moved to close the door. "Get out of here."

"Oh. The letter is for—"

"I said I don't want it. What are you, deaf, old man? Unless you're delivering *her* and not some useless paper, you can take your goddamn letter and get out of here."

Henry stood, mouth agape. The door slammed in his face and he recoiled, closing in on himself.

Behind him, Roger rushed forward, scooping down to retrieve the discarded mail. "Sir!" He handed Henry his cane. "Let's go."

A cat cried in the dark.

Roger laid a hand on his trembling arm, guiding him toward the car.

Henry yanked his arm away. "I don't need help." His legs shook. His heart galloped.

Roger started the engine, stealing looks in Henry's direction. In the side mirror, Henry watched as the house got smaller before disappearing.

"I wish I had been there," Roger said. "Sir, I really wish I had been there; you should have woken me up. I could have gone with you to the door and helped. And then I—"

"It's fine. There was no way for us to know he would react that way."

"I know, but—"

"It would have been the same outcome, even if you'd been there."

"Yes, but—"

"Enough," Henry exploded. "Kid. He didn't want it." He could feel the weight of the final letters settling on his shoulders. Words he didn't write digging into his skin like razors. He clutched the unwanted mail with its torn envelope, wondering what it said, who it was from. The sting of a thousand paper cuts sliced his heart. He wanted to curl into a ball in the footwell.

Roger stayed silent. Twitching his fingers, jiggling his leg.

It didn't take long before he started again. "Well, I should have punched him. Or kicked the door. Or at least said a few choice words to him, but my words tend to dry up when I'm dealing with confrontation, and I never have the courage to say anything in the moment. My mom says I need to get better at handling adversity, but, I don't know, I just . . . freeze. That's probably why I've built so many radios, now that I think of it. I've never stopped to explain that I just get the work done so fast. And then I want to talk to someone about it. Instead, the minute I open my mouth, I'm relegated to the back of the room with only wires and pliers and breadboards for company." He shook his head. "And I shouldn't have tried to help you get back to the car; it's just—"

"It's fine."

"I know, but I should have left you alone."

Henry leaned against the door. "No, I should have let you. It's just . . . I'm not the best at accepting help." He exhaled through his nose. "Since Elsie died, my mind feels like it's a sieve. There are parts of my life I remember so vividly it makes me gasp. Everything else? It falls straight through, and all that remains is a feeling I can't quite articulate. I can see the pity in everyone's eyes." Roger shot him a look. "Yes, even yours, and the desire to help the senile old man who hobbles with a cane and can't recall whether he's coming or going half the time. And I appreciate the help, I do, but it's just so . . . I can't think of the word. I guess it makes me feel small." The road stretched out before them. "And these letters? They make me feel bigger. Worthwhile. Like I'm *doing* something for once. But the reality is, they're not expecting me, these people. I'm a stranger, turning up out of the blue, with something for them I can't explain." He stared out the window. Roger's leg continued its dance. Miles passed.

When Roger spoke, his voice vibrated. "I wonder what it says. Maybe it's an envelope filled with money. Lunch is on that guy if it is."

Henry chuckled, appreciating the attempt at lightening the mood. "Let's find out." He tore open the envelope.

"Oh. Sir, I was joking . . ."

Inside was a double-sided sheet of lined paper, folded in half. Henry scanned the words on the page and rolled down the window.

As Roger took a bend, the car curving around the road, Henry opened his hand and let the letter go. Behind them, it tossed on the breeze and landed, without a goodbye, in the ditch.

619 W 38th Street
Kansas City, MO

Phillip,

I'm writing to say good-bye. By the time you get this letter, I'm sure you'll have started a search party. No doubt you've already sent mail to my mother and Lila and called round to all the men at the club. It's too late for apologies; I won't be reading anything you write. Please don't come after me.

You can be a decent man, Phillip (when you choose to be), and I'm sure you will make the future Mrs. Blythe incredibly happy. But we both know I was never meant to be a housewife, and I fear I've never quite lived up to your high standards. Your anger and disappointment at the blackened meals, stained trousers, and ripped draperies . . . it's suffocating. I cannot marry you.

Please send my love to Lila. She has been a lovely friend, trying ever so desperately to teach me her etiquette ways. But I fear I have disappointed her as well. She once told me I was forbidden from wearing a skirt without stockings, so I drew lines up the back of my legs and dared her to feel my new, ultra-thin hosiery. She nearly fell over in shock. I've never felt as free as I did in that moment.

Wishing you a lifetime of happiness and more laughter than you're used to. Do try to laugh now and again, won't you?

Maisie

77

Friday, October 28, 1966
5:30 AM

In the early morning hue, Shelbina, Lakenan, and Monroe City passed by without notice. Sleepy towns on a sleepy interstate. By the time they came to a stop on the edge of the Mississippi, they had been driving for hours.

At Hill Street, Henry said, "Let's stretch our legs."

A light fog filled the air, and he could hear the roar of the river better than he could see it. A cool breeze kissed his skin. He inhaled deeply.

"Look, sir."

Henry turned to see Roger pointing left. Squinting through the trees, he could just make out a dim light above the horizon. On and off it pulsed through the dawn fog.

Roger set off in its direction.

Cane in tow, Henry followed Roger's brisk pace with a slow, more arthritic one. After a hundred yards, they arrived at the base of a hill. A bronze statue of two young boys marked the start of a steep incline. Henry couldn't make out the plaque in the limited light, but he knew what it said.

"Tom Sawyer and Huck Finn," he explained, continuing past the immortalized characters. A set of stairs led the way, and they followed, pausing every few feet to catch stolen breath. Halfway up, they learned they were climbing Cardiff Hill. Two hundred yards beyond, they learned Henry's knees—especially the one still harboring shrapnel like a lost treasure—didn't agree with hills.

More than an hour had passed by the time they reached the lighthouse. Henry peered up at the round white building and watched its light circle the sky. His chest hitched; his legs burned. His knee hated him completely. "Stars and shadows ain't good to see by," he said with a smile.

"What's that?" Roger was slumped at the foot of the building, breathing hard.

"Mark Twain. *The Adventures of Huckleberry Finn*," Henry said. "This was their hill. And this"—he waved an arm at the building—"was Twain's lighthouse. The magnificent Mississippi, rolling its mile-wide tide along . . ."

He sank onto a bench.

Roger sat down beside him. "I always hated the ending."

"Ah. Most people did. Though it wasn't really an ending, was it. It was a bridge to the next chapter in the story. To his next life."

"But we don't know what happened. Did he stay or leave?"

Henry rubbed his palms together against the morning chill. "Not every line needs to be written. You have a duty, as a reader, to keep the story going. To write the next line yourself."

Roger turned to face him. "What do you mean?"

"An author can only take a story so far. It's up to those who read it, who fall so far into the story they can't escape, to keep it alive. What do you want Huck to do next?"

"Well," Roger mumbled, "I suppose I want him to return to Aunt Sally."

"So make it happen. In your mind, you can send Huck off on his adventure *and* bring him home. You can imagine the best of both worlds for him, with the ending you're looking for. Me? I want Huck to explore. I want him to climb mountains and swim seas and find everything his spirit is crying for."

"Like you?" Roger said it so quietly that Henry almost didn't hear him. "If you don't mind me saying so, sir, you seem to be looking for something with all these letters. Perhaps something more than self-discovery?"

Henry let the question settle.

"My son, William," he said eventually, once the memory formed beyond a feeling of overwhelm. "He sent me a letter from the front before he died. I remember it was so . . . ordinary. He didn't speak of the horrors we knew he must be experiencing; the same ones I, too, had experienced. He didn't talk about missing home. He wrote to us about a game of cards he'd won. Pinochle, I think. Or maybe poker. They played it all the time, he said, a small group of them. And this was the first time he'd come out on top. William wasn't competitive, you see; he couldn't care less about who won and who lost, war notwithstanding, of course. What he loved most was being with others and getting caught up in the game. 'I just like the feeling of being alive,' he wrote in that letter. A week later he was gone."

Henry turned to face Roger. "I used to find Elsie sitting on his bed, clutching his words, tears streaming down her face. I tried to get her to stop reading it. It was making her more upset, doing more harm than good. But she looked at me, that fiery wife of mine, and told me it reminded her that our son had *lived*. It stayed in her bedside drawer for years, that letter. An important reminder of how miraculous even the simplest life can be. I suppose, really, that's what these letters represent to me. That every life, no matter how big or small or commonplace, is worth being etched onto a page. Even my own."

He shook his head, willing some truth from his own existence to break free. "Perhaps it's still in there. That letter from William." He desperately wanted to read it. It would be the first thing he did when he got home. "Even if I have a few of the facts wrong, the memory feels . . . sharp."

Roger sat on his hands. "Sharp?"

"Like swallowing bleach and being unable to stop." He shrugged. "It's hard to explain. But every moment of my life is wrapped up in feelings I can remember more vividly than anything else."

In front of them, the water flowed steadily, shimmering in the pulse of the lighthouse. He thought again of Huck and his desperate desire to escape confinement.

It felt, though he couldn't admit it out loud, a little like the unending entrapment of a broken mind.

78

Friday, October 28, 1966
6:56 AM

Roger watched the river. He knew it would eventually flow into the Gulf of Mexico, traveling more than two thousand miles to get there. He'd read once that it took a single drop of water three months to flow from one end of the Mississippi to the other.

Beside him, Henry was lost in his own thoughts and feelings.

Roger thought about what his life had felt like up until now. Sure, there had been some big emotions over the years. When his dad left. When Pete moved. But since then? He hadn't felt much of anything. Did that make his existence commonplace?

They had four letters left to deliver.

While Henry slept, Roger had looked at the letters and memorized each address, just in case. Rubbing his thumb over the seal on the back of one, he had felt excitement fizz through him from head to toe. He hadn't told Henry he'd looked at the letters. The old man was as protective of them as he would be a small child. "A man must protect what matters most," Henry had said the day before. It was his motto, apparently.

Now Roger understood why letters were what mattered most to Henry.

Roger thought about the note from his own father. A handful of meaningless lines he couldn't get out of his head. Not an apology. Not even an explanation.

Just a useless invitation to go camping.

A tightness clawed at his chest. He pictured the door slamming in Henry's face, the sound of the man's shouting, and he wondered deep down whether his own family would react the same way. If he turned around and traveled to the Badlands, would it all be for nothing?

"I hope not," he pleaded, his voice low so Henry wouldn't hear. "It *can't* all be a waste of time."

The lighthouse circled past them. Roger's leg never stopped moving. In the distance, a bird chirped, and he was grateful for the sound.

79

Friday, October 28, 1966
7:16 AM

Brenda pressed a fist into her lips. "It wasn't a waste of time," she said as Stokes stared at nothing, practically cross-eyed. Beside her, Fletcher swayed. She turned to bring him into the conversation, but he wouldn't meet her eye.

The security guard hadn't said a word to her in days.

Fine. So be it.

While the two men had been trying to catch Walton, the van had been loaded a dozen more times. Every time Brenda watched it drive away, she felt invincible. As if nothing could stop her from fixing the problem. The minute she'd mentioned to the receiving crew that orders had come from Stokes's office, they did whatever she asked. No one questioned her or looked down on her. For the first time in her life, people were listening to her.

She needed to keep Stokes distracted so she could keep going.

"I think," she said, clasping her hands in front of her waist, "if you understand what's happening at that address, you'll know what to expect. Isn't it better to be prepared? If you—"

The cigarette dangled between Stokes's lips. "Ha! Absolutely nothing is happening there. We stayed for hours, and all we saw were a bunch of Blacks coming and going."

Brenda thinned her lips. "If there are people there . . ." She spoke slowly. Why could the man not grasp even the most basic concepts? "It means if Walton makes it there before you, he'll deliver the letter."

Stokes looked up at her.

"But if you expand your surveillance to the street, taking in everyone and not just the occupants at that address, you have a better chance of seeing him before he gets anywhere close to the door."

"And how does that help me?"

Brenda felt as if she might implode. "If you find Walton before he gets there, you can take the letter from him and deliver it yourself. Think about how good that will look, Reginald. The manager of the post office prioritizing presidential correspondence despite dealing with a major issue. You'll be the hero."

The last word made her want to gag.

Understanding flitted across Stokes's face. Good, now they were getting somewhere. If she could just get him to focus on Walton for a few more days, she could—

"No," Stokes said, the corner of his mouth twitching. "I have an even better idea."

80

Friday, October 28, 1966
7:24 AM

Stokes lit another cigarette and leaned back in his chair. Brenda always did come up with a good plan. Even if the ideas were his first.

"When Walton turns up at that address, we're going to intervene, like you said."

Brenda nodded. In the corner, Fletcher looked up.

"But we're not going to deliver it," Stokes said.

"Sir?" She looked even uglier when she frowned.

What did the woman not understand? It was a good thing he was around. He hoped O'Brien knew just how important he was. How much the post office needed him to clean up every mess. "We're going to take the letter and destroy it, so no one knows it ever existed."

Why hadn't he thought of this earlier? Sure, the idea of obliterating an actual piece of mail made his chest feel a little tight, but what other option did he have? He rubbed at his sternum. Letters had done nothing but give him a headache his whole life, and this one from the White House was making everything worse. He needed to get rid of it.

In front of him, Fletcher had started to sweat and kept looking at Brenda, who stood with her mouth open, not saying a word.

"Once we get rid of this letter and take care of Walton, everything else will fall into place. Just you wait and see. We won't even need to lift a finger."

He couldn't wait to teach everyone who had ever doubted him a lesson.

81

Friday, October 28, 1966

7:45 AM

Henry turned to Roger. "I'll demonstrate, and then you can deliver the next one." They were parked in front of a small house in Hannibal. Roger had helped him navigate his way down Cardiff Hill an hour before. Going down with a cane was harder than going up, and it had taken Henry longer to descend.

Roger's nervous leg asked the question first. "Me? Deliver one?"

"Of course." Henry had a feeling Roger hadn't been asked to do anything lately except build . . . what did he build? Rockets? Radios? Anyways, he didn't think Roger got asked to do much. He seemed ready to burst with an eagerness that made Henry proud.

As Roger watched through the car window, Henry made his way up the front path to a wooden door with a brass door knocker in the shape of a horseshoe.

Flo would call that lucky.

Henry smoothed down the front of his shirt and knocked.

He hoped the kid had a good view. Henry knew he'd be leaning forward, jiggling his legs and his hands and his ears, waiting to see what happened next.

Henry could already picture him letting out a whoop and telling Henry how amazing it was to see a letter get delivered to someone. The joy on their face. The skip in their step.

The door opened.

Henry's hands flew to cover his eyes, cane tucked under his elbow. The letter fluttered to the ground. Oh heavens.

A woman stood before him, buck naked.

"Can I help you?" she asked.

Henry spoke through his hands. "I'm so sorry. I'm just delivering a letter."

"Wonderful," she said. It was possible she jumped a little with excitement. Her voice certainly did. "I love letters."

His own voice was muffled. "Me too. It's there"—he nudged his foot to the left—"or there." He swung it to the right. He couldn't see which direction the letter had fallen and didn't dare remove his hands. That would make everything worse.

"You can lower your hands," she said with a laugh that made his pulse race. "No shame here."

"Oh no. No." He shuffled back a step. "I'll just leave you to it, if that's all right. And be on my way." Hands still firmly in place, Henry spun around. Taking a peek to make sure he was headed in the right direction, he moved to the car.

In the passenger window, Roger didn't blink.

"Thank you," she said to his back.

Every part of him burned. "You're welcome, my dear," he called over his shoulder.

Only when the door closed with a click did he lower his hands, gaze fixed on the car and nowhere else. He tripped on a crack in the pavement and caught himself before falling. Pinching his lips together, Henry told his old heart to slow down.

510 Olive Street,
Hannibal, MO

Patsy,

Look at this dress I found in the Montgomery Ward catalogue. Don't you just love it?

This pattern will really show off your curves. When Leroy sees you in it, he'll be sorry he ever left. That's for sure.

I was thinking of getting a similar one in olive. Do you think it would complement my eyes?

Let me know. I can put in an order for us both.

Speak soon,

Ida

82

Friday, October 28, 1966
8:54 AM

"Are you ready to give it a try?" Henry rubbed a thumb over the front of the envelope. They hadn't stopped laughing since the last house, both men stammering and squirming side by side.

"Oh yes. Yes, sir," Roger's knee was on the move.

Henry gave a slow smile. "It's simple, really. But it must be taken seriously. You never know what you're dropping into someone's hands and how it will make them feel. Case in point: last night." He handed Roger the envelope. "Sometimes we bring joy, other times we bring sorrow. It might be good or bad or even embarrassing. Like the last house. It all depends on what's inside, and we have no way of knowing that. We're just the messengers."

Roger unclipped his seat belt and opened the door.

Henry turned to face him. "Don't knock too loudly; it's still early. But don't knock too soft that they don't hear you. If no one answers, you can slip the letter through the slot. It *is* anticlimactic when that happens, but it's still rewarding. You'll see."

He watched through the windshield as Roger approached the house.

83

Friday, October 28, 1966
8:57 AM

The letter burned in Roger's hands. He couldn't believe Henry was actually letting him do this. At home, his mom had told him not to worry about cleaning because, apparently, questioning the impact of sodium dichloro-s-triazinetrione dihydrate on the skin was not helpful. At school, the teachers told him not to worry about answering questions because *he didn't know when to stop talking.*

No one ever trusted Roger to do anything meaningful.

Until today.

He bounded up the path and had to force himself to slow down right before the door. He hopped from one foot to the other before knocking. Not too loud, not too soft.

A thin layer of frost coated the front lawn and weighed down the flowerless ninebark that ringed the porch. Roger pictured the soft white blooms that would arrive with spring and waited for someone to open the door.

Around him, the street was waking up. A car started three houses down. A bus ambled past on its way to the school. Roger looked back at the car. Henry, framed in the passenger window, raised a hand that told him to wait. Roger turned back toward the door and gripped the letter tighter. He heard a voice inside and the sound of a door closing. He wondered how many people were home.

The handle turned, and Roger held his breath.

A woman stood behind the screen and peered out behind round glasses. "Yes?" she asked, one hand holding the door.

"Hi . . . hi, ma'am," Roger stuttered. "Hi."

"I'm not buying anything." She made to close the door.

"Oh no." He bounced. "I'm not selling anything."

She kept the screen closed. "What can I do for you?"

He exhaled and held up the letter. "I'm looking for Norma. I mean, a Mrs. Norma Handler." The envelope shook.

"I'm Norma," she said, pushing the screen open with a slippered foot.

"Oh great. That's great." Roger handed her the envelope. "I'm so glad you're home and I'm so sorry to disturb you, only my friend and I"—he turned to look at Henry in the car—"are delivering letters, and this is the first one I've got to deliver and . . ."

He stopped talking.

Norma leaned against the screen door and pushed a thumb under the flap. "Let's see what we've got, shall we?"

Roger bobbed. "Oh, you don't have to—"

"It's no problem. If it's your first delivery, you should have a chance to know what it says." She scanned the contents. "It's from my friend. Ruby. She moved to Illinois. For a man, no less." A small smile touched her lips. "It seems she's having a rather hard time with his family. It says here his daughter is behaving rather immorally and she's had to bail the girl out financially a number of times." Norma folded the letter and tucked it back into its envelope. "I suppose I should write her back with some solutions to her problems."

Roger grinned and gave her a salute. She laughed and returned the gesture. With a farewell, she closed the door.

He practically sprinted back to the car.

Dear Ruby,

I must reply to the letter I just received from you. It's postmarked a number of weeks ago, but it only now arrived on my doorstep. It was a rather surprising delivery, to say the least. I answered the door with my curlers in, that's how little I was expecting a knock to come. And it was a teenage boy delivering it. Normally I would have shooed someone like that off my porch in a hurry, but there was something about him, an eagerness, a bubbling over of excitement, and I found myself accepting what he was offering. Much to my surprise and delight, it was your letter. I have a feeling it's been on a spectacular journey to get here.

Now, on to the matter at hand. I fear that unless Kathleen shows any improvement morally, I don't think you and Daniel should be burdened financially to provide her with a place in which to continue her affairs with men and drink. You need to cut her off. It's a hard decision to make, especially for Daniel, but I fear young Kate needs to be taught a rather strict lesson.

It will be up to you to teach it to her. I'd help if I could, you know that. I miss you dearly, Ruby. How I wish you were still a few doors away. Give my love to Daniel and the kids (yes, even Kathleen), and please write again soon.

Yours,

Norma

84

Friday, October 28, 1966
10:30 AM

"Pull in over there," Henry directed, pointing to the Golden Bear parking lot. He'd spotted the large sign advertising pancakes a block away.

Roger slid into an empty space. "Do you need the restroom?"

"No. We need breakfast." Henry pushed open the door. Roger scrambled out the other side.

"Breakfast? Sir, we ate before we left Hannibal. After the house with the . . . you know." Roger dipped his head, trying to hide a grin.

"No we didn't. We haven't eaten anything since last night."

"But . . . but sir. We had eggs and bacon at the Roadside Café. You asked for egg whites, no yolk . . ."

"Hmmm," Henry mumbled, "I don't remember." He tapped his cane on the ground, looking at the pancake house. He didn't feel hungry, but surely he would have felt full if he'd eaten already. He hovered between the building and the car.

Roger closed the gap between them. "If you're still hungry, we can eat here."

"Yes. I must still be hungry," Henry said. "We'd better have some breakfast." Roger took his elbow and steered him toward the front door. Henry let him. Above them, a welcoming billow of smoke puffed from the chimney.

* * *

He wasn't hungry. At least, not hungry enough for a full stack of pancakes. He pushed the food around his plate while Roger shared more about his delivery to a woman named Norma.

"She had curlers in," the kid said with a laugh. "My mom always answers the door in curlers." He spun the saltshaker between his hands.

Henry swallowed another bite, tuning the kid out. He'd heard all about the delivery on the drive to Springfield. He'd been proud at first, but the more Roger talked about Norma and her correspondence with Ruby, the more Henry's palms began to sweat. That had been the third-to-last letter, and he felt, guiltily, as if he'd thrown something important away by letting Roger deliver it. He moved a piece of pancake from one side of the plate to the other. He couldn't help feeling as if he'd lost something he couldn't get back. A sigh escaped his lips.

"Sir?" Roger set the saltshaker down. "Are you finished?"

Henry looked at the food he hadn't eaten and shoved the plate away. He felt too full to even look at it, as if it were his second meal of the day. "I don't know why I ordered this. I'm not hungry." Roger's eyes widened, and he picked up the salt once more. Twisting, twisting. "Stop moving already." Henry banged a fist on the table. Every head in the dining room turned their way, and he turned the color of the crimson tablecloth.

Henry closed his eyes and gripped the side of the table. When he opened them, Roger had pushed the seasoning away and sat like a statue.

"I'm sorry," he whispered. "I shouldn't have snapped."

"Oh no. Oh no, sir." Roger moved his hands to his lap. "I take no offense."

"I don't think I'm quite ready for it all"—Henry waved a hand absently—"to end."

"Ah, I understand. I'm not quite ready for this to end either." Roger's hand flew to his lips and tapped erratically. "After this, I . . . I don't know if I can face turning around and heading back to the Badlands. I don't think I'm strong enough."

"Of course you are. Just look what you did with . . . what's her name? Norma."

"Yes. Yes, that was nice. I'm glad to have done it. It's the first real memory I've made in a while, to tell you the truth. But I'm worried it won't feel quite so . . . rewarding . . . with my dad. It feels unnecessary, like we should all just let the past be the past." Roger stared absently at the still-full plate of pancakes in the middle of the table. Henry looked at him closely and realized, with a start, he hadn't noticed before just how golden the boy's eyes were, flecks of gold dust mingling with light brown. They reminded him of Elsie. He studied Roger's features, trying to commit them to memory.

"It *will* feel different with your dad," Henry said after a pause. "But if you don't go, you'll never know. What's worse? Always imagining the worst possible outcome or taking a chance on the best? I'm not excusing your father for leaving—not at all. But . . . if I could have one more moment to talk to William, to see the man he was at the end . . . I'd give anything for that. Sure, your dad might disappoint you again. Or he might be everything you've been looking for." He lifted a shoulder. "Besides, doing what you say you will, having integrity, is important."

The gold sparkled in Roger's eyes.

All we can do is keep moving, Henry thought. It was his . . . what was the word? Reaching for his cane, he stood up.

"Before that, though, we have a mission to complete, you and I."

85

Friday, October 28, 1966

11:57 AM

Fletcher took another bite of his sandwich, a dollop of mayonnaise landing on his shirt. He wiped it away with greasy fingers.

He'd been surveying the house all morning, leaving only to grab lunch down the street. He was due to report back to Stokes soon, fill him in on all comings and goings.

Fletcher finished his sandwich and let out a belch in the empty car. He tasted pastrami on his breath. With a thick hand, he wiped the sweat from his brow.

Across the street, someone caught his eye. An old man, walking at a snail's pace with the help of a gnarled wooden cane.

Walton!

Fletcher jumped up in his seat, thighs jamming into the steering wheel. With a humph, he extricated himself onto the pavement. Scrambling to stay on his feet, he saw the man walk in the direction of the house he'd been watching. It must be Walton, coming to deliver the letter. Fletcher crossed the street as fast as he could, grabbed Walton by the arm, and spun him around.

The cane clattered to the ground. "Gotcha," Fletcher exclaimed to the surprised face.

"Wh . . . what?" the old man stammered.

"Oh, don't play coy with me, ol' Henry. I know it's you." He held tight to the man's arm. "Out to deliver the letter, are you?"

"What? I'm not Henry," the man cried. "My name is Harold."

Fletcher studied the man's face. Around them, people were turning to stare.

The man was clean-shaven with a whiskey nose. His eyebrows were thick and gray and unruly, sticking straight out. He didn't resemble the picture from the wanted poster. But he had a cane. And he was here, on this street.

Fletcher glanced around wildly. He could feel the sweat building under his arms. With a gasp, he let go of the man's arm and stumbled back a step.

It wasn't Henry Walton.

"I'm sor . . . sorry. Sorry, sir," he said to the startled man. "Just a misunderstanding," he called to the street, reaching for the man's cane. "A simple misunderstanding."

The man was shaking, eyebrows twitching. "Now see here—"

"Yes, yes, a misunderstanding." He pressed the cane into the man's hands and snarled, "Move along. It was a simple mistake."

The man glowered at Fletcher before turning to continue his slow walk. He passed the house without a glance, cane tapping his forward progression.

Fletcher watched him go, trying to figure out what he was going to tell his boss.

86

Friday, October 28, 1966
1:09 PM

Stokes leaned back in his chair and thumped his feet on the top of his desk while Fletcher spoke.

Spitting a sliver of fingernail onto the floor beside the security guard's feet, he rolled his eyes. "Well, that was useless, wasn't it?"

Fletcher winced and hung his head. "I didn't mean to grab the wrong man, sir. I swear he looked identical to Walton."

Stokes agreed that one old man with a cane looked exactly like the next. That was beside the point, though. Fletcher had still messed up.

"I was trying to be more hands on. So we can wrap this thing up as fast as possible." Fletcher touched a thick hand to his forehead and wiped away beads of sweat. "I was thinking we could . . ."

Stokes tuned him out. Something Fletcher said set his mind racing. *Hands on.* Could that be the answer to their solution? Instead of just grabbing the letter from Walton, should they actually be grabbing the man himself?

He lifted a hand to shut Fletcher up. "You're right."

Fletcher's head snapped up. He cocked his oversized skull and opened his mouth to speak.

Stokes said, "Walton has been tormenting us for days now. Weeks. Brenda made a snide comment yesterday about public opinion shifting in his favor. How people have come to that conclusion is beyond me. Anyways"—he wagged a finger in Fletcher's direction—"you're right. We do need to be more hands on."

Fletcher blinked. "What does that mean?"

Stokes lit a smoke. "We're going to keep staking out that house." He puffed. "And we're going to wait for Walton. But we aren't going to politely tell him we need his help and convince him to get in the car and give us the letter and send him on his merry way." He came around the front of his desk and leaned in close. "We're going to take that slippery old man and make him pay."

The color drained from Fletcher's face. "But . . . sir."

"Tomorrow morning. Be ready."

87

Friday, October 28, 1966
1:22 PM

Brenda listened in as Fletcher bumbled his way through the incident with the lookalike and Stokes latched on to a new idea.

How could they be so useless?

A headache wrapped itself around her temples. She longed for the day when she no longer had to hover outside a closed door. If only Stokes had paid attention to her last week and stopped obsessing about the break-in. This wouldn't be happening right now. Instead, they would have spent days working through the backlog and trying to get the facility back up and running.

Now they were making plans to . . . do what exactly?

She didn't like the sound of Stokes's manic laugh. If they were going after Henry, she would need to stay close to make sure they didn't cause any additional chaos. The last thing any of them needed was to get caught.

Not when they were so close to the end.

88

Friday, October 28, 1966
2:07 PM

Springfield was a sleepy town. It didn't have the hustle and bustle Roger expected from a capital. It was as if everyone, confident in their place in the state, moved without worry. Henry and Roger sat on a bench across from the state building. Roger rolled the Batman marble between his fingers, taking in the building's domed roof. He wanted to circle it and count the columns. He wanted to touch the brickwork, feel the history.

"So many stories," he whispered.

Henry turned to face him. "Pardon me?"

"Oh, nothing, sir. I was just talking to myself."

"You do that a lot."

Roger tapped his thigh. Bounced his knee. "Yes. Sorry. I don't usually notice when I'm doing it. My mom always thinks I'm talking to her from another room."

"But why?" Henry asked with a slight shake of his head.

"Oh. Well, I guess it's just nice to have someone to talk to sometimes," Roger reasoned. "Even if that someone is yourself."

Henry harrumphed. "I prefer silence."

I know you do, Roger thought with a small smile. He let the quiet linger and went back to studying the building. They had one letter to deliver in Springfield and then a final letter for an address in Chicago. It was incredibly important, Henry had said the day before, that letter for Chicago. It was the most important thing he'd ever held. But when Roger tried to guess what the letter with the presidential seal contained, Henry had said he didn't know what Roger meant.

Roger wanted to hazard another guess but decided against it. The last thing he needed was to confuse Henry any further. Roger knew memories faded as you got older. His own grandfather was a testament to that. But with Henry, it felt different.

Deeper.

Henry had fragments of facts surrounded by full feelings. Earlier, he'd told Roger a piecemeal story of the time he met his good friend Flora. He couldn't remember all the details, but, according to Henry, the vision was very pink and filled with awe.

Roger didn't know when he'd last felt awe, before meeting Henry.

A mother and young daughter crossed the street. The young girl gripped her mother's hand tightly, little legs trying to keep up with an adult pace. He wondered if that was how Henry felt: always struggling to keep up. Roger cast a sideways glance at his companion. He knew Henry could sit there all day, watching the world go by, safe in the knowledge that if he didn't speak, he wouldn't make a mistake. It would be up to Roger to push them forward.

With a last look at the capitol, he rose from his seat.

"It's time for the second-to-last letter, Henry." He helped the old man to his feet.

89

Friday, October 28, 1966
2:31 PM

Something about the house felt familiar. As if he'd walked its halls, heard its stories. It wasn't special, this yellow-brick bungalow. It looked like a thousand other houses Henry had passed in his lifetime. But there was something that made him feel at home. A warmness that seeped from under the front door and down the path.

Henry knocked.

He looked at the letter in his hand, addressed to a man whose name he couldn't pronounce. He wondered where they were from. With a name like that, they couldn't possibly be from Illinois originally. Perhaps they had traveled from faraway lands, deciding Springfield was the place they needed to be to achieve the American dream. He scanned the street. If this place helped them achieve their goals, he could be proud of that. There was something comforting about people coming to America and finding a home for themselves.

He knocked again, hesitating on the doorstep.

The idea of not delivering this letter straight into someone's hand left him breathless. There was only one more after this. He needed to deliver it. He needed to pass it over and know it had made it to the right person and that the person was grateful for his journey.

If no one answered the door, the letter was as lost now as it had been on the overflowing receiving platform.

Henry leaned closer to the door, but all he could hear was the wind rustling the leaves on the street behind him. He knew Roger would be watching him, waiting to see what happened with this letter. He wondered if Roger was talking to himself in the car. Giving a pep talk to no one and everyone. Henry's thoughts rarely escaped through his lips. They circled his mind, going round and round in their quiet, calculating manner. Except more and more lately, they halted unformed between one ear and the other. Fragmented ideas and ideations stilled in his gray matter and disappeared; thoughts that had started and ended within a single breath.

No one answered the door.

Henry looked at the letter in his hands. It had started to crumple in his grip. He smoothed it out. Tried to pronounce the name. The wind picked up around him, and Henry adjusted his collar. Leaning on his cane, he considered his options. It took every fiber of his being to not open the letter and consume the words. They were so close he could taste them.

Henry inhaled. Exhaled. Pushed it through the letter slot and turned his back on the American dream.

They would get the letter when they were meant to.

There was nothing else Henry could do.

1966 Lee Street
Springfield, IL

Mamá y Papá,

I'm not coming home. I know you're desperate to have me come back, but I just . . . can't. There's nothing left for me there. I'll always be grateful for the sacrifices you made, moving to a new country, giving up your whole lives, so we could have a fresh start as a family.

But it's time for me to have a fresh start, on my own.

Now that I've experienced the mountains—just the sheer scale of them is enough to take your breath away!—and the ocean, I know I can't come back to our small little community. It's too suffocating for me (and I don't mean that as an insult to you).

And I know what you're saying, that only jipitecas live out West, but Mom, if you could just see it out here, I know you would understand.

I WILL be home for Los Posadas, though. I promise. I can't wait to see Alejandro's face when I tell him how short the girls' shorts are out here. He'll be booking the next train, jajaja! But seriously, I am so happy. I hope you know that. I love my little apartment overlooking the ocean. I fall asleep listening to the waves every night, and I've never slept so soundly. It doesn't hurt that I don't have Alejandro's snoring coming through the wall and keeping me up all night.

Don't tell him I said that!

And Maria got us both interviews at a law firm as typists. We go on Monday, and I'm going to wear the blazer you made me with those striped pants. Maria is going to lend me her orange platforms, because she says they make the outfit.

Fingers crossed I get it! I can just picture it now: Little Gabby Aguirre, the Legal Typist from Springfield. Don't tell anyone until I write back and let you know I got the job, though. I don't want to spend the holidays telling people I let my family down.

Te amo,

Gabriela xo

90

Friday, October 28, 1966

2:47 PM

Fletcher didn't know which way was up. He was still shaken from the mix-up on the street, and from the offhand comment Stokes had latched on to. That wasn't what he'd meant about being *hands on*. Sinking into a chair, he felt the cold metal pressing into his sides. His office on the second floor was smaller than a broom closet. A fat brass ring of keys hung beside the door, giving Fletcher access to every room in the building. He should find one to hide in instead of going with Stokes.

With a sigh, he rubbed his lower back, kneading out a knot that felt like a permanent addition to all his other health issues.

He hadn't slept properly in days. All he could think about when he closed his eyes was the night of the break-in. He wished he could go back to the night in question and do things differently. For starters, he wouldn't have checked the print shop four times in an hour just to be on the safe side. And he wouldn't have chased the men down the stairs instead of using the elevator. He knew those were the decisions that had set this whole chain of events in motion.

If only his daydreams could turn to realty.

Fletcher wondered, not for the first time, where Walton was now. Was he back in Chicago? Or miles away, delivering letters to their rightful owners? He felt a flash of pride at what the old man was achieving, not that he would admit it to anyone. Fletcher flinched at the thought of all the letters that would never end up in the right hands. The ashes that plumed into the sky, never to be read.

It made him sick.

If only there was a way for him to stop it all before things got out of control. He gave a sad laugh at the thought. He might have a knot on his spine, but even he could admit he didn't have a backbone.

7043 S Paulina St
Chicago, IL

Vince,

Well, I never. ECT wasn't my idea, you foolish man. I simply asked for a tincture. Which you do need, if you want to make something of yourself.

Flora in my sewing group (you know, the one who made those terrible orange curtains and tried to sell them to me?) says a special cedarwood and frankincense ointment will do wonders for your confidence.

I'll see if I can get some off her, shall I? For the next time you visit?

By the way, I finally got that gravy stain out of your white dress shirt. It took ages. Maybe I'll keep it here for a while, just until you need it again. And please try to use a napkin next time.

Go forth and use your voice, dear boy!

Ma

91

Friday, October 28, 1966
2:57 PM

Vera's reminder to cover her tracks rang in Brenda's ears as she yanked open her bottom drawer. Memos and letters and half-drawn charcoal sketches were stuffed inside. She grabbed them by the fistful and shoved them into her handbag. A clipped ad for the crematorium fluttered to the floor.

She tucked it into her bag as well.

92

Friday, October 28, 1966
3:41 PM

Roger picked at a spot on his left cheek. Beside him, Henry watched the passing signs, most likely trying to confirm they were headed in the right direction. They hadn't spoken since Roger had turned back onto I-72. For the first time ever, words cracked in his throat, refusing to escape. He gripped the wheel with both hands and tried to focus.

A fifth blue car drove past, more cobalt than navy.

He estimated Chicago was less than five hours away, by way of Bloomington. He'd committed the address of their final letter to memory but knew he would need to look at a map once they were in the city to find it.

They passed a cemetery, etched tombstones emerging from the manicured grass at odd angles.

Roger tapped the steering wheel, chasing the dead away.

He wished the radio was on, but the first thing Henry had done when he climbed back into the car after attempting to deliver the letter at the little yellow house was turn the sound off.

Roger wanted noise. Henry wanted silence.

He stole a glance at his elderly passenger, who was deep in thought beside him. Roger knew Henry was thinking about that last letter. It wasn't the only door that had been unanswered; Henry had told him about many over the past couple of weeks. Knocks that went unheard. Lonely letters passed into the abyss through slender mail slots. Neighbors who yelled that so-and-so was away and they could keep hold of the letter if needed, promising to pass it off to the right hands as soon as they saw their good-for-nothing neighbor—had they mentioned they had a bone to pick with them anyway?

No, it wasn't the first unsuccessful attempt on his journey. But somehow, this one hit differently. Roger pushed down on the accelerator, trying to put some space between them and Springfield. *Clarity comes with a little space,* his mom always said.

What Henry needed now was the type of distance that made everything feel okay again. "One more letter," Roger whispered to himself.

One more letter and it would all be over.

93

Friday, October 28, 1966
4:31 PM

Something was wrong, but Henry couldn't quite put his finger on what it was. They'd been somewhere. A house, he thought.

Yes, a lovely little yellow house.

Henry had a soft spot for yellow houses. There'd been one at the end of his street growing up, and the woman who lived there, a Mrs. Misener, used to sit on her front porch and call out to everyone who passed by. For the kids, she always had a bowl of boiled candy beside her on a small wicker table, and inevitably the parents would be stuck asking Mrs. Misener about her day while their child sucked away on a hard treat.

Henry had liked the lemon ones best, the sweet tang against his tongue.

His mother used to bring Mrs. Misener groceries every few days, rescuing other women who got trapped talking longer than they wanted. When Mrs. Misener died, the bowl of candy was refilled every day for a month, though none of the neighbors knew who was doing the filling.

"Oh, I'm sure someone just wants to make sure all those kiddies still get their candy from Irene," his mother would say. When Henry pointed out that there were more lemon-flavored candies than usual, his mother would toss him a wink.

A car sped past in the opposite direction and tugged Henry's mind back to reality. What was it he'd been trying to remember?

There was a little yellow house (not unlike the one Mrs. Misener had lived in) and a letter. A letter he hadn't been able to deliver. Was that new? He didn't think so. Surely there had been other letters that had gone undelivered—left with a farewell on a doorstep, placed with care against an unanswered door.

Silence ballooned in the car, filling the space between the seats, tucking itself into the glovebox, draping lazily over the dash. Why was it so quiet? It wasn't normally so—

"Oh." Henry gripped the door handle.

The car swerved into the next lane as Roger clawed at the wheel. "Are you okay?"

Henry's knuckles were white. "It wasn't the last letter." He turned to look at Roger. "That little yellow house. It wasn't the last letter, was it?"

His mind scrambled to put the jumbled pieces together. The letters, Roger, the next stop on their journey. He was missing something.

Roger let out a breath and stared out the window, two hands on the wheel. "No," he acknowledged. "There's one more letter. Remember? The one with the seal?"

"From the ocean?"

Roger snorted and looked his way. "No, Henry. Not the animal. The presidential seal. Your last letter to deliver—it's from the White House."

Henry whistled low and slow. The White House. He couldn't picture the seal. "Is it here? Do we have it?"

He needed to see it for himself.

Roger nodded toward the glovebox. Inside, tucked with care on top of an old pack of gum and a wrench that was erring toward rusty, was a single envelope. Henry pulled it out and held it with both hands. Turning it over, he gasped at the sight of the round mark.

It was so very . . . official.

He turned it back over and read the address once more. "Chicago," he said, his throat dry. "We're going back to Chicago."

"Yes. We'll get there tonight."

"It will be late," Henry said, still clutching the letter. "Too late to deliver it tonight. Best to wait until morning."

"Sir?" Roger raised an eyebrow in his direction. "Don't you want to—"

"No." He was firm. "It will be too late. There's a hotel, the Shubert Hall . . . or something like that. We can go there and then we can take this"—he held it up in front of him—"to its rightful owner in the morning."

Roger gave a small nod and kept driving. Fields rushed past the windows, and Henry leaned forward to turn on the radio. He was glad Roger had agreed to a hotel. He needed time to think. Time to plan for his final delivery. Besides, *a good night's sleep is the key to a successful day,* Henry always said.

He thought maybe that was his motto.

94

Friday, October 28, 1966
7:40 PM

Flora sucked on the end of her pen, a pile of loose paper spread out in front of her. She pushed the top one aside, scanning the contents of the page below. "Jupiter," she muttered around the pen. "The moon is squared." She scribbled a note on the blank page beside her and kept reading.

Across the table, Stan drummed a patient tune.

"When that happens, the moon squared with Jupiter"—she leaned back in her chair—"it can cause a lack of forethought. A carelessness."

"Hmmm." Stan's fingers kept up their drumming. "But I thought Jupiter is benevolent."

Flora raised a painted eyebrow at the accuracy. "Yes." She chewed the end of the pen. "But there are very rare times when it can result in dramatic events."

Stan's laugh rumbled. "Dramatic events? This whole thing has been a dramatic event. I don't think the moon squaring off with Jupiter in the sky could make it any more intense."

She studied the paper in front of her, frowning. Flora knew the impact of Jupiter was generally positive. It resulted in success and a feeling of well-being. Jupiter was a planet she paid close attention to, to trace the happiness of her days.

But this?

"It just feels . . ." She met Stan's gaze.

He gave a shrug. "Well, I for one don't think there's anything to worry about. Jupiter will bring luck, like it always does."

He left the room, humming to himself. If Stan could be calm, she could too. She was overreacting. Gathering the papers, Flora tapped them into a neat pile and set them on the edge of the counter, out of the way.

Stan was right. Surely things couldn't get any more dramatic.

95

Friday, October 28, 1966
9:09 PM

Roger was driving in circles.

Henry's directions, while clear, didn't make any sense, and with every new turn Roger feared they were getting more and more turned around. He slowed at the next intersection and turned left, as instructed. Continuing east on Monroe, Roger tried to take in the buildings as he drove past. CLOSED signs hung limply in every shop window, their shadows cast by streetlamps every few feet.

"Left," Henry said with a nod. "It's left here."

"We've already—"

"Just go." Henry signaled, and Roger made the turn. A park sprawled out beside them for three blocks. At Randolph, Henry made a noise in the back of his throat that sounded like a swallowed gasp. "Left," he cried. "Left here."

Roger obliged. He was quite sure they had already been down Randolph, but he didn't see anywhere to stop and ask for directions. He wished the radio were on, but Henry needed it off to think clearly.

"I swear it's around here somewhere. Perhaps try a right?"

Roger ignored him and kept going straight. Up ahead, he could see the faint glow of a sign. It couldn't be a coincidence. Pulling to a stop in front of the hotel, Roger peered out the window. "Henry," he said slowly, "is it possible the hotel is called Sherman House? And not Shubert's Hall?"

"Hmmm." Henry leaned forward to look at the building in front of them. "I suppose that could be possible, though I am quite certain there is another hotel close by called Shubert's Hall. It must be a strange coincidence, but this will do."

Roger carried both suitcases into the lobby while Henry shuffled ahead of him, cane tapping out each step on the tiled floor. At the reception desk, a young woman sat reading a magazine. Her face was awash in freckles, and Roger wondered if she was ever self-conscious about them.

He thought they made her skin shine.

Clearing his throat, he nearly tripped over his own feet when she met his gaze. Her eyes were the color of her lightest freckle, rimmed by a deep brown that was almost black. Towering over her, Roger felt small.

"We need a room, please." Henry spoke up, cutting through the magic of the moment. "A room with two beds."

The young receptionist rolled her eyes at the sight of Henry. There wasn't a Shubert's Hall hotel after all. Spinning to the wall behind her, she grabbed a set of keys from a dainty hook. There were two identical keys on a small brass ring. She set them on the counter with a smack. "Welcome back." Roger watched as Henry counted out the money to pay for the room, already familiar with the price.

He doubted the older man had connected the dots.

She counted his money twice, tongue sticking out between her front teeth. When she was satisfied he had proffered the proper amount, she dismissed them with the room number and went back to her reading.

With a whispered thanks, Roger followed the tapping of Henry's cane up the stairs.

96

Friday, October 28, 1966
9:43 PM

Henry frowned at the identical brown beds and wondered what was wrong with a little color. Color evoked feeling, memory. Or at the very least, a simple white spoke of cleanliness. Brown blurred everything together in a jumbled heap with no start and no end. He hated brown.

Roger, seemingly nonplussed at the monotony of it all, sprawled out on the bed farthest from the door. His eyes were closed, his chest rising and falling with even breaths.

Henry pulled the items from his bag. He placed the clothing in the dresser, tucked his shoes side by side by the door, laid out various toiletry items by the sink, including a razor he desperately needed to use, and set a single white envelope on the small (brown) table beside the bed. He thought about the seal on the other side and felt a flutter in his stomach.

A scrap of paper in his wallet reminded him what Stan and Flora's number was, in case he forgot. Which he hadn't. He just couldn't quite recall the last digit right now. Or the first. As the operator placed the call, he waited for Stan to pick up on the other end.

Roger let out a snore and rolled over, away from Henry.

"Hm, hello." Stan's voiced boomed down the line.

"It's me." Henry leaned back on the pillows, the phone cord dangling off the bed. "I'm back in Chicago."

Stan sounded glad to hear from him. "That's great news. Are you at home? Flo and I will pop—"

"No, no. I'm not at home. I'm at a hotel." He tried to remember the name of it to tell Stan but got stuck. "Something beginning with *S*, I think."

"Mmm, okay. Do you want me to come there? I can try to find out what one you're at. Do you need anything?"

Henry assured his friend that he was fine. Roger was making sure he was safe and fed.

"Roger?"

"Oh yes, my friend Roger. Just a young boy, really. He picked me up from the side of the road in Kansas. Or maybe Montana. He almost ran me over but didn't. Then the car was stolen, and he's been driving me around ever since."

The silence on the other end of the line was loud.

"St-stolen? Run over? What the devil is going on?" Stan's voice had tightened to the point of strangulation.

"Oh, so much has happened. Too many things to recall, if I'm completely honest. I can picture them happening, but I'm not sure I could say them out loud. Do you know what I mean?"

Stan sighed. "Yes, Henry. I know what you mean."

"But Roger has been a great help to me. I'm sure of it." Henry watched the soft rise and fall of the kid's back. "And he got us back to Chicago. There is only one letter left to deliver, Stan, and you'll never guess where it's from."

"Hmmm, where?"

"No, guess."

"Henry—"

"Just try to guess. You never will, but just try."

"Mmm, okay. Is it from the—"

Henry cut him off. "The White House. Stan, it's from *the White House*. It's got a presidential seal on it and everything."

"Wow." Stan's breath was a whoosh. "That's remarkable. What was the post office doing with a letter from the White House on the receiving platform? Letters of that caliber are always sent to the eighth floor."

"I don't know. I didn't discover it until a couple of days ago. Roger is going to take me to deliver it in the morning, and then that's it. I'll be done." He traced the edges of the envelope. "Can you believe that?"

"I've been having a hard time believing almost everything that's happened so far," Stan said with a laugh, "but it doesn't surprise me that a letter like that has ended up with you."

"Why?"

"Mmm, because it's you, Henry. Things like this just seem to happen to you."

"What happens if I can't find a way to deliver it?" He couldn't bear the thought.

"Knowing you, you'll either find a way or you'll make one. You're the most determined person I know."

Henry couldn't admit the real reason he wanted to deliver the letter. Why he'd set off in the first place. As his mind drained like a sieve, he couldn't help feeling as if, piece by piece, he was slipping away. Soon there would be hardly anything left of him. If he could just get this important piece of mail to its destination, he could close out this final chapter with dignity. Meaning. No matter how many things he forgot, he knew this would be something he always remembered. His fingertips tingled at the thought.

"I hope that's true. Say, what does Flora say about the planets right now? Because if I ever need a day where I can put things right, it's tomorrow."

"Oh. Yes. The planets are fine, she says. The planets are just fine. Benevolent, even." Henry thought he heard Stan choke, but it must have been static on the line.

"That's marvelous. Benevolence makes the world go round. That's my motto."

Henry cut off Stan's chuckle as he hung up the phone. Creeping into the bathroom, he reached for the razor. Tomorrow was a monumental day, and he wanted to be ready.

97

Friday, October 28, 1966
9:56 PM

Stan turned to Flora, who was hovering beside him.

"Do you have your diary?" he asked.

She nodded and flew to the front room, skirt flapping behind her, to retrieve her diary. She'd been writing things down since he met her, though he'd never stopped to consider her words. Sometimes she wrote a single line; other days she filled multiple pages with things she never wanted to forget. The top shelf of their closet was lined with old diaries, each with the year penned on its spine.

She cracked the latest one open as she returned, pen at the ready. "What do we need to write down?"

Stan told her about Henry's presidential letter. She let out a low whistle and committed it to paper. He asked her to write down that Henry was at a hotel beginning with *S*, and with an accomplice named Roger.

"Apparently, he's just a kid."

"A kid?"

"Mmm. Obviously one old enough to have a license, given the Ford broke down who knows how long ago and he's been driving around with this Roger ever since."

Flora wrote it all down.

"And it's his last letter?" she asked, tucking the pen inside the diary and closing it. "This one from the president?"

"That's what he says."

"Good, one more letter, and then he can come home." She turned to return the diary to its drawer in the bureau. Stan sank into his BarcaLounger and stared at the muted television, drumming out a tune on the edge of the chair.

"One more letter." He repeated Flo's words softly. "And then you can come home, Henry."

And Stan could tell his friend just how proud he was.

98

Saturday, October 29, 1966
8:16 AM

The weekend hustle was getting under Brenda's skin. People streamed past her car in an endless flow. Mothers with crying children. Teenagers trying to outdo one another. Gaggles of girlfriends hoping to find the latest fashion before anyone else. Men with low voices. Men with loud voices. Men with heads sinking into wide shoulders who didn't use their voices at all.

If only Stokes could refrain from using his.

All morning, Brenda had strained to see the house through hordes of people.

Now she watched as a group of young boys skipped up the sidewalk, coming precariously close to the bumper of her car. The shortest of the group was being pushed around by three others. They sneered at him while they shoved him out of their way and ran a few paces ahead. She wished their mothers could hear the names they were using.

It would be a bar of soup in the mouth if she were in charge of any of them.

The short one righted himself and stumbled after the others. He would need to learn to defend himself if he was going to survive the world. When he caught up to them, Brenda watched as he kicked the tallest one in the back of the knee and kept walking. She cracked a smile and sipped from her steaming Thermos.

She'd been parked down the street since before sunrise.

The house had stayed quiet, no one coming or leaving so far, and Brenda probably hadn't needed to get there so early, but she had wanted to know what time Stokes and Fletcher felt it appropriate to turn up.

Just before eight had been the answer.

An unseemly hour to begin a stakeout. Henry could have been and gone before sunrise without her boss being any the wiser. Just when she thought he couldn't get any more incompetent, he went and showed up at eight o'clock.

"Useless," Brenda muttered to herself.

Up ahead, a dark-green Datsun began to slow. She watched it pull over, a hundred yards from the house, and kill its engine. It was the first car to stop on the street all morning, and Brenda felt the hair on the back of her neck rise. Moments passed and nothing happened. She was just about to pull her gaze from the car when the passenger door opened and Henry Walton emerged, cane in one hand, crisp white letter in the other.

Brenda slammed her Thermos down and leaned forward as Henry began to walk, leveraging his cane for support.

"Come on," she hissed. "Notice him."

There could be no turning back now. They were all in too deep.

Up ahead, the white van that had been there since just before eight o'clock was still. As Henry moved down the sidewalk, Brenda held her breath.

99

Saturday, October 29, 1966

8:16 AM

Fletcher's thighs pressed into the steering wheel as he stared at the house across the street. They'd traded the Caprice for a boxy white Econoline this morning, but it didn't seem to offer any more space up front.

Beside him, Stokes suffocated the limited oxygen with a cigarette, window cracked an inch. Fletcher knew his boss would go through a whole pack while they waited, flocking ash onto the floor as if it were a landfill, before demanding Fletcher go buy him more.

Fletcher huffed quietly and shifted to the left, trying futilely to move away from the smoke. He turned his gaze to the cloudless sky.

It was a soft periwinkle and reminded Fletcher of the Monet print he had above his bed at home. He was just wondering if they would get clouds today—because that meant they might get rain, and he didn't have his umbrella—when a group of small boys passed the van. Fletcher watched as the smallest boy kicked the tallest boy, and something in him crumbled.

Vincent Fletcher had never been the kicking type. No, he was the one who got kicked. Over and over and over. For a brief moment, he tried to imagine what it would be like to kick the person trying to keep him down, but the thought dried up the minute it entered his brain. There was no point trying to picture a different outcome.

With a sigh, Fletcher closed his eyes and hoped the day would be over soon.

100

Saturday, October 29, 1966
8:17 AM

Stokes barked out a laugh as he watched a small boy kick a tall boy. "Don't suppose you've ever kicked anyone in the back of the knees, have you, Fletcher?" He flicked ash onto the floor of the van and inhaled deeply. "Can't ever see you defending yourself."

Fletcher, eyes closed, mumbled a response that Stokes didn't try to hear. He watched the kids move farther up the street.

"I'm sick to death of watching this house," he said, voice sharp. "Where the hell is Walton? I don't want to sit here all goddamn day."

"I don't know." What a useless response.

"Pffft. Of course you don't. I wasn't asking you." In the side mirror, Stokes watched as a Datsun pulled to the curb a few cars behind them. He started listing all the reasons he hated Datsuns—and any Japanese models, for that matter—to occupy the time.

Lighting another cigarette, he added four more reasons to the list.

101

Saturday, October 29, 1966
8:19 AM

They were going to miss him. Goddammit, they were going to miss him! Brenda gripped the steering wheel as Henry Walton tapped his way closer to the van.

102

Saturday, October 29, 1966

8:19 AM

A tapping sound brought Fletcher back to the present. He glanced at Stokes, who was muttering under his breath about the Japanese, and peered through the windshield at the street.

He couldn't see anything that would explain the tapping. With a quick look in the side mirror, Fletcher gasped the same time his boss swore.

Henry Walton was coming their way.

103

Saturday, October 29, 1966

8:19 AM

Stokes slammed his cigarette into the overflowing ashtray. "Don't just sit there. Do something!" he screamed.

Fletcher pulled his bulging form from the driver's seat into the back of the van. Stokes shuddered as the security guard's skin grazed his as he squeezed past. "Do I just—"

"Grab him." Heat crept up Stokes's neck, burning the lobes of his ears. He leaned forward to look in the side mirror.

This was it.

"Fletcher, you massive waste of space, don't mess this up."

Stokes closed his eyes and waited as he heard the van door scrape open.

104

Saturday, October 29, 1966
8:19 AM

Roger turned the Datsun off to wait. He had parked a hundred yards or so from the address and had a good view of the house. He wanted to watch Henry deliver the final letter. He couldn't quite explain it, but knowing this was the last letter made him jittery. More jittery than normal. The fluttering in his stomach felt both positive and ominous.

He knew it was because he wasn't ready to set off on his own again.

He was used to Henry and the uneven way his mind worked. Roger pulled the compass out of his pocket and ran a thumb over the front. With a click, he opened it and took in the intricate face. Henry had given it to him that morning. Roger had protested, of course. He couldn't take the compass from Henry. It had been a gift from Elsie. No, he couldn't accept such a generous gift.

But Henry had been insistent.

He no longer needed a compass, he'd said. He'd found his way to places he'd never dreamed of visiting and back again. That was enough. Now it was Roger's turn for an adventure.

Roger had tried to offer the Batman marble in response, but Henry had politely declined.

Roger leaned back in his seat and tried to steady his breathing. The uneasy feeling must be because he wasn't ready to say goodbye to Henry. He would deal with that later.

First, it was time to witness Henry complete his mission.

105

Saturday, October 29, 1966

8:20 AM

Henry leaned on his cane and moved the letter to the inside pocket of his jacket. He was holding it too tightly. It wouldn't do to deliver a crumpled letter with a presidential seal. When he was confident it was secure, he ambled forward.

Up ahead, a large white van was parked almost opposite the house.

Rather than cross behind it, Henry decided to walk in front of the van so he had a clear view of any oncoming traffic.

He felt charged, his skin electric as he got closer to the house.

He'd needed this adventure, he knew now. Something to shake him out of his boring routine and breathe life back into his existence. Yes, this adventure was the best thing to ever happen to Henry Walton.

"One more letter," he whispered with a smile. "Just one more letter." He looked briefly at the bright sky before everything went dark.

106

Saturday, October 29, 1966
8:20 AM

Roger must be seeing things. Surely.

One minute Henry was there, and the next, he was gone. Shaking his head, Roger scrambled to figure out what had just happened. Henry had been on the sidewalk. Henry had stopped for a brief moment before continuing on his way, ahead of the white van . . .

The white van.

He watched as it jerked away from the curb and accelerated down the quiet street.

With shaking hands, Roger turned the key and pressed on the gas to follow. Henry was in that van. The letter with the presidential seal was in that van. Roger could not let that van out of his sight.

He couldn't lose Henry. Not now. Not when they were so close to completing this mission together. Not when he finally felt like he could be his full self around someone, accepted for every quirk and tic and rambling thought.

Gasping at the air, Roger took the next turn at full speed and followed the van.

107

Saturday, October 29, 1966

8:20 AM

They had him.

Within seconds, the van was tearing away down the street. And so was the Datsun. With a muffled curse, Brenda left the house behind and joined the pursuit.

108

Saturday, October 29, 1966
8:21 AM

There was a bag over Henry's head. Or rather, there was something dark over his head that felt like a bag. Either way, he couldn't see. He touched a hand to his chest and felt the letter tucked safely inside his jacket. Reaching out, he tried to make sense of his surroundings. The floor underneath him was hard and cold. Most likely metal. Given that they were moving, he knew he was in a vehicle. And since he couldn't feel anything around him, he assumed it was a larger vehicle, like a utility van.

It clicked in his mind. The white van he had been trying to walk in front of.

Somehow he'd ended up inside.

Crime wasn't so bad in Chicago that random old men were snatched (cane and all) from the sidewalk in broad daylight. Which meant someone had been waiting to apprehend him.

But who?

Whoever it was, they were driving at breakneck speeds through the city.

"Who are you?" he cried, reaching a hand out to steady himself as they turned left. "What do you want?"

Silence.

He heard the click of a lighter before the putrid scent of smoke filled the air. He tried to pay attention to the route they were taking, but it was a futile effort. He couldn't remember which direction they had just turned, let alone what maneuvers the van had made before that.

Henry thought of Roger, waiting in the Datsun for him to deliver the letter. And, with a crushing sense of disappointment, he thought of Martin Luther King Junior and the letter he was probably expecting.

Gripping his cane, Henry hung his head and waited for what would come next.

The door squealed as it was flung open and cool October air filled the inside of the van. Henry swung his cane out. And again.

"Calm down, old man," a voice sneered in front of him. "No need to get all upset." Henry swung his cane in the direction of the voice and heard a satisfying thump.

"Goddammit. Give me that." The cane was ripped from his hand, and Henry's insides went cold. A hand yanked him from the back of the vehicle, and he swayed on the uneven pavement.

He tried to see through the bag but could only make out shadows.

One to his left, one to his right.

Someone shoved him. "Move." Without his cane, and with one knee that moved normally and one that didn't, Henry wasn't steady on his feet. He tripped forward before a hand gripped his arm, balancing him.

It wasn't the same hand that had pushed him. This one was meatier. Sweatier. More gentle.

The shadows led him around the side of what looked like a large building. He tried to picture where they were, but it was no use. The bag, and the erratic driving, had all but rendered him completely lost. The sound of an unoiled door filled the silence, and he was shoved, yet again, into an open space. With a final push, Henry was forced onto a chair. The bag stayed on his head. One of the shadows reached down to tie his legs to the legs of the chair before moving up to secure his wrists. He wished he knew who was doing this to him.

"Who are you?" he asked again, his voice small in the large space. "Why are you doing this to me?"

No answer.

He tugged at the rope around his wrists. The sound of four shuffling feet filled the air as his captors moved away from him.

"Don't want to—"

"Have to tell him—"

"No! You do it—"

Henry craned his neck to hear. "Tell me what?" he yelled through the bag. "What do you need to tell me? I don't have anything for you. If you let me go, I can get my wallet. It's at a hotel called the . . . it's at the . . . Shu House. Yes. It's at the Shu House hotel, and it's filled with cash. Filled! I'll get it for you. Just let me go . . ." He strained at the rope again, feeling it give just a little. "If you would just take this damn bag off my head and untie these ropes, I can get you cash." Henry was twisting his head side to side, trying to throw the bag off, when, with a flourish, it lifted.

He blinked in the bright morning light that filtered through sheet metal walls.

Squinting, he looked around.

Concrete floor spread out around him, cracks cutting through the tough surface in an uneven pattern. Stone pillars rose from the ground around the space in intervals, holding up rotting wooden beams high above their heads. The door they had entered through wasn't closed properly, and it banged lightly in the wind. The back wall was at least three hundred yards away. Piled up in front of it, Henry could see stacks of boxes, rusty old car parts, and what looked like half a tractor. He thought he saw a small door in the far corner, but he couldn't be sure.

The rope cut into his skin as he tugged, red marks snaking their way around his wrists.

He looked at the two men in front of him. One was short and fat, with an uneasy look atop his triple chin. The other was shorter and less fat. His eyes sneered above a nose that had seen too many bar fights. He leaned down and blew smoke into Henry's face.

Henry coughed and twisted his head to the side. "What do you want?"

"The letters," the smoker snarled. "Where are the letters?"

"Letters?" Henry frowned. "I don't have any—"

"Shut up," the man exploded. "We know who you are, Henry Walton"—he made Henry's name sound like a problem—"and we know that you stole letters from the post office. Now, where the hell are they?"

Something niggled at the back of his mind, but Henry couldn't grasp the thought long enough to make sense of it. It was a feeling, a wisp of a memory that he wasn't sure was his. "I don't have any letters."

It was the wrong thing to say.

He didn't see the hand coming until it slapped him across the face. The impact made his body jerk, which made the ropes cut into his wrists even deeper.

Henry let out a strangled cry.

"You do have letters, you useless old man. And I want to know where they are." The man, clearly in charge, spat on the ground beside Henry's foot and leaned down. His eyes were bloodshot. The scorn on his face did nothing to improve his appearance. "Tell. Me. Where. They. Are." He spit the words out like poison.

Henry recoiled, eyes wide. He didn't have letters. Why did this man think he had letters? He'd been out for a walk, and then suddenly he was here. It was a classic case of mistaken identity. "I don't—"

The second slap was harder than the first. Henry's eyes watered. As he shook his head, he heard the fat man whispering frantically.

"Mr. Stokes, you can't—"

Stokes. Henry racked his mind for where he knew that name from. The husband of one of Elsie's friends? No, that wasn't it. Someone from the club? No. How did he know the name Stokes?

Just as quickly as the fog had descended, it lifted. Reginald Stokes was the manager of the post office. And Henry did have letters. Or at least, he'd *had* letters.

"Stokes," Henry said, watching the surprise catch in his captor's eyes. "Reginald Stokes. You're right. I *did* have letters, but I don't have them anymore. They're gone."

"Gone?" It was more scream than question, so Henry didn't answer. Which angered Stokes even more, because he got right in Henry's face, nostrils flaring, to say in a low growl, "Explain *gone.*"

"I delivered them all." Henry smiled proudly, looking from one man to the next. "At least, I think I did. My mind goes a bit hazy at times, you see . . ."

Stokes went three shades whiter at that, and Henry had to force himself not to smile. He watched smoke dance through the dust motes.

In a strangled voice, Stokes asked him about his final letter. For Lake Street. "We know you had a letter to deliver there this morning. It's why we were waiting for you."

Henry remembered the letter. He could picture the seal on the back. And he remembered the kid pulling the Datsun up on the street in front of the house. "Yes, I did have a letter to deliver this morning," Henry said cheerfully. "And I did just that."

"What?" Stokes stamped his smoke out.

"I delivered it."

"That's not possible."

"What's not?"

"You couldn't have delivered it. We saw you arrive."

"When?"

"What?" Stokes's eyes narrowed. "We saw you arrive right before we took you."

"Oh," Henry said, "but that was my second arrival, not my first." He ducked away from the slap this time, anticipating it before it happened. "I delivered the letter at sunrise."

Henry explained he had woken before the sun, determined to finish his mission. "So, after breakfast, I made my way over to Lake Street and slipped the letter through the mail slot in the door. I would have knocked, but it was too early. Then we left to go have breakfast again, because I couldn't actually remember having the first breakfast—nerves, you see—and you know the rest."

"Who's *we*?"

"Pardon me?"

"Who was driving the Datsun? Who were you with?"

"Oh, the kid. Randy. No, no. That's wrong. I keep getting it wrong. Roger! It's Roger driving me around since my Ford got stolen. Have you ever had a car stolen while in the middle of an adventure? It was a huge inconvenience, let me tell you. Luckily, Roger almost ran me over but instead picked me up and helped me deliver my letters."

Stokes blanched. "They're not your letters, Walton. You broke into the post office—a federal building," he added with a snarl, "and *stole* them."

"Did I?"

Henry figured the slap was deserved this time. It still stung.

"I don't remember," he admitted. "I do remember a lovely woman who built a fire to keep me warm, but her name keeps escaping me. And a short man, like you, who tried to bully me. But a lot of the other things seem to have . . . dimmed. Sorry." Henry shrugged. "Why do you hate letters so much?"

Stokes glared at him. Beside him, the fatter man swayed on his feet, sweat pouring down his brow.

Henry looked at Stokes. "Your man looks ill," he said as the fatter man fainted onto the hard concrete floor.

109

Saturday, October 29, 1966
8:31 AM

A scattered pile of leaves blew across a parking lot, curled brown edges catching on bumps in the pavement. Roger had watched as Henry was shoved through a metal door on the side of the building, accompanied by two hefty men, one shorter than the other in a way that probably bothered him.

Now Roger was circling the building looking for another way in. He couldn't just barge in on the scene; he needed to scope things out first. Like Batman would.

The brick facade was crumbling in places, and Roger stepped gingerly over piles of rubble. The windows above his head were all smashed, jagged pieces of glass sticking up at odd angles. He watched as a pigeon flew into the third-story window, followed by another.

In the far corner, a slender silo rose high into the sky, towering above the abandoned building like a beacon. The apex was painted in red and white circles, the red now faded to a rusty hue. A metal ladder ran from bottom to top.

"There is no way I'm climbing that," Roger muttered, continuing his stakeout and moving past the silo. He tugged himself away from a copse of brambles clinging to his pant leg and edged along the west wall. He thought he saw a door behind the towering bush, but there was no way to get to it. Pulling himself up, he tried to look through a cloudy window on the first floor.

He couldn't see or hear anything.

Above him, a third pigeon entered the building. Roger felt a pang of jealousy.

If he couldn't get into the building from the ground, he would have to go higher. Eyeing the silo warily, he exhaled in a huff.

Henry needed him. He would have to climb.

110

Saturday, October 29, 1966
8:38 AM

Someone was stuck on a ladder outside the building. Brenda watched in fascination as a young man attempted to make his way to the top. He'd climbed the first ten rungs before lowering himself to the ground and cowering against the building. He'd tried twice more with the same outcome. Now he was higher than the tenth rung and still climbing. Brenda couldn't tell if his legs were shaking or if it was the wind.

She turned her attention back to the van, which was parked haphazardly in front of a heavy metal door, the driver's door still ajar. Behind it, the dark-green Datsun was parked at a neat angle.

Both vehicles were empty.

The rundown warehouse sat on the edge of town in a heap of faded brick and broken windows. A concrete parking lot snaked its way around three sides of the building, decades of weeds trying to claim the territory for themselves. Given how high some of them were, it was clear who was winning.

She looked at the climber. He'd made it five more feet. Now he was clutching the ladder with both hands and, if she wasn't mistaken, talking to himself wildly. His head shook as if he were caught in a one-man argument. Brenda watched as he took another step, casting her gaze to his destination. A solid platform sat under a row of open windows near the roof of the building. He was trying to get inside.

Pulling off her button jacket, she tossed it onto the driver's seat. She gave a tut of disdain to her kitten heels and A-line skirt, but there was nothing she could do about her attire now.

It would have to do.

Once again, it was up to her to sort out the mess Stokes had made.

Brenda picked her way through the abandoned lot to the silo and started to climb.

111

Saturday, October 29, 1966
8:51 AM

"Oh, for the love of—" Stokes rolled Fletcher over with his foot. "Get up, you useless—" It was no use; Fletcher was out cold. Stokes scrubbed a hand over his face and turned back to Walton. "Stop lying," he said, jaw tight. "And tell me what happened to all those letters."

Henry stopped squirming and gazed up at him. "I told you, I—"

"Yeah, yeah. You don't remember. You're just a senile old man who can't remember what he had for breakfast, am I right?" He kicked at the dust by his foot.

"A banana, I think," Henry said, lips twitching.

Stokes clenched his fists, kicking up more dust. "I need to know where you've been," he snapped. "Where did you take those letters?"

Henry's shoulders slumped. "I think—"

"No. No thinking. Just tell me where you've been."

"To Canada."

"Wh . . . what?" Stokes leaned down and gripped both of Henry's wrists tightly, peering into the old man's eyes. "What do you mean, Canada?"

"I took a letter to Canada. I had to go through the right door to get there. Or was it the left? I'm not exactly sure, if I'm honest."

"Get to the point," Stokes hissed, squeezing Henry's wrists tighter. "Where did you go in Canada?" He couldn't keep up with Walton's story. The men on the receiving platform hadn't mentioned Canada.

They hadn't even mentioned a different state. They'd been so focused on the letter with the presidential seal that they hadn't stopped to think about what other letters Walton had taken.

"She was dead." Henry's answer landed like lead on the hard floor. "I think she was dead before I got there."

Stokes didn't know what to do with that information. He stepped back and nearly tripped over Fletcher, who was still sprawled on the floor but seemed to be coming to, if the soft moaning was any indicator. "Where else?" he ordered.

"Oh, well. Let me think. There was a baby who wouldn't stop crying, and the poor mother looked ready to give up. And a nice man who was lonely, and a woman with no eyebrows who I feel like I knew from somewhere else." He kept listing random people. "There were a few colored men and one colored woman who refused to answer, so I slid the letter under her door. There was a family who made me sit down on the sofa while they crowded around to read the letter together. It made me feel special, but also like an intruder. And there was—"

"Enough," Stokes snapped. None of these stories told him anything. Turning around, he kicked Fletcher in the ribs. "Get up." The security guard opened one eye and stared up at him. Stokes moved to kick him again, and Fletcher held out his arms. He kicked the dirt instead, sending it flying in Fletcher's direction. He couldn't understand why he was always surrounded by idiots.

What had he done to deserve this? He treated people fairly, and in return, what did he get?

He spun around and eyed the old man, who'd had no right to deliver his letters. "I don't care about the people you delivered letters to. They mean nothing."

Henry tried to interrupt, but Stokes ignored him.

"I only care about the one from the White House." He studied Walton's face for a hint of recognition.

"I don't—"

"Shut up. I know you didn't deliver it this morning. That means you have it on you. Fletcher"—he snapped his fingers in the security guard's direction—"search him."

Fletcher whimpered. "Mr. Stokes, I—"

Stokes let out a low growl. “I said, search him.”

Fletcher rose to his feet like a bear awakening from hibernation and came to stand beside him, swaying slightly. Stokes nodded at Walton. “Go.”

“I don’t have anything,” Henry said with a soft chuckle. “Except a compass. Unless . . . did I give that away? I might have. I do remember giving away Elsie’s handkerchief, which I don’t think she would have minded. I also gave away quite a lot of my time, but seeing as I retired from the post office more than a decade ago, I have time to spare.”

Fletcher moved forward to carry out the command, but Stokes held out a hand to stop him. “What?”

“Pardon?” Henry raised an eyebrow. Stokes didn’t know if it was an admonition or a question.

“What did you say about retiring from the post office?”

“Oh. Well, when I was sixty-five, I retired. Hung up the ol’ hat, as they say. This was a few years ago . . . more than a decade, I think.”

“You retired from the post office?” Stokes glanced at Fletcher, who held out his palms.

“Yes.”

“The Chicago Post Office?”

“Of course. Where else? I’m a Chicagoan through and through. Though I can’t say I’ve always agreed with Daley’s tactics. But that’s by the by.”

Stokes stared at the man. “You’re saying you worked at the Chicago Post Office and retired, when, the early fifties?”

“Yes.”

“Doing what?”

“I was a mailman.” Henry’s grin filled his whole face. “Back to my roots now, you could say.”

Stokes roared with laughter. “A mailman? You? Don’t be ridiculous. You never worked at the Chicago Post Office. You’re just a—”

“Yes I did.” Henry’s smile started slipping. “I started working there when I was twenty-one.”

“No you didn’t. I don’t know what you did with your life,” Stokes said with a snarl, “but it wasn’t working at the post office.”

"But . . ."

"I've been at that post office for thirty years. I started on the second-floor receiving platform, and when it was clear I was far smarter than anyone else in the building, I was promoted to management. Couple years later, and I was head honcho. I've been head honcho ever since, and I'm telling you, you never worked there."

"I don't understand."

"What else is new?" Stokes looked at Fletcher. "Search him," he said with a nod in Henry's direction. "I want that letter."

Fletcher moved forward the same moment the door crashed open.

112

Saturday, October 29, 1966
9:03 AM

Brenda shoved the intruder forward. "Walk."

The kid tripped over his feet before moving into the warehouse. Behind them, light spilled across the floor, catching dust motes in a midair dance. Ahead of them, she could see Henry Walton tied to a chair, Fletcher hovering awkwardly beside him.

Stokes's face looked more blank than normal. Could he get any more pathetic? "What the hell are you doing here?" he asked, sounding like someone who had lost all control of a situation.

Her heels clacked as she made her way across the concrete floor. "I found this young man attempting to scale the building."

The young man in question bounced on the balls of his feet. He hadn't stopped fidgeting since she'd forced him off the ladder.

"You clearly didn't realize you were being followed, though it's not the first obvious thing you've missed." Fletcher's head jerked up. Brenda looked away. "It's a good thing I've been doing my own following today."

Stokes let out a mirthless laugh. "You're the last person we need help from. We've got everything under control. Don't we, Vince?" He smacked Fletcher on the back. The security guard rolled his shoulders forward but didn't say anything.

"To come in here and suggest otherwise," Stokes said, coming toward them, "is grounds for dismissal. How does that sound?"

Brenda stood taller and looked down on her boss. "You want to fire me? Go ahead. See how fast everything falls apart without me. You have no clue what I've had to do these past few weeks . . ." She clamped her mouth shut. Stokes didn't need to know about the letters.

No one did.

She glared past him at Henry, who sat immobile in the center of the room. "And you," she said, "have made everything worse."

"Me?" Henry asked, eyebrows raised.

"Him?" the kid asked, still bouncing.

"If you had just stayed away, Stokes would have been forced to do his job for once and clean up the mess he created."

Walton tried to lean forward. "What mess?"

But Brenda didn't hear him. Blood pounded through her eardrums. She wanted to lash out at them all. "Instead," she said, throat hoarse, "I've had to take care of everything myself. I always have to take care of everything myself. Do you think anyone notices? Do you think I've ever received a *well done* or a *thank you* or even a goddamn pat on the back?" Her face burned. "Of course not. I show up daily and make more of a difference than you two combined"—she jabbed a finger at Stokes and then at Fletcher, who stepped back—"and you don't even notice."

Cutting herself off, she inhaled sharply.

Stokes squinted. "You want a thank-you?"

"Yes. I want a thank-you once in a while."

"Gratitude does have significant benefits," the kid said. They all turned to stare at him. "Whenever my teacher sends me to the back of the room to build a radio, I always work harder the next time if she pauses to appreciate my hard work."

"I could really use a thank-you too," Henry called from the chair. "For all my efforts. I don't think it's been easy on me, though I can't be one hundred percent sure."

Brenda's gaze darted around the warehouse. She couldn't read the look on Fletcher's face. "You see?" She pinned Stokes with a glare. "You should be thankful for everything I've done. Like Henry said, it hasn't been easy. You don't even know half of what I've had to do. If you would just pay attention for once—"

"Enough." Fletcher threw his hands in the air. "No one is going to thank you for burning mail, Brenda."

She froze. What did he say?

"Burning what?" Stokes rounded on the guard. "What did you just say?"

Fletcher puffed out his cheeks. "She hasn't just been destroying magazines and circulars. She's been shipping actual mail off to the crematorium as well. Thousands and thousands of letters have been burned on her watch."

Brenda recoiled. "You useless piece of—"

Before she could finish her sentence, the kid shoved her toward Stokes and sprinted to Henry's side.

113

Saturday, October 29, 1966
9:16 AM

Roger's whole body shook uncontrollably. He knelt beside Henry and gripped his hand. "You okay?"

Henry offered a half smile. "I think so, kid."

Standing up, Roger rounded on the other three. "You've been burning mail?" He couldn't have heard that right. There was no way the largest post office in the world would deliberately dispose of people's words. It was unheard of.

It was the opposite of everything Henry had set out to do.

Color rose in the woman's cheeks, an ugly rouge that didn't suit her. "Don't listen to him. It's not what it looks like." Her movements were jerky as she tried to wave away the accusation. "We had permission, and—"

The shortest man's voice thundered around the room. "Stop." Thick stubble spread across his chin, contrasting with the pressed suit he wore.

Roger squeezed Henry's shoulder. What had they got themselves into?

"Stokes, listen . . ." The woman crossed her arms.

Stokes got in her face. "Listen to you? My incapable assistant?" He spun around to look at the security guard. "Fletcher, explain."

The guard mumbled toward the ground, arms loose by his side. "I saw her the other day, sir. Loading more than magazines into the back of a van. That's how we've been able to move through so many."

Roger shuddered. How could someone be so cruel?

"Look," Brenda said, palms out. "I did it for the good of the establishment because you have refused to take action. What's done is done. We're here for a different reason." She gestured at Henry before asking Stokes, "Do you have it?"

"Not yet," Stokes said, fists clenched. "Fletcher, grab the letter."

"You're not grabbing anything." Roger took a protective step in front of Henry's chair. "Unless you go through me first."

Stokes looked him up and down, cracking his knuckles. "Who the hell are you?"

"Roger."

"How do you know Walton?"

"I found him on the side of the road. Outside Elk Point. His car was stolen—"

"I told you." Henry cried, "I told you my car was stolen."

"Shut up," Stokes snapped. "You picked him up in Elk Point, and then what? What have you two been up to, Roger?" He made Roger's name sound like an alias.

"Well, we delivered letters, I suppose."

"Suppose?"

"I mean . . . yes . . . we delivered letters. Henry had letters to deliver, and I, well, I had time to kill, so I helped."

"You've been a great help," Henry said from the chair. "I couldn't have done it without you."

Roger's cheeks burned.

"Why did he have so many letters to deliver? Did you ever wonder that?"

"He told me," Roger said, "about how he used to work at the post office and it was his mission to do this last delivery."

Stokes's laugh hurt Roger's ears. "Look, old man," he said, looking past Roger at Henry. "Like I said already, you never worked there. You didn't work on the receiving platform, in the print shop, or in the money order section. You *definitely* didn't work on the sixth floor, where they rewrap damaged parcels, or the seventh floor, which handles mail from foreign countries. You weren't a security guard, a letter carrier, or even a janitor. I'd bet my life on the fact that the first time you ever entered the Chicago Post Office was the night you broke in to steal hundreds of letters."

"But I . . ."

"You're a deluded old man who committed a crime."

"That's why I couldn't find my hiring letter," Henry said, more to himself than the others. "It didn't exist." A hollow sigh escaped his lips.

No one moved.

"Sir," Roger said, breaking the silence. "You might not have been a mailman before, but you are one now." He pumped the air with his fist. "Think of everything you've done. The letters you've reunited people with, the joy you've brought to their lives. You've made me realize just how important letters are to—"

Stokes cut Roger off. "Enough of all this *letters are amazing* bullshit. They're not amazing. They are an utter waste of human time and brain power. A relic from the past we should be doing away with. The number of letters that come through our post office is ridiculous. All these sad, pathetic people, reaching out to someone who doesn't care about them. It's a joke. I hate . . . no, that's not the right word . . . I *despise* mail. I'm not even mad you've been burning it"—he turned to Brenda—"I'm mad you did it behind my back."

His words hung in the stale air. Above them, a pigeon cooed.

"You despise mail?" Henry's voice was strangled. "But it's your whole life."

Stokes's gaze hardened. "Ha! My whole life? Not a chance."

"No," Henry pushed. "There must be a reason. You can't have always hated letters. It's incomprehensible for the manager of the post office to have always hated letters."

They all waited for an explanation.

When Stokes spoke again, it was to the floor. "You want the truth? I sent a letter once. A long time ago." He paused briefly. "I was six . . . or seven . . . and it took me days to write the perfect letter. I worked so hard on making sure my writing was clear, every word legible. I remember licking the stamp and placing it painstakingly in the top corner. And then I slipped out of the house, after my mother . . . it doesn't matter. I went down the street by myself and stood in front of the bright-blue box." He drew a line in the dust with the toe of his shoe. "I never heard back. I became *obsessed* with mail after that. Every time the mailman came to the door, I would race down the stairs to greet him first. The years crept by, and nothing ever came. I could have given up, done something different, but I didn't want to feel like he'd won. So I got a job at the post office myself, on the receiving platform, responsible for sending the mail up the chutes, so I could keep an eye out. Always hoping that one day—" He stopped, realizing what he was saying and cringing. "Caring about getting a letter is weak. It's a waste of time, and the people who sit around, like I did, waiting for an answer, are fooling themselves. We're better off without the whole construct."

"You're wrong," Roger said, taking a hesitant step forward. "Sometimes a letter does come. I waited *years* for something from my father too. But it came. And I think . . . no, I know, after this, I'm going to go set things right. Because of Henry." He nodded in Henry's direction. "But also because of that letter. They're important. They're tiny parcels that make up the whole of who people are, what makes us human, and you should feel privileged working with them every day."

Stokes quaked with laughter. Or rage, it was hard to tell.

"I don't feel privilege. I feel disdain. Now, get that goddamn letter." He turned to Fletcher. "Or I will."

The response the pigeon gave was one hundred percent more positive and obliging than the response from the security guard.

114

Saturday, October 29, 1966
9:35 AM

"No."

All eyes turned toward Fletcher. He wanted to disappear through the stone floor. His stomach clenched and sweat pooled in his lower back. He thought about his mother's letters. About tinctures and ECT and the need to stand up for yourself.

With a shaky exhale, he forced himself to stand taller and meet Stokes's stare head on.

"What did you say to me?" Stokes's voice was deep.

"I said"—Fletcher narrowed his eyes—"no."

"You self-righteous . . ."

Fletcher tuned Stokes out. He wasn't here anymore; he was up with the pigeons, ready to take off. He was looking down on them all from above, not fully part of his substantial body. He was somewhere else far, far away.

". . . and if you think you're coming back to work on Monday, you've got another thing coming."

Fletcher's hand went to his chest. But it wasn't fear he felt, it was freedom. For the first time in a long time, he felt truly happy. "Okay," he acknowledged. "If I no longer work for you, I don't need to act as security for you."

And with a small spin that embarrassingly caused him to reach out for balance, he positioned himself in front of Henry and folded his arms across his chest.

From the corner of his eye, he caught Roger pumping an arm in the air.

Brenda, though she said nothing, looked incredulous, and Stokes . . . his expression would haunt Fletcher's daydreams for quite some time.

Fletcher didn't care.

"This is the stupidest, most ill-conceived kidnapping of all time," he said. "The letter should be delivered, if it hasn't already, and the fact that you want to get your hands on it to destroy it is despicable. Enough letters have been burned, Reginald. It's time to stop."

Reaching down, Fletcher untied Henry's wrists.

115

Saturday, October 29, 1966
9:39 AM

Time stood still for Reginald Stokes. The air around him felt heavy, weighted. His ears rang. Brenda, face flushed, shook a fist in his direction, demanding that he take action. Do something. Man up.

He rocked back and forth, his left hand gripping his right wrist. Above him, the pigeon squawked incessantly. And then it shit on his shoulder.

Stokes hung his head in defeat.

September 1923

To Dad,

Please can you come home? I'm sorry I'm too little to play pitcher. I'll try harder.

Mom says you met another woman and want nothing to do with us. She only says it at night after she's had whiskey. I keep telling her not to drink all your whiskey, Dad, 'cause you'll want some when you get home, but she won't listen.

Her eyes get all black and she throws things.

But it's okay. I know she's just sad like me.

Maybe we could mail a letter to your lady so you could say goodbye. I could help you. I know where the post office is. They're not done building it. They said it won't be completely ready for another few years and they've even kept a big hole open at the bottom because one day they say they're going to build a road straight through the building.

We could drive on that road together, Dad!

Wouldn't that be neat? If Mom's feeling better, we can bring her too. I think she'd like that. Driving under all those words.

Will you come home? Things would be better if you were home.

Love,

Reginald

116

Saturday, October 29, 1966
9:40 AM

Henry rubbed at his wrists where the rope had been. He looked up at the round man who had freed him. His face was familiar, but Henry couldn't place him.

"I think," the man said, his voice low, "that you have one final letter to deliver, Mr. Walton." He shot Henry a wink before turning back to the others. Henry lifted a tentative hand to his chest, feeling for the envelope.

". . . so don't even think about it," the security guard was saying. "All I have to do is put in a little call to O'Brien and let him know what's been going on inside the post office." The threat, though foreign to Henry, seemed to hit the mark. Henry watched as Stokes's shoulders tightened. The woman lifted a hand to her mouth.

The wind whistled like a laugh.

Roger leaned down. "You okay?"

Henry nodded. "I think so." His head was spinning with the events from the past few weeks and the news that he wasn't actually a retired mailman. He racked his mind for a memory to cling to, but everything floated through like sand in an open fist. Bits and pieces shone brighter than the sun—Elsie's hair, William's first steps, the taste of lemon hard candies—while others felt like half-formed thoughts that drifted just out of reach.

He tried to feel angry.

What kind of mind gave up on someone so slowly and yet so swiftly? What kind of mind abandoned its closest friend before their time was up?

The anger never came. Nor did the defeat.

It's never too late for the adventure of a lifetime was Henry's motto. Even if you couldn't remember why you'd started.

He reached for the letter, pulling it from his pocket. There was a collection of gasps as he ran a finger along its edges.

"I love letters," he said, looking at each of them. "I don't know why, really. They're just so . . . special. They can be filled with hope or sadness, anger or joy. Every piece of the human experience can be folded in half and sent around the world. It's magical. So maybe I didn't, according to you, work there." He shrugged and carried on. "But I think I've made a difference these past couple of weeks." His ears were ringing with everything he wanted to say.

There would be time for that later.

Pushing himself up from the chair, he reached out for Roger's help. The kid gripped him tightly, taking most of Henry's weight onto his own.

"This letter is important. Even if it didn't have a fancy seal on the back, it's still important. I think it scares you, having all these pieces of people's lives stacked up in your post office." Stokes's eyes widened. "I think it overwhelms you to hold such an important responsibility. So you treat them as if they're nothing. Mere scraps of paper that can be sent out with the trash. You're crumbling under the weight of their meaning, and so you lash out. You destroy. You do everything in your power to get rid of the thing that's crushing you. But it's not working, is it?" Henry met Stokes's eyes head on. "You still can't sleep at night, can you?"

No one answered. Unless the birds counted.

Leaning heavily on Roger, Henry tucked the letter into his pocket once more, making sure it was safe. He opened his mouth. Everyone watched him expectantly.

. . . and it was gone.

Henry racked his brain. He knew there was one more important thing to say. It had been there, fully formed. Oh, why had he put the letter away for dramatic effect before saying what was on his mind? He wasn't a dramatic type of man. Now he would never get to speak his mind to the man before him. He tried to grasp the gist of it, but it was no use. Whatever words Henry had wanted to say no longer existed in his mind.

That was the hardest thing, he realized.

He could handle the feeling of being lost, of always being one step behind the rest of the world. He could even handle the forgetting of meals, though these days his waistline spoke of the opposite. Not remembering people's names? Fine. Having notes sprawled throughout his life? Sure. Even the idea that he needed to rely on people more had stopped making him feel uncomfortable.

But forgetting his words?

That pushed him to the breaking point. Because we are what we say. The words we say too quickly and regret, the sentences we labor over, the beautiful ideas that drop into our mouths.

And the ones we put down on paper.

We are our words. What happens when we forget them?

Henry looked around at the expectant faces. The lines between the woman's eyes cut deep. The boss wore a scowl that made Henry want to giggle. The guard was still breathing heavily. And Roger, dear Roger, was looking down at Henry patiently.

There was so much he wanted to say to the kid. So much he wanted to say to all of them.

He nodded toward the door.

It was time to go.

117

Saturday, October 29, 1966

9:51 AM

Roger stole glances at Henry as he drove, trying to gauge how he was feeling. Henry stared out the window and gave nothing away.

Outside, the streets of Chicago were in full swing.

Children laughed and cried, people ran here and walked there. Young, not so young, elderly. They all existed together on the streets, moving in their own directions, sliding in and out of each other's lives without a thought.

Roger squinted into the brightness, making a right turn.

They couldn't see the warehouse anymore, but he could feel it, like a pulse, behind them. As they left, the security guard rounded on the other two, not letting them leave. Roger hoped they would pay for everything they'd done.

He looked at Henry again. The letter was clasped in the old man's hands. His mom was never going to believe all the stories Roger had to tell.

"Roger?" Henry had turned from the window and was looking at him.

"Yes?" Roger glanced sideways quickly before focusing his attention once more on the road. He was trying to remember which way to go next.

"Thank you." Henry gripped the letter tighter. "I'm not sure I can name all the things I'm thankful for, but just know I am filled with endless gratitude."

Henry seemed smaller than normal. A little less there. Roger thought it was a trick of the light.

"It's nothing—"

"I can assure you, it's not nothing."

Roger shrugged. "I know, I'm just . . ."

"You're just not good at receiving compliments, I know. But when a man uses his voice to say something positive about you, you accept it. A man's word is the most important thing he has, I always say. It's my motto."

Roger grinned and turned left. "Thank *you*, sir."

"Me?" Henry's eyes widened.

"Yes, thank you as well. For everything." He pulled up, for the second time that day, across from the brick house and cut the engine. "What will you do, after you deliver it?"

"Oh, I haven't stopped to consider that." Henry's eyes were wet. "I think I need to leave myself a note about Elsie. And William. The pain of suddenly remembering is much more agonizing than a heartbreaking reminder every morning. It's time I let reality settle itself around my shoulders, no matter how difficult it is to bear."

He turned to look at the quiet house.

"You ready?" Roger asked.

Henry nodded and pushed open the door. The wind had died down, and a light breeze floated across the dashboard. Roger unhooked his seat belt and reached for his own door handle.

"Let me do this," Henry said, voice low.

"But, sir, your cane—"

"Is something I no longer need." Henry exited the car with only a couple of wobbles and straightened himself to full height. He looked across the street at the house, and something Roger couldn't quite describe shone in his eyes.

"I'm so proud of you," Roger whispered. But the door had already closed, and Henry had already taken his first step.

When he was level with the house, Henry paused, looking down at the letter clutched between both hands. Roger watched as he rubbed the seal on the back, tracing the raised edges. After a breath, Henry squared his shoulders and took a tentative step off the curb.

Halfway across the street, he turned to look at Roger, a wide smile spreading across his face.

Roger grinned back and dug into his pocket. He needed to show Henry something. A symbol of his admiration and joy. A message between the two of them. He held the Batman marble high and tried to show it to Henry through the glass. As he waved his hand, the yellow flashed. And then it slipped from his grasp and rolled under his feet.

Bending down, Roger gripped the marble in his palm.

A screech of tires filled the air.

As he straightened, a single envelope floated into the bright sky.

118

Saturday, October 29, 1966
10:03 AM

There was no blinding light, nor was there total darkness. For Henry Walton, there were memories and words that flooded back like a tsunami, a rushing tide of everything he'd lost finally returned to him.

And of course, there were letters.

Monday, October 31

Celebrating the Life and Legacy of Most Wanted Mailman Henry Walton

By: Robert Howard

Henry Walton's face was splashed across a tri-state area on wanted posters for the better part of two weeks.

Dubbed the "Postal Pickpocket" by the Chicago Police Department, Henry was, according to post office management, at the center of the postal crisis and the reason for its spectacular downfall.

But it would seem, as is often the case, that there's more to the story.

There's no arguing that a crime was committed.

Henry Walton broke into the postal facility in downtown Chicago and stole hundreds of letters.

And he delivered them.

Setting off across Chicago, Rockford, Davenport, Minneapolis, Fargo, Sioux Falls, Sioux City, Hannibal, Springfield, and even Canada, Henry took the backlogged mail and brought each and every piece of correspondence he carried to the unsuspecting hands of its rightful owners.

One such delivery was to a woman named Delwyn Davies. "Henry was remarkable," Delwyn crowed. "He was so passionate about mail and getting letters to people. The backlog at the post office tore at his heart, and he wanted to do something about it. And," she said with a laugh, "I'm so glad he did. He brought hope to so many people in such a short amount of time."

We estimate that Walton delivered 268 pieces of mail over the course of two weeks.

As his face graced the unseemly posters, he continued on, battling car trouble and a failing memory.

"He was so determined," said Roger Knight, who joined Henry for the final leg of his journey. "When I met him, his car had been stolen, and still he was committed to getting people their letters. To Henry, letters were life."

Roger, a 17-year-old from Chicago, offered to drive Henry to his final deliveries. The pair spent two days together and delivered the remaining mail. "Henry was the most extraordinary man I ever met," said Roger. "He left everyone's life a little better. Especially mine."

Before setting off on this grand adventure, Walton worked at the Ferrara Pan candy factory for his whole career. When he retired, he was awarded the Lifetime Achievement Award, honoring his dedication to the factory.

"He used to joke they named the *Oh Henry!* after him," recalled close friend Stanley Byrd. "He loved working with candy, always sneaking a few into his pockets to hand out to local children."

"He started as a packager, on the line," said Flora Byrd, wife of Stanley and dear friend of Henry. "He loved the repetition and being able to focus on his own thoughts while he worked." After that, Henry went on to become a floor supervisor, a shift supervisor, and finally associate warehouse manager.

"He was always so dedicated to whatever role he was given. Though letters have always had his heart," said Flora.

According to the Byrds, Walton was a foot messenger during the First World War, responsible for delivering letters between two camps stationed three miles apart. His job was to get from camp to camp undetected, bringing instructions, responses, and orders with him.

"He's always loved delivering messages," said Stanley. "Though at the end, he couldn't remember much of what he'd done in his own life. Not at the candy factory or during the war. Aside from his old injury, he had little recollection of all the important memos he transported."

Continuing, Stanley said, "It's as if his mind clung to what he cared about most and not what was true. I've spent my whole career at the Chicago Post Office. So, when his mind started failing, Henry's memories got mixed in with mine. He sort of assumed my identity. Because of that, Henry believed he'd spent *his* whole life at the post office and that by delivering these letters, he was repaying the institution he loved so much."

"Stanley was so important to Henry," Flora said, "I think, in the end, he unintentionally adopted Stan's life story as his own. Stan's memories became his identity and his mission. Who were we to tell Henry he was wrong? Watching him with those letters, it was as if the spark had come back to him and he was alive again."

If Henry wasn't a mailman back then, he certainly is one now after everything he's achieved. Which is why we are saddened to also report that, while delivering his final letter, Henry Walton was killed in a traffic accident.

A service is being held to remember the life and legacy of Henry Walton at Egan Funeral Home on Saturday, November 12.

As we wait to see what becomes of the largest postal facility in the world, one thing is clear: Almost 300 people had their lives touched by the actions of one unforgettable (mail) man.

119

Wednesday, November 2, 1966
2:43 PM

"This is a devastating situation for the people of Chicago, who have trusted the sanctity of the postal facility for decades." The police chief's voice crackled through a small wireless in the common room. Stokes would have turned the volume down, but three thick men sat in front of the radio, listening intently.

"We've uncovered proof that post office management burned thousands of letters in response to the backlog."

"Who the hell would do that?" the largest one growled, spitting a wad of tobacco on the ground.

The police chief continued. "While we don't believe we'll ever uncover the extent of the destruction, we are committed to uncovering as much as we can."

Stokes leaned back, making himself smaller.

"Letters were moved from the facility to a crematorium over the course of a week. At the time, post office manager Reginald Stokes went on record to say they were closed to properly sort through the backlog so they could ensure Chicago citizens received their mail."

Stokes blinked rapidly. Did these men know his name? The guards did, but what about everyone else? He shot a furtive glance around the room and stood up slowly.

"Stokes, who has worked at the Chicago Post Office his whole life, rising up the ranks to upper management, has declined to comment. His lawyer insists that his secretary, a Miss Brenda Taylor, is the one responsible for the cover-up and shared that Stokes will be pleading innocent to all charges." He *was* innocent! "Only time will tell. A trial has been set for February. The Chicago Post Office will remain closed for the foreseeable future, and a Mr. Aldo Lombardo has been appointed interim manager."

Stokes crept toward the door.

One man pounded the table while another shushed him and said the bulletin wasn't over yet.

"While it appears the city has been failed by those in charge of the postal service, Henry Walton dedicated his time and energy to delivering mail to the people of Chicago and surrounding areas. This, if nothing else, speaks volumes about Walton's character."

Stokes swore under his breath and fled the common room.

Walton continued to receive posthumous praise on every news channel while he was left saying *no comment* to everything. It made Stokes want to lash out. Hate mail had started piling up, and the guards delighted in sliding it into his cell every morning, daring him to burn it.

And he would if he could.

That much was certain.

6400 Kimbark Ave, Apt 103
Chicago, IL

Vera,

I'm still not allowed any visitors. They said I have to wait until after the trial. I'm *not to be trusted*, apparently.

Which, really, is fine by me. While I'd love to see you, I know there are hordes of people who would try to visit just to spit in my face if given the chance.

So it's probably for the best that I'm in here.

Gives me time to relax for once, surrounded by smart women. We've started studying the patterns and habits of all the guards, sharing information through the toilets. You never know when it will come in handy.

Besides that, I've got a new pen pal. A woman in Ohio who burned mail from her husband's mistress and feels a kinship.

I keep all her letters under my mattress. Some things are too precious to destroy.

Love,

Brenda

120

Friday, November 4, 1966
8:59 AM

Fletcher tucked his shirt in before entering. He'd started a diet and hoped the results would be fast. His mom's friend Flora had given him some herbs to try. They were bitter, but Fletcher was willing to try anything.

On the receiving platform, he greeted the men with a wave. "Morning," he called, climbing onto a stool by the door.

Since Aldo had been appointed interim manager, things had really turned around. The sorting staff had been there around the clock to work through the backlog, and Fletcher was finally able to see parts of the floor. Even the conveyor belt looked emptier.

The men had even started receiving full overtime pay after Aldo met in private with O'Brien.

Fletcher had needed to explain himself for quite a long time after everything happened. He'd admitted to nabbing Walton and trying to steal the letter with the presidential seal. He'd even told them about the stranger he had grabbed by accident. Aldo had listened intently, asking the occasional question. When he was done, Fletcher hung his head and said he'd accept whatever punishment they had in mind.

"Will you stay on and guard the sorting?" Aldo had asked.

Fletcher, confused, had bumbled his answer. "Wh . . . what do you mean?"

"We need a security guard to make sure this doesn't happen again," Aldo had said with a smile. "And we can't think of a better guard than you. The way you saved Walton and turned on Stokes and Brenda . . . everyone's talking about it."

Fletcher had blinked many times to clear the wetness that had suddenly welled up in the corners of his eyes.

And then, without hesitating, he said yes. He would guard the post office for many years to come.

Ignoring the rumbling of his stomach (two breakfasts were not allowed on this diet), Fletcher settled in to guard people's precious letters.

For once, there was nowhere else he would rather be.

121

Saturday, November 12, 1966
1:01 PM

Roger looked out at a sea of faces. In the front row, he saw Stan and Flora. Stan's fingers played a slow tune while Flora's worried at a tissue. Roger felt a swell of love for the couple. There had been a surge of activity—planning the funeral, answering police inquiries, talking to the press—and they'd included Roger in it all without question.

The front two rows were filled with Henry's closest friends and those who had known him best. For anyone else who had outlived their family and lived a relatively quiet existence, two full rows would have been the extent of it.

Today, the funeral home was filled to bursting.

Roger looked at the people who crowded the space. Young and old, some were together as a family; others had come on their own. Light streamed through the stained-glass windows, painting them all in a rainbow of bright colors. Even his mom was in attendance, giving him a wave from a seat near the back.

Beside him, a choir was finishing the last notes of "Amazing Grace." Roger watched as Flora dabbed at the corners of her eyes. Her hair was a commemoratory shade of flamingo pink. When he'd told her Henry remembered that moment, their first meeting, with awe, she hadn't been able to speak for hours.

The music faded and silence filled the room, broken by the soft hubbub of children squirming beside solemn parents.

Roger stepped to the microphone.

"We're all here because one man changed our lives. Whether you knew him for decades"—he nodded at the front row—"or you met him once, Henry Walton changed your life. Maybe in ways you don't even know about yet.

"Henry made me feel whole. He filled in the cracks in ways I can't even begin to explain. When I first met him, he was on the side of the road, in the middle of his mission. He was so determined—filled with a tenacity I'd never seen before. Nothing could get Henry Walton down. Not the theft of his car, the momentousness of his adventure, or his failing mind." Roger paused, scanning the room. "No matter how much Henry forgot, there was one thing he always remembered: Words matter. Spoken words, written words, they all matter. And what he cared most about was that everyone got the opportunity to receive the words that were meant for them. He was so dedicated. So passionate. It didn't matter that he kept forgetting, kept misremembering. Kept losing the very words he loved. He never stopped. There are so many parts of our journey that will stick with me, but the one thing I will carry forever is one of Henry's mottos. Of which he had many."

A soft chuckle rose from the front row.

"It's this: *You don't have to remember an adventure to know it happened.* To me, it means you don't have to have perfectly formed memories—where you can see and smell and taste every detail—to know you've lived a good life. Done a good thing. Had a good time."

Roger thought about the past few days before continuing.

"Our minds bend and move, year over year. Some of us remember everything, while others find their minds are like Swiss cheese, filled with too many holes to count. Henry's mind was like that. It was vibrant and broken. He remembered nuanced details from his childhood but forgot we'd already eaten lunch. He could paint Elsie from memory, but he couldn't remember her laugh. He could tell me what William spoke of but couldn't describe the tone of his voice. I've learned that memories are puffs of smoke, twisting and shifting until they're gone. But just because a mind can't make the smoke reappear doesn't mean it wasn't there in the first place. You don't have to recall a face to know that you loved it. That feeling will never disappear."

Roger looked into his mom's eyes, thinking of all the good moments they'd had before his dad left. She gave a small nod.

He took a deep breath. "More than anything, this is what I will take with me into my life. Because that's what Henry taught me in the end. Even if there is a chance you might forget it all, you still have to live."

Hours later, after consuming many small sandwiches cut into triangles, some sickly sweet pastries, and more tea than he knew how to politely decline, Roger stood on Stan and Flora's front path clutching a letter. Through the door, he could hear the soft pulse of music and laughter. Their house was full, and stories of Henry passed from room to room on the lips of old friends and new.

When he'd said goodbye to his mom earlier, for a second time in only a few days, she'd tucked a handful of Oh Henry!s into his hands with a smile. They were now in the bag at his feet.

"There you are," Flo said, coming to stand beside him. A bright floral shawl covered her shoulders. Little tassels hung from its edges, swaying as she moved.

Stan closed the door with a click, fingers drumming against the wood. Roger couldn't place the tune. Before his time, he figured.

"Mmm, all set?" Stan asked.

"I think so. How're the planets?"

Stan shot him a wink.

Flora said, "The moon was conjuct Neptune earlier, which can make you feel unbalanced. And sensitive. Which . . . you know. Of course." She peered up at him. "It's a time to be alone, really. When the sky is like this."

The soft tinkle of Delwyn's laugh drifted through the window as she retold the fire story.

Roger met Flo's gaze with a smile. "I don't feel quite so alone anymore."

She pulled him into a hug, wrapping her arms around his neck. A tassel tickled his cheek. After a moment, Stan joined in, his bear arms circling the pair of them. He hummed in their ears, and this time Roger knew the song.

"To the stars above, if you hear me . . . hear my plea," he sang, voice too low to hear, "for I don't want to say . . . say goodbye."

When they separated, Flo grabbed his hands. "We're so proud of you, Roger. For everything you've done and everything you're about to do next." She gave a squeeze. "You'll visit?"

"Of course," Roger promised. No one had ever asked him to stay in touch before. He bounced up and down, already eager to feel connected.

"And you have everything you need? Car's okay? You've got gas?" Stan tapped his chin.

Roger nodded. "Yes, yes, and yes," he said, checking the items off in the air.

With a final hug, they slipped back into the house, leaving him alone on the path. He glanced up at the night sky. The North Star pulsed in the distance. A beacon. Slipping the compass from his pocket, he watched the dial spin and settle. He tucked it away, beside the marble, and reread the name on the front of the envelope, absently running a finger over the seal on the back.

It was time to deliver it.

After that?

Roger would go visit his father to put the past behind them. From there, he'd go wherever life took him. And he'd always remember to live as if he'd never forget.

He thought, perhaps, that would become his motto.

Author's Note

The United States Post Office Department was established in 1792, and by 1833 the first post office existed in Chicago. Throughout the 1800s, the city became a critical distribution hub for mail going east-west, and at the turn of the century, the Plan for Chicago outlined the need for a greater facility.

Construction began in 1921 and continued to expand as more stories were added. In 1932, the Chicago Post Office was touted as the largest post office building in the world—spanning two full city blocks and containing more than 2.3 million square feet of interior space.

The walls were grandiose in design; however, the Post Office Department suffered greatly from management and sorting issues throughout the 1930s and 1940s. And while a new emphasis on technology came in the 1950s, the postwar economy created an explosion of mail.

By October 1966, the Chicago Post Office was overwhelmed. Ten million pieces of mail were backlogged, and a three-week shutdown was issued to deal with the crisis.

Afterward, President Lyndon B. Johnson formed a task force. The commission's final report, released in 1968, called for a government-owned corporation to operate the Post Office Department and for the removal of the position of postmaster general from the presidential cabinet. These findings became the basis for the Postal Reorganization Act of 1970.

While Henry's heist is my fictional creation, the facts surrounding the post office and the backlog in the story are historically accurate.

This includes the depictions of all postal processes, details on the inner workings of the postal system, and the architecture of the building. They really did leave a hole in the bottom of the building to facilitate the eventual extension of Congress Street across the river, accomplished with the completion of the Congress (now Eisenhower) Expressway in 1955. The history of the Zone Improvement Plan is also accurate, including Mr. ZIP, as is the destruction of mail: Postal workers were forced to destroy circulars and advertising during the crisis, though, to my knowledge, they never secretly burned anyone's letters.

The 1960s offered a rich backdrop of civil rights for the story, though I have extended the sequence of events for the narrative by postponing the initiation of Lyndon B. Johnson's Great Society Agenda in 1965 to 1966. And while Johnson did send correspondence to Martin Luther King Junior, the letter with the presidential seal in the story is fictional.

Lawrence O'Brien was the postmaster general at the time. And while he really was in the motorcade when John F. Kennedy was assassinated, all other depictions of him are fictional.

Throughout the story, I have used letters to demonstrate the importance of connection. The letters are mostly fictional, though Elizabeth Taylor really did respond to her fans, and the 1918 letter from Elsie to Henry is an almost word-for-word recreation of a letter my grandmother-in-law, Betty, sent my grandfather-in-law, Elwyn, during World War II. Additionally, it saddens me to say the hate mail Mr. Lewis received in the story is based off a real letter MLK received in 1964.

Henry is a fictional character, though his war injury is inspired by my grandfather-in-law. During World War II, Private Elwyn Hancock (6094433 of the 7th Armoured Division Desert Rats) was a foot messenger stationed in Northern Africa and Italy. One day, he cut a mile off his route. A German tank fired at him, and more than 80 percent of his body was hit by shrapnel. During the attack, his elbow was sliced off at the joint. Elwyn lived into his nineties, though his injury meant his left arm was permanently frozen at a right angle, with his bone exposed for life. He was awarded numerous medals of bravery, and a tin that contains letters sent between Elwyn and Betty during the war remains one of my most cherished possessions.

Acknowledgments

This story has been many (many!) years in the making and there are several people to thank for their support, encouragement, and wisdom along the way.

First, I am deeply grateful to you, my readers, who picked up this book and followed Henry on his journey. I hope you've enjoyed reading his story as much as I've enjoyed writing it.

To my wonderful agent, Laura Heathfield, thank you for believing in me and my writing every step of the way. Your meticulous eye for commercial fiction helped shape and elevate the story. I am so honoured to be a Greenstone author and have endless gratitude for the entire Greenstone Literary team.

Thank you to my co-agent, Mary Darby, who has ensured Henry will be loved in multiple languages around the world.

To my brilliant editor Faith Black Ross: Your comments and suggestions brought this story to a whole new level. It's thanks to you that Roger takes up more space on the page and in our hearts.

Thank you to Rachel Keith, copyeditor extraordinaire, for your meticulous attention to detail.

Thank you to the entire Alcove Press and Crooked Lane teams. Special thanks to Thaisheemarie Fantauzzi Perez for your patience with every email, question, and follow-up. No doubt I've already sent you an update to these acknowledgements. And to Julia Abbott and Rebecca Nelson for being so wonderful to work with.

To my husband, Matthew Howells: After sixteen years, you're still my biggest supporter. Thank you for all your edits, ideas, and support. Who would have thought a "couple of kids" in their 20s, from opposite sides of the world, would be where we are now!

Thank you to my parents, John and Sharon McIntyre, for instilling a love of reading and storytelling in me from the beginning. To my sister, Crystal McIntyre, thank you for chatting through every plot hole and character arc. You've been championing the story for years and I can't thank you enough. Additional gratitude goes to all the members of my extended family who have cheered me on and provided the best inspiration (if you know, you know).

Thank you to Liz Hammond, my incredible beta reader. Liz's writing has been featured in Vogue, Today's Parent, Huffpost and more, and you should definitely go read every word she's ever written. I'll follow you anywhere, Liz!

To my critique partner, Aurrice Duke: Thank you for your wisdom and your support. I will always get excited when your name pops into my inbox from the other side of the continent.

Thank you to all the incredible authors who took the time to blurb this story. Your kind words mean more than you could ever know.

I would also be remiss not to thank the internet strangers on Reddit who helped me craft a query letter. You know who you are and I'm so grateful to be part of our online community.

The Purpose, Vision, and Goals program at lululemon has quite literally changed my life. To everyone who has checked in on my goal to write a novel and encouraged me over the past decade: Thank you.

My heartfelt appreciation goes out to postal workers around the world for all you do to keep people connected.

And finally, thank you to my late grandmothers, Doris Hodgins and Elizabeth (Beth) Burdick, and my late mother-in-law, Joyce Howells, for the experience and courage to write Henry. It broke my heart to burden such a passionate character with my second-hand knowledge of dementia. My heart goes out to everyone who has experienced, or is experiencing, this syndrome. In the words of Henry Walton: *You don't have to remember an adventure to know it happened.* My hope, above all else, is that his character will remind everyone to live.